I0747977

# This is the Way the Story Ends

An"almost-but-not-quite-true" story

PATRICIA J. PARSONS

MOONLIGHT PRESS | TORONTO

Copyright © 2022 Patricia J. Parsons

This is a work of fiction. Unless otherwise indicated, all the names, characters, businesses, places, events and incidents in this book are either the product of the author's imagination or used in a fictitious manner. Any resemblance to actual persons, living or dead, or actual events is purely coincidental.

ALL RIGHTS RESERVED.
No part of this publication may be used or reproduced in any manner whatsoever – including electronic, mechanical, photocopying, recording, or otherwise stored in a retrieval system – without written permission of the publisher except in the case of brief quotations embodied in critical articles and reviews.

ISBN   978-1-7779032-3-7

For information or permissions:

Visit www.moonlightpresstoronto.com
Or email moonlightpressinfo@gmail.com

*This book is for Mom*

*and*

*The 2007 graduating class
of Canada's National Ballet School*

# Some Other Books by Patricia J. Parsons

**The "almost-but-not-quite-true" stories**

*The Year I Made Twelve Dresses* (Book 1)
*Kat's Kosmic Blues* (Book 2)
*The Inscrutable Life of Frannie Phillips* (Book 3)
*Something I'm Supposed to Do* (Book 4)

**"Lit-for-Intelligent-Chicks"**

*Plan B*
*Confessions of a Failed Yuppie*

**Historical Fiction**

*Something More Than Love*
*Grace Note: In Hildegard's Shadow*

# First, a word from the author about books and spelling

This is the way the story ends.  This book is the fifth in the "almost-but-not-quite-true" series and begins where *Something I'm Supposed to Do* ends. If you haven't read that one, it's okay—this one will stand alone. The books each stand alone. But if you want to know why this is the way the story really ends, you might want to read its prequel.  Either way, I hope you enjoy reading the story.   And that brings me to spelling.

I write all my published work using Canadian English. For example, that means I spell neighbour and harbour with a "u," closer to British English than American. So, I would write about the Halifax harbour. But I will always use the spelling of how a place or institution is actually spelled, regardless of its location. So, if one of my characters lives in or visits Bar Harbor in Maine in the USA, then I will spell it the way it is typically spelled in that country. Confusing? Maybe, but it's how I do it, so don't bother writing a review that says my spelling is inconsistent. It's consistently correct in an inconsistent way.

*"I have lived my life according to this principle: If I'm afraid of it, then I must do it."*
~ Erica Jong, *Fear of Flying*


*"Those who cannot change their minds cannot change anything."*
~ George Bernard Shaw


*"Good and evil both increase at compound interest. That is why the little decisions you and I make every day are of such infinite importance."*
~ C.S. Lewis

# Charlie

I SHOULD HAVE PAID CLOSER ATTENTION to the young woman in the art gallery that day. I had walked in with one goal: to see if I could find out more about the characters in the unfinished manuscript I had discovered among my great-grandmother's belongings long after she died. The young woman in the gallery began telling me a story, but I couldn't seem to focus on her words. I don't know how my mind could have wandered off like that. All I could hear was the thrum of my own thoughts leading me in a different direction—to a different story with a different ending. But when a writer writes a story, is the writer in charge of connecting a series of events? Or are those events already connected? The answers to these questions turned out to be important—very important—and the questions begin with the writer.

I'm a writer—I have always wanted to be a writer. I dreamed about it as a teenager, trying my hand at short stories inspired by all the angst a teenage girl could muster. I studied writing in university, hoping to one day become a famous novelist—just like everyone else in my classes wanted to do. What I learned is that being a writer isn't easy. Writers write hoping that readers will read their words, but what if no one wants to read what they write? Is that person still a writer? Maybe or maybe not, but I know one thing: if you don't have a story to tell, don't say anything. A writer shouldn't have to ponder about what to write. If you have nothing to say, you shouldn't write. The truth is I didn't have much to say for a long time, but everything changed for me the year after my mother died.

I found myself in a strange place in my life—I was untethered from everything that came before. Because I was free, I finally had something to say. So, I wrote a book about family secrets, and people read it. Then one thing led to another, and I discovered that I had only just begun. I had so much more to tell.

I wrote stories about my mother and my great-grandmother, but I ran into trouble when I tried to finish a story that didn't belong to me. Perhaps even worse, it turned out to be a romance—not something I have much to say about, I'm afraid. Although I tried, I realized that my idea of a romance was unformed, influenced by what everyone else said a romance should be.

So, what exactly is a romance? Maybe it's the characters between the covers of the schlocky novel that the woman is reading on the beach. Or maybe it's those star-crossed lovers in a Shakespearean tragedy. You know the ones. They all die in the end.

There's a weird organization that romance writers belong to these days, and they have a lot to say about what a romance story is. They say a romance has to have a happy ending. They say it has to be satisfying and optimistic. They say there can be no tears or sadness at the end (presumably, they permit sadness on the road to happiness). But, of course, this is all nonsense because happily ever after is a relative thing. Relative. It all depends on where you're sitting when you're looking at the story's ending.

It seems like romance is defined by people who make things up for a living—writers who fall asleep, dream up a story and then vomit it out onto the page for you to read. But I finally discovered that romance might be something else. It might be something more fundamental—something more authentic.

You know all this, though, don't you? Life isn't all optimism and satisfaction, and just because a writer wants a romance to connect events so that the story ends with the lovers strolling off happily into the sunset doesn't make it so. Life is messy—often chaotic. It is sometimes noisy and often unpredictable, no matter how banal and unoriginal you think your life is. But that's the only way it can be an adventure. Even poor Helen Keller said that life is either a daring adventure or nothing at all.

This particular adventure started that day in the art gallery when all I could hear were my own thoughts. It was in my hometown of Halifax, Nova Scotia, on Canada's Atlantic coast. But the story started in New York City. I should have paid more attention to that story. I may not know a lot of things for sure, but I know one thing. Everything in life has a beginning, a middle and an end. And I know that life is a series of stories. So, stories also have beginnings, middles and ends.

This is how it really ended. But first, you need to understand how it really started. In 1989.

# 1

# Antonia

## 1989

*Anger is an acid that can do more harm to the
vessel in which it is stored than to anything on
which it is poured.* ~ Mark Twain

I WAS SO ANGRY AT TIM FOR LEAVING. I was angry the moment he told me he had to get away to clear his head. I was still angry when he slung his coat over his shoulder, picked up his suitcase and walked out the door of our apartment. And the fury built day by day in the month that followed when I heard from him only twice. Both times, Tim could say only that he hadn't finished his research and didn't know when he'd be back. The old saying that hell hath no fury like a woman scorned was on the money. And I never fancied myself the kind of woman to be scorned by anyone—much less my roommate, lover of five years and soon-to-be business partner. But now I had to talk to him. It couldn't wait.

Tim had driven out of Manhattan on that April evening en route to somewhere called Halifax. He told me it was in the Canadian province of Nova Scotia. I'd barely heard of it and certainly had never thought I'd ever need to know anything about it, much less set foot in it. But something happened, and I cracked. Before I knew it, I was on the phone with my travel agent, who was booking me a flight once he got over the confusion about my destination.

"You want to go where?" Alan said to me, sounding more confused than I'd ever heard him in the past five years that he'd been my travel agent. I could hardly blame him for the confusion. He'd booked trips for us to islands in the Caribbean, Paris, San Francisco and beyond. I never once mentioned a hankering to visit anywhere north of the forty-ninth parallel. Once I convinced him I was serious, I started packing a small suitcase, threw everything else into my trusty brown leather satchel and called Nathan. Nathan Harrison was my long-time friend and soon-to-be business partner, along with Tim. I gave him an update.

"I'm coming with you," Nathan said. Nathan had almost as much riding on Tim's speedy return to the city as I did. Almost. And Nathan knew why. I let him come along.

Once on the ground in Halifax, I had to see Tim as soon as possible. This conversation about our future business plans—not to mention our lives—couldn't be put off any longer. So, Nathan and I checked into a hotel on the city's waterfront, and Nathan said he'd meet me in the bar later. I then commandeered a taxi driver to help me find the address I'd managed to charm out of our boss Ken. It seemed that Tim had checked out of the hotel two weeks ago and was temporarily renting a cottage of some sort somewhere outside the city. Ken had been a bit light on the details. It occurred to me that Tim had probably also been light on the details when he told Ken, so I could hardly blame him for withholding information he didn't have.

I sat in the back seat of the taxi as it made its way out of the city and then along a narrow secondary highway full of twists and turns. The lights of the city gave way to blackness. More than once, I had to hold my breath to keep myself from puking in the back. I knew if I did, the driver wouldn't be inclined to take me back to the city, and I had no intention of spending any more time than necessary in the sticks.

"St. Margaret's Bay, eh?" the driver said as we emerged from an especially dramatic curve.

I could now see lights dotting the edge of what appeared to be a giant black hole, which I assumed was the bay to which he referred. It made me wonder who could live in such a seemingly god-forsaken place like this. I missed the bright lights of New York City already, and I'd been gone less than a day.

"It's a right pretty place in the daylight," he said, continuing his monologue while I continued to concentrate on keeping down my dinner. I supposed I shouldn't have eaten that airline food. They said it was risotto, which I loved, but it felt more like mush, and now I was suffering for it.

"How much farther?" I managed to say.

"Oh, about ten more minutes, I reckon," he said.

"I expect to be no more than an hour," I said. "Can I count on you to come back and retrieve me?"

I could see him shrugging in the front seat. "Suppose I can. Got a friend out this way. I'll have a quick cup of tea, and I'll be back," he said as he pulled off the road, the taxi's tires crunching along on a gravel surface. I could see him peering at the house, which was in darkness. "You sure you want me to leave you here?"

I was already opening the car door and getting out for air. "I assure you I can take care of myself," I said. But my stomach did a slight lurch as I noted that the house was in darkness, and Tim's black Supra, which he had driven out of Manhattan on his way north, was not in the driveway. I just hoped that wherever he was, he'd be back soon.

I walked toward the porch, the taxi's lights as it backed away, lighting my way. I walked up the steps and peered into the darkness. I stood there contemplating the absurdity of my situation, and as I stood, my fury at Tim returned. "Damn you, Timothy Sinclair," I said out loud to no one. "What the hell are you doing in this outport?"

There was a window flanking the door on each side, so, of course, I did what everyone on TV did. I moved toward each of them in turn and peered inside. Not a single light. Or a living soul. Then I tried the door.

"What the hell?" I said. "It's open?" And so it was. *Who on earth leaves their front door unlocked?* I thought. Evidently, Tim did—presuming I was even in the right place.

I opened the door and walked inside. As soon as I moved over the threshold, I knew this was the right place. I could smell a faint, lingering aroma of Ralph Lauren Polo, Tim's cologne of choice. I dropped my satchel on the floor near the door and moved toward the archway leading to where I could see a dim light. As I walked into what I supposed was the living room, I could see the light from the moon shining over the water outside the big picture window. I shrugged. *Okay*, I thought, *that's impressive.* But then I looked around at what the light revealed in the living room. I could make out a few meagre pieces of furniture—two oversized chairs flanking a massive stone fireplace and a drafting table beside the window. Tim, the creative genius he was, had told me he was here to research Titanic memorabilia for an advertising campaign he was working on for our current employer. That drafting table must hold the evidence, although I could also see an easel beside it which seemed a bit odd to me. Was Tim painting again? I certainly hoped not. We had business plans that didn't include a walk down memory lane when he used to do watercolour painting. I sighed. Tim's artistic genius would be put to much better use when he and I and Nathan (who, like me, was a Harvard MBA, but he was the business wizard, and I was the marketer *extraordinaire*) got our agency up and running on Madison Avenue.

I turned back toward the fireplace and realized I was tired, so I plopped into one of the chairs. I would simply have to wait for Tim to return. I only hoped he got here before my taxi driver returned. I didn't have to wait long.

Less than ten minutes later, I heard the door open, then close, then swearing just before the light in the hall came on. I gathered Tim was home and had tripped over my satchel. My bad.

"Finally. You're here," I said, getting up and making my way toward the hall.

"Geezus, Antonia," Tim said, clutching his chest as I stood in the archway as if he might be having a heart attack. "What the hell…?"

"What the hell am I doing here? Nice to see you, too," I said. "You know the old saying—if the mountain won't come to Mohammed—well, you know the rest." I walked back into the living room and turned on a lamp before taking up position in the chair beside the fireplace again.

"Geezus, Antonia," he repeated.

"You already said that. The proper follow-up might be hello," I said as I looked around the now-lit room. My eyes rested on the easel and drafting table. The image on the easel suggested that he had, indeed, been painting again. I'd have to nip that in the bud. I wasn't spending the best years of my life with an artist in a garret—or cottage, in this case.

"Sorry," he said. "Hello. You just took me by surprise."

"Good," I said. "That was precisely what I intended. There's nothing quite like a good surprise."

"You hate surprises, Antonia."

"People change, Tim," I said, shrugging. "Anyway, it's clear to me that you can't be planning on spending any more time here." I could feel my nose twitching just slightly as my head swivelled to take in the entire living room tableau. "I'll just wait for you to throw your things in a suitcase, and we'll go to my hotel. I took a suite at the Harbour Plaza Hotel in town. I was surprised they have such nice hotels here. Anyway, I'll just wait."

Tim looked puzzled. I'd seen that look many times over the five years we'd been together. "Why would I want to go to a hotel?"

"I mean, Tim," I said, sweeping my arm around, "just look at this place. It's so not you." I was truly appalled that a young man like Tim, so used to the finer things an urban life can offer, could live here.

He threw his car keys on a table and sank into the sofa facing the water. "And just what would be me, Antonia?"

"Oh, Tim, let's not get into that now. I haven't seen you in a month, and we have a lot to talk about."

"How did you get here, anyway?" he said, cutting me off. God, I hated it when he did that. "I didn't see a car outside. And how did you even find me?"

"Believe me, it wasn't easy," I said as I examined my nails. "It almost seemed like you didn't want to be found. But, as you know, I have my ways. And Ken is so easily manipulated. You did give him your mailing address. Then I managed to find a cabbie in town who seemed to know this area and was willing to take me out here for a reasonable price. I must say I had no idea it was this far outside town." I stood up and walked over to the small window overlooking the driveway. "You know, I've even missed that nasty Supra of yours." I stopped for a moment as I looked out into the driveway, which was now lit by the light from the porch. "Where is it?"

"In the garage—getting fixed."

I looked out the window again, where all I could see was a minivan. You know. One of those nasty vans mid-west moms use to ferry their kids around. It looked like an old dodge Caravan with that fake wood trim along the sides. They just screamed, "I've given up!" A shiver of revulsion traversed my neck. I turned to Tim. "How did you get home?" I said, looking out into the driveway again. Then the penny dropped. "You haven't been driving that disgusting minivan parked out there?" It hadn't been there when the cab dropped me off.

"Why not?" was all he said.

"God, Tim. Only carpool parents and hicks drive vans, for god's sake. Remember what we used to say about them?" He shrugged. "Condoms prevent minivans, if you'll recall." I shook my head in complete disbelief. "I cannot believe your standards have begun to deteriorate in such a short time. Things are more desperate than we thought. You've got to come home."

"I can't," he said, walking over to the drafting table. "I'm not finished here yet."

This visit was not going as I had planned or hoped. Could it get any more difficult? I had no idea.

"From what I've seen of this hole so far," I said, "Canada is a refuge for the dull and the commonplace."

I watched his face. I knew him so well that I could recognize a tide of anger as it rose. What was he so angry about?

"Where do you get off—" Tim started to say, but he was interrupted by a loud knock on the door.

"Expecting someone?" I said, sitting down once again.

"Tim?" I heard the door open, and the voice sounded like a young woman if I guessed correctly. "Tim, am I early?"

*Well, well, well,* I thought, *this evening is beginning to get a whole lot more interesting. And potentially complicated.* "Expecting company, Tim?"

I looked at Tim's face. It was a mask of sheer horror. I almost rubbed my hands together. "I guess our talk will have to wait a bit, won't it?" I couldn't even imagine what this was all about—at least I hoped I couldn't. I stayed sitting placidly in my chair, the rapt audience.

There are moments in our lives when things change in the time it takes to breathe in. It's that breathing out that's the dangerous part. I suppose that's why it seems we hold our breath.

She came into the living room. I looked her up and down, comparing her chinos, white T-shirt and scuffed espadrille sandals with my go-to travel outfit I was still wearing—black Escada jacket with power shoulders, black T-shirt, black slacks and boots. Whoever this young woman was, her sartorial selection for this evening was sorely lacking. Then I watched her as she made directly for Tim, who was standing across the room, framed by the window and the moonlight beyond. She hadn't noticed me yet.

The young woman threw her arms around Tim's neck and started to speak. "Tim, you'll never guess what…" She must have noticed me out of the corner of her eye. I watched her turn her head abruptly away from Tim toward me, and I looked at her face. I saw her eyes—the eyes that had only a split second ago been looking into Tim's. And I breathed out.

"Oh, I'm so sorry, Tim. I didn't know you were expecting anyone else," she said, pulling away from him.

I could smell danger in the air. Whatever happened next was destined to change—well, everything. I had never been one for melodrama, but I could feel something shifting. This situation was going to require more finesse than I had expected.

"I wasn't," Tim said quietly as he turned toward me. "Meg, this is Antonia St. John. Antonia, meet Megan McMaster."

Tim was staring at me, and I knew he had no idea what was coming next. He had often mentioned I was a bit of a loose cannon. I don't think he really had any idea how much. I didn't immediately get up, so Megan walked over to where I was sitting by the fireplace and extended her hand in greeting. I looked her up and down again, this time for Tim's benefit. He always hated it when I appraised other women this way, but it was just who I was. To tell you the truth, it was also who everyone I knew in New York was. So sue me. I saw no reason to be subtle. But I noticed on this second once-over that this Megan person was young. I mean really young. She couldn't have been more than twenty-one. I only hoped there was a good reason she was throwing her arms around Tim's neck, and by good, I mean platonic. But I knew women well enough to recognize that look. There was no doubt in my mind about what had been going on.

"Charmed," I said, reaching limply for the extended hand.

"You must be one of Tim's New York colleagues," Meg said.

I could feel that bitter taste of—what exactly was it? I refused to believe that it was jealousy. How could I be jealous of someone like this? "You could say that," I said. "And you must be one of Timothy's Canadian—"

"Antonia!" Tim almost yelled, cutting me off mid-sentence.

"I was just going to say one of Timothy's new friends." I gestured toward the small sofa near the chair where I was sitting. "Please, Megan, sit." Megan sat down. I looked at Tim. "Timothy, why don't you get us a glass of wine? Megan and I can get to know one another a bit." I knew how much he hated it when I called him Timothy. He said his mother was the only one who could get away with it.

As Tim stepped into what I suspected was the kitchen, I turned my attention to Meg. "What is it you do in this part of the world, Megan?"

"I'm just finishing up my PhD in environmental science."

"I didn't know you had such brilliant friends, Timothy," I called to him. "Soon, you'll have to call her Dr. McMaster." I could hear glasses clinking in the kitchen. I almost giggled when I considered how rattled he must be at this point. I turned back to Megan. "Environmental science. How fascinating. So, you're an activist?"

Megan shrugged. "Not really, although I think we all ought to be. My master's research was on the damage oil tankers are doing to the whale population off the Atlantic coast, but my doctoral research is moving in a slightly different direction."

*Well, well, well,* I thought, *now this is a fascinating revelation.* I smiled benignly at this naïve young woman. "And has Timothy been helping you with your work?"

Megan shook her head, looking puzzled. "No, of course not." Just then, Tim appeared in the doorway. He moved quickly over to where we were sitting, gave each of us a wine glass, and poured.

"Pity," I said, taking the glass. I glanced at my watch, calculating how much time I had before the taxi returned. I shrugged off my jacket as if I might be planning to stay a while and placed it carefully on the arm of the chair. "Just before you arrived, I was telling Timothy that we're all looking forward to his imminent return to New York, wasn't I, Timothy?"

Tim was looking daggers at me, while Megan simply looked confused. I was gaining ground here.

Megan turned to Tim. "This is sudden. Are you leaving Halifax already, Tim?"

"No. I mean…"

Tim was losing control of the situation. *Score one for me*, I thought. *Perhaps it's time to go for the jugular.* An environmental science nut? This was too delicious to let go. I had found my route to checkmate.

"Do you mean yes?" Megan said, frowning at Tim.

I took a long drink of wine, draining my glass. "A nice wine, Timothy. I remember it well. I'm a bit surprised you can even find it here." I put my empty glass on a side table and stood up. "Good heavens. Where are my manners? It seems I'm interrupting your evening here. I do apologize. I'll just get my things and call a cab." I picked up the jacket I'd just removed and began putting it back on, then continued, not caring in the slightest that sarcasm was beginning to drip from every word I spoke. "I'm sure you two have a million things to talk about. And I'm sure Megan must find the work you're doing for your latest client fascinating."

"We don't really discuss Tim's work," Megan said.

I looked at Tim, whose face seemed to have drained of all colour.

"Antonia, that's enough!" he said, controlled fury dangling from every word.

"Oh, Tim, I don't think so. I don't think it's *nearly* enough," I said through clenched teeth as I turned to Meg. "You really should have a look at the new work he's doing for Eastern Oil. I'm sure an environmental scientist such as you would be fascinated. I do believe that they might have been indicted last year for oil spills—not as substantial as that recent Exxon disaster, mind you, but deadly, nonetheless." I hoped I didn't look overly smug as I turned to Tim. "Weren't they responsible for all those dead whales that washed up on the beaches in Maine?"

I heard the sound of gravel crunching on the driveway.

"Well, what do you know?" I said. "Just in time, my cabbie has returned."

Checkmate.

# 2

*We're all islands shouting lies to each other across*
*seas of misunderstanding.*
~ Rudyard Kipling, *The Light That Failed*

HOW OFTEN HAVE YOU GOTTEN OUT OF BED in the morning thinking that everything about to happen to you will change your life in ways you can't even comprehend? You probably don't believe this, but even those minor, everyday things that happen can have far-reaching effects. You know—it's the butterfly effect.

It's all about that slight, invisible vibration of those tiny butterfly wings that can move even the tiniest bit of air, affecting something on the other side of the world. That tiny change, magnified by space and time, compels more changes—changes you never saw coming. That's every day. And then there are the days when something happens—and everything changes. That's what had happened to me the morning I decided to book that airline ticket and fly north to find Tim.

I now had almost forty-five minutes to think about this—to relive it in my mind—as the cab made its slow journey back into Halifax over those winding roads in total darkness, taking me back to the hotel where Nathan was waiting in the bar.

I remembered the morning when everything shifted for the first time—when I knew I couldn't wait any longer. I'd have to talk to Tim. I was already awake, staring at the ceiling, when the alarm rang. I could still feel my left arm flung across the empty space in the bed beside me while my body clung to its own edge. My edge. My side. By then, it had been three weeks since Tim had left on his "sabbatical," and I was thinking about how odd it was that we all seem unable to sleep in the centre of a bed when a previous occupant isn't there.

That was the moment my thoughts about that empty space dissolved into simmering anger. I was angry because he should be here. Timothy Sinclair, my boyfriend, roommate and business partner, should not have driven away from New York City—and me—on a research trip to the wilds of Atlantic Canada. He should not have found it necessary to clear his head and put some space between us. We had plans.

I remembered sitting up abruptly and looking at the three books on my bedside table. I had reached for the top one—a favourite book that I'd read for the first time at age seventeen. I guess I'd been a bit like the protagonist in this novel when I'd first read it. Like Isadora Wing, Erica Jong's heroine in *Fear of Flying*, I'd been trying to find my place in the world. And all that sex (Isadora's, not mine) hadn't hurt either. Remember, I was seventeen. But now I was thirty-three, almost thirty-four, and I'd discovered a fascinating truth about life. You'll never find your place by looking for it. You have to create it yourself. And that was what I thought I was about to do. Yet, Erica's book still held me captive—I was rereading it for about the eighth time.

I had flipped it open to a sentence I'd highlighted many years ago. "Anger is really disappointed hope," it read. I had held that to be true until that very moment of my life. I didn't want my festering anger at Tim to represent hope of any kind, especially not disappointed hope. But I knew Erica was right. I hated myself for that weakness but didn't have time for these thoughts that morning. I had places to be.

My usual morning routine started with a quick workout thirty-five stories below me in our building's well-equipped gym, followed by a smoothie, then a shower, and dress in whatever suit I'd picked out the night before. Then I was ready to head downtown to my office at Madison Avenue and 24th Street. Tim and I usually shared a cab since we went to the same office. But that day, I was skipping the workout and the smoothie in favour of a quick espresso while I stood at the sink in our white-on-white kitchen and reviewed my notes for an eight am breakfast meeting. I was pitching a new client.

The client was a famous vodka maker—Absolut, if you must know—but this pitch would be different. This one was an off-the-books pitch, by which I mean off my employer's books. You see, Tim and I and our friend and colleague Nathan Harrison, the business wizard of the ad firm where we all worked, had been planning our exit to self-employment for the past year or so. I'd been thinking about it since my first day with Moffat, Green, Berger and Partners, a behemoth of a New York ad firm eight years earlier. No, scratch that. I'd been thinking about having my own business since I was seventeen, right about the time I'd been introduced to *Fear of Flying*. And I needed Tim.

But it was the events of later that day that had really propelled me to make that call to Alan, my travel agent. Now, as I sat in the taxi, about to disembark in front of that Halifax, Nova Scotia hotel, I checked my watch, clocked the time, then figured out how long it would be before Tim showed up here tonight, and I could tell him what I'd come to tell him.

~

I dropped my large satchel in my suite, freshened up a bit and headed downstairs to the bar. There seemed to be some convention going on, so I had to make my way through throngs of overly happy, slightly inebriated people with lanyards dangling around their necks. *God, how stupid people look when they leave those things on after hours*, I thought. *Have they no self-respect? No sense of aesthetics?* After looking around, I sighed and concluded that I was in the one place in the world where plaid shirts and fisherman-knit sweaters constituted a fashion statement.

I found Nathan in the back of the bar, where he had grabbed a booth. I slid in across from him and told him what had happened.

"So, you didn't have a chance to talk to Tim at all?" Nathan said, draping his Brooks Brothers-clad arm over the back of the red-faux-leather banquette. Nathan was the most elegant man I knew. Never a hair out of place and the best-fitting clothes money could buy. That's what would make him a terrific business partner. In my view, it made him hungry, and hungry ad executives were the most successful ones.

I shook my head while the waiter took my order. I was still feeling a bit ill from the drive back and thought I would prefer water, but I allowed Nathan to order my usual Cosmo. "Not really. I did, however, meet a young woman called Megan McMaster." Nathan looked puzzled, so I told him how she had arrived unexpectedly. At least I had not been expecting her, although clearly, Tim had been.

"You don't suppose Tim's having a fling, do you?"

I thought about this for a moment. "Yes," I said finally. "I do suppose. In fact, I'm certain of it."

"This might make things a bit trickier here, you know, Toni," Nathan said. Nathan was the only person in the world I allowed to call me Toni, and only when no one else was around. I'd made that clear to him some years ago, and he never tripped up.

Then I told Nathan about Megan's work as an environmentalist and how I might have let it slip about Tim's oil company clients.

"Let it slip, Toni? You never let anything slip. What were you thinking?'

"Nathan, my darling man, I think you know me well enough to know exactly what I was thinking."

He shook his head and looked at his watch. "How long do you think it'll be before he shows up here?"

Nathan knew Tim almost as well as I did. I glanced at my watch. "I give him another half an hour," I said. "There's a whole lot of unfinished business here."

"Are you sure it was a good idea to antagonize him by telling that girl about his client?"

"You should have seen how she looked at him, Nathan. She's smitten, as only a very young, naïve and idealistic woman can be. And that's irresistible for someone like Tim, who seems to be going through an early mid-life crisis. I suppose it might even be flattering to him. Anyway, her knowing the truth about Tim's work may be the only way to get him to come home now."

Nathan looked alarmed. "You don't suppose he had any notion of staying here? Toni, Tim's a city boy."

I told Nathan about the watercolour painting I saw on the easel in his living room. "You remember when we first met Tim six years ago?" Nathan nodded, and I continued. "He had stars in his eyes. He knew he could make a living as a graphic artist, but deep down, I've always felt he harboured a dream to be a famous artist. A real artist, you know—painting what he wanted instead of bowing to clients' whims. He used to talk about Wyatt Lee every once in a while. Remember him? We went to a gallery opening of his a few years ago. He's one of three of Tim's classmates whose artwork is internationally recognized. Anyway, he always seemed a bit jealous of Wyatt's success as an artist."

"I remember him, "Nathan said, sipping his martini—extra dry two olives. "He was a bit of a twat, wasn't he?"

I laughed. Nathan had a way of getting to the heart of the matter. Wyatt was, indeed, a twat, so full of himself. I hadn't liked him, but Tim revered him. I looked up and thought I saw a familiar face heading past the door. "Be right back," I said to Nathan as I slid out of the booth. "I think I saw Tim out in the lobby."

I stood in the doorway of the lobby bar and looked around. I saw Tim over by the house phones, about to pick up the receiver, presumably to call me. "Tim," I said, walking toward him. "It's okay, Tim. I'm here. I knew you'd come." Tim put the receiver down and looked at me. "I saw you as you walked by. Nathan and I are having a drink. Come join us."

"Nathan? He's with you?" By the sound of his raised voice, I wasn't sure whether he was confused or annoyed—probably a bit of both.

"You didn't seriously think Nathan would leave it entirely to me to bring back our business partner, did you? You know Nathan better than that. He has the crazy idea that our rather intimate history might cloud my otherwise impeccable judgment."

I took Tim by the arm and led him into the bar and through the boisterous crowd to where Nathan was waiting.

"Well, old man, I have to admit I didn't really think she'd pull it off this time. Do have a seat. You look like you could use a drink," Nathan said, gesturing to the passing waiter to bring two more martinis—one for Tim and one more for himself. I hadn't touched my drink.

I knew Tim hated it when Nathan called him "old man." Nathan was aware of his feeling about this and only did it to push Tim's buttons, and it worked every time. I also knew Tim's drink of choice was not a martini. He was a scotch man, but he didn't say anything.

I slid into the seat beside Nathan so we could both have direct eye contact with Tim. We had to make him see reason about our business plans, and he and I needed to have a private talk about our personal plans.

"I didn't expect to see you here, Nathan," Tim said. "Antonia hardly needs a caretaker."

Nathan shrugged. "Quite right. Look, Tim, we all like to explore our options once in a while, but we've been talking about starting our own agency for ages and seriously over the past year. Our time has come, and we need all our talents. Antonia's sales genius, my business wizardry and your creative brilliance." He made a grand hand gesture to include all three of us. "Regardless of what you might think, you are important to us—both of us. And I think it's fair to say all three of us made a commitment to this project."

I leaned across the table toward Tim. "Listen to him, Tim. Nathan and I started worrying about you a couple of months ago when you started questioning every little thing about our lives—nitpicking, really. First, you started questioning the type of clients we'll be representing. Then it was the networking parties, even though you know how important those are and will be in the future. Then you questioned taking clients—*our* clients, mind you—from Ken." She leaned back against the banquette. "I suppose I shouldn't have been surprised to find you at home packing after that fiasco with the gallery opening the night before. You didn't have to be so rude about that young man's work."

Tim fiddled with the napkin, then looked up and said, "The work looked like some kid had puked on the walls." Then he started laughing—a laugh that sounded like a demon had possessed him.

I shivered, remembering his ferocious reaction to the artwork and the whole event that evening. He complained (loudly) that no one would be falling all over this young man's art if they didn't have something to gain by being in the good graces of the kid's father, a hotel tycoon. Tim had been loud, and when he had downed several glasses of champagne (I had lost track.—it was hard enough to keep track of my own consumption at those events), he didn't seem to care who overheard him. I knew he had a point, but I, for one, was willing to debase myself (Tim's words) and make nice to the dad about his kid if it helped us with our business plans—which we expected it to do in spades.

The waiter appeared and placed martinis on the table in front of Nathan and Tim.

"You know, guys, I don't know why I came here this evening," Tim said, knocking back the martini and gesturing to the waiter for another.

"I think you're ready to come home," I said, surprised to see Tim chugging a martini.

"Don't put words in my mouth." Tim reached over, picked up my untouched Cosmo—something he would never touch—and downed it. "There is something I want to say to you, though, Antonia." I looked at him, anticipating an apology. "I wanted to tell you that you're a damn bitch. That little scene you put on earlier was out of line."

I shook my head. "You've always known I can be a bitch, Timothy Sinclair. I always thought it was one of the things you liked about me. I see what needs to be done, and I do it."

"Come on, you two—"

"Just shut up, Nathan," Tim said with a vehemence I'd seen only a handful of times before. "No, Nathan. Now I see things a lot more clearly than I have for the past six months."

Nathan gestured toward the two empty glasses in front of Tim. "Too many more of those, and you won't be seeing anything clearly."

I put my hand on Nathan's leg under the table in a vain attempt to stop him from antagonizing Tim any further. Too late.

"Shut up!" Tim's voice was rising, and I could feel eyes from other tables begin to settle on us as the waiter placed another martini in front of Tim.

"Tim, keep your voice down. You're making a scene."

"Why should I care, Antonia? Everyone around here is…," he looked around the bar at the tables full of people, "…how did you put it? Oh yes. I remember your words exactly. It was dull and commonplace. Surely that means that whatever they think can't possibly count."

I rolled my eyes as Nathan began to rise from his seat. "I think we've taken this as far as it can go this evening," he said.

Tim stood up quickly, stumbling so that he had to catch himself from falling by hanging onto the pillar behind the banquette. He was out of control. He leaned over and grabbed Nathan by the collar, pushing him back down in his seat. "No, Nathan, I don't think we have. Sit down, you pompous ass."

People were starting to gape. Nathan sat down quickly. I hoped Tim would calm down, but he seemed to be on a roll, and I was at a loss as to how I could stop him.

"Here's the way I see it," he began. "First, you two need me for your little business venture. Second, neither of you is above stealing clients you have no right to steal, and, finally," Tim stared at me, "I know that you, Antonia, have been cheating on me with Nathan for months."

"That is not true, Tim," I said, but Tim wasn't having any of it.

"Be quiet and listen. I chose to ignore your little dalliance until I could figure out what to do about it. I may not have handled it well, but I handled it."

"Dalliance? Whoa. You've got it all wrong, man," Nathan said. Tim snarled at him.

If I thought I'd been angry at Tim before, that was nothing compared to the fury rising in me now. "You're hardly one to be taking the moral high road," I said. "You, the wounded lover? As if. I saw you looking at that Megan girl. And I saw how she looked at you. A little young for you, isn't she?"

"Shut up, Antonia. I'm not finished. The two of you have it all figured out, don't you? You know you can't make your business plans work without a creative, and I'm the best in the business. Clients trust me. They see my vision. They see my artistry. And they won't agree to go with you if I'm not on board. So, you need me."

He did have a point, but I couldn't let him get away with this. "Well," I began languidly, "from the reaction I got out of your little friend Megan, I'd say you don't have any reason to stay here any longer. I'd say we have a pretty good basis for a working relationship." I did sound a little bitchy, but sometimes circumstances demanded a level of bitchiness that I had perfected over the years.

I guess that was too much for Tim. His ears were beet red, a sure sign he was about to explode as if he hadn't already done so. He stood above us as Nathan and I remained sitting in the booth, still shoulder to shoulder. "Go to hell, Antonia." Then he turned to Nathan. "Thanks for the drinks, *pal*. Enjoy your conquest."

Nathan started to protest, but it was too late. Tim was already halfway across the bar, staggering into surprised bar patrons who must have been wondering what had just happened.

I put my hand on Nathan's arm as he arose from the booth as if to follow him. "Let him go. Just let him go."

"Antonia," he said, "you haven't told him, have you? He's completely oblivious to everything."

I swallowed hard as I looked toward the doorway through which Tim had just disappeared. "No, I haven't. I haven't told him anything." I wondered how long it would be before I had a chance to set the record straight.

# 3



*The wise adapt themselves to circumstances as*
*water moulds itself to the pitcher.*
~ Chinese Proverb

IT WAS HOT THAT SUMMER IN NEW YORK. Sizzling. I spent the entire time running from one air-conditioned space to another as much as possible. Some days, as I rode home in a taxi (air-conditioned only insofar as the windows were open), I watched the tourists staggering along the streets, sweltering in the heat and wondered what it must be like to be a mother with three kids in tow. What was it like dragging children through the streets of a strange city where they so clearly didn't want to be? It seemed to me I could see more vacation squabbling than enjoyment, and I shivered at the thought.

I put my nose to the grindstone and produced more work in two months than in the previous six. Even Ken, my boss at Moffatt, Green, Berger and Partners, noticed. Through a million little things, though, I perceived that my single-minded focus on my work was making me difficult to work with. I knew my secretary, Lisa-Marie, was becoming increasingly anxious whenever I was around. I suppose a child in her early twenties, working in New York at an ad agency with a laser-like focus on finding a husband, found me difficult (I knew this was the case from listening to her inane conversations with Ken's secretary Joannie whenever she dropped off papers for me). I was always hard on Lisa-Marie, expecting her to produce more and more. But I never expected anything from anyone I didn't expect from myself. I hoped my demands might sharpen her or at least help her see that there was more to life than husbands and babies. At least she had to know that there wasn't any glass ceiling I wasn't willing to shatter, which would pave the way for the next decade of women, of which she was a member. But alas, it didn't seem to be working.

"When is Mr. Sinclair coming back to the office?" Lisa-Marie said to me nonchalantly one morning in late August as she delivered my mug of creamy orange cappuccino, a concoction made from instant, flavoured coffee crystals. I'd been addicted to this beverage since we'd done the ad campaign a few years earlier. Lisa-Marie never looked me in the eye when she talked about Tim. I suspected she had a massive crush on him and was jealous that we were involved. Of course, when I thought about it, she never seemed to make eye contact with me much at all, a sure sign she was frightened of me. At least it kept her on her toes.

"I'm not sure, Lisa-Marie. Why? Is someone looking for him this morning?" I said as I took the offered mug and set it on the desk beside the massive pile of file folders I was reviewing.

"Well, Joannie says Mr. Berger mentioned he needs him here in the office. She said Mr. Berger didn't seem happy about Mr. Sinclair being away." She looked away as if gazing at something on the far wall. "There's been talk."

"What kind of talk?" I said, sitting up straight and paying attention.

"Well…" Lisa-Marie seemed increasingly uncomfortable with this line of conversation. Perhaps she even regretted bringing it up, but her crush on Tim had likely motivated her.

"Well, what?" I said. I could hear the impatience in my voice.

"Well, people are saying he's planning some kind of coup. That he's gone away to get a new business set up. That would mean he'd be leaving, wouldn't it?"

Dear god, I was going to have to put a stop to this immediately. It was ringing a bell a bit too close to home.

"Lisa-Marie, that sounds like office gossip to me. Doesn't it sound like gossip to you?"

Lisa-Marie nodded.

"I'll speak to Mr. Berger to clear this up. I can assure everyone that Mr. Sinclair is not up to anything nefarious and will return soon." I was not assured of either claim, but no one in the office must know that anyone was planning independent forays into the Madison Avenue advertising scene. Not yet, anyway. "In the meantime, I'd advise both you and Joannie not to participate in any further office discussion about this. Are we clear?"

She bobbed her blonde head up and down like a bobblehead on the dashboard of a pick-up truck and backed out of my office. After she closed the door behind her (at least she remembered to do that after being told more times than I could count), I picked up my phone and punched in Nathan's extension. His secretary told me she was sorry, but Mr. Harrison was at an outside business meeting. She wasn't sure when he'd be back. Of course, she knew exactly when he'd be back, but she didn't like me and seemed to have made it her career mission to protect Nathan from the office bitch. Well, we'd see how that worked out.

After I put down the phone, I thought about calling Ken's office to see if he had a moment, but it was likely Joannie would be just as protective of her boss. What was all this about protecting the men in the office from me? Anyway, I decided I'd just drop in.

I lifted my jacket from the back of my chair, arranged the shoulder pads in the perfect place, and glanced in the mirror I kept in my desk drawer to be sure my lipstick was immaculate—the deep red shade I favoured was another hold-over from an ad campaign I'd worked on a few years back. I remembered coming up with the slogan that these lipsticks were the difference between looking good and looking great. I favoured the latter, so I continued to use my favourite—it helped that the company had sent me a year's supply every year since. It was called fire and ice. It was so very me.

I opened my office door, breezed past Lisa-Marie, who quickly hid the nail file she'd been using on her lap under her desk, then headed down the hall. The leather soles of my new Salvatore Ferragamo pumps made a satisfying smacking sound as I passed by the open office doors and through the lobby, the sound muffled only momentarily as I stepped across the cream-coloured shag rug in the reception area where several young men sat uncomfortably waiting for job interviews. I only hoped Ken wasn't looking for a replacement for Tim.

I breezed past Joannie, saying, "Is Ken in his office? I'll only be a minute," while she quickly stood up behind her desk and was immediately pulled back by the cord of the telephone receiver she had plastered to her ear. The cord wasn't quite long enough. I was in.

"Antonia," Ken said, looking up from his desk, his reading glasses perched on the end of his nose. He shrugged them off, and they dangled from the ever-present black leather cord around his neck. "What's up?" He put the glasses back on and reached for his fat leather-bound appointment book, opening it presumably to today's date. "Did we have a meeting?"

"I'll just be a minute," I said, sinking quickly into one of the two brown leather chairs across from him. These, along with the leather-covered pencil cup, the leather blotter and the leather sofa along the wall behind me, along with the dark wood wainscoting and green paint on the walls, gave the impression of being inside a New York men's-only club, the kind of place I despised, for reasons you can probably guess.

"Have a seat," he said, entirely after the fact.

"Ken, I just wanted to give you a heads-up on Tim's return to the office."

He seemed to perk up at that. "So, you've heard from him? That's wonderful. I've been sending him those new-fangled electronic messages, and we've had a few telephone conversations, but it's not the same as having him right here in my office. Can't seem to get him on the phone very often. Glad to hear you've had better luck."

"Yes, of course," I said, lying through my teeth. "Of course, I've heard from him. He'll be coming back to New York very soon." I certainly did not know this for sure, but I had already figured out that he would need to come home at some point if only to tie up loose ends. After all, we were joint owners of the apartment we had both called home until a few months ago. And the lying was justifiable. After all, I had to protect my business partner, who I had no intention of letting move anywhere, much less Canada. Once I had him back in New York, I would have the upper hand. I just wondered how long it would take to get it.

When I left the office a few minutes later, Ken seemed slightly mollified, but this wouldn't last long if Tim didn't appear soon. Later that afternoon, I closed my office door and put my feet up. I was so tired in the afternoons these days. *Perhaps I shouldn't have worked all weekend*, I thought as I picked up the phone and punched in Tim's phone number at the cottage in Nova Scotia. All I got was an answering machine. What would I say?

"Hi Tim, it's me." A reasonable start. "I miss you. We all do. I know you're angry, and you probably have a right to be…" Did that sound like an apology? I hoped so because it was as far as I was willing to go. Even I have principles. "Any chance you could let me know when you'll be back in New York? Even if it's just for a short time. Call me." I almost hung up, then added, "Please."

I didn't have to wait long for an answer.

# 4



*Life is not a problem to be solved, but a reality to be experienced.*
~Soren Kierkegaard

TWO DAYS LATER, IT WAS A SATURDAY AFTERNOON when I heard the key in the lock. I was sitting in the living room and was expecting Tim. After I left my message on his answering machine, he called Lisa-Marie, asking her to tell me he'd be back on Saturday afternoon. Lisa-Marie could hardly contain herself when she realized Tim had called her instead of me. I just rolled my eyes at her.

Now, I reached for the September issue of the *Vogue* magazine I'd been reading, placed it carefully on my lap and opened it to a random page. I must have looked slightly startled when Tim walked into the living room and threw his keys on a side table, as was his habit. The article I was pretending to read was about abortion rights.

Tim stared at me as I unthinkingly put the magazine aside as quickly as possible.

"Tim," I said, the calmness in my voice belying the rate at which my heart was racing. It was time. "It's wonderful to see you."

He said nothing, staring at me as if he had seen a ghost. But the minute I looked down at my T-shirt—designer, of course—pulled tightly across my mid-section, I realized that it was not a ghost that he'd seen.

"Antonia, are you…" He couldn't even say it.

"Pregnant," I finished his sentence for him. "Yes. I am that."

Tim took in a deep breath, then forced it out as he collapsed into the chair opposite where I was on the couch. "How long?"

"Twenty-two weeks. The baby's due December 27."

"I think I need a drink," Tim said, getting up and going to the liquor cabinet beside the floor-to-ceiling window that looked down over the Hudson River in the distance. He poured himself a big glass of scotch and gazed out the window for a moment before returning to his seat. I said nothing—although there was much I wanted to say. But there would be time.

"Does Nathan know?" Tim said. Then he shook his head as if to clear cobwebs. "What am I thinking? Of course, he knows." He took a big gulp of scotch and then sat back, still staring at me.

"Of course, he knows," I said. "I had to tell someone. Nathan and I have been friends for years."

"And much more than friends recently."

"About that," I said. "You've got things all wrong, Tim."

"Do I? How do you think I felt watching the two of you so chummy? You, the woman I love...loved...love." He ran his hands through his hair and reached for the glass again.

"Tim," I said, "I can assure you that any jealousy you feel is seriously misdirected. I have loved you from the first moment I laid eyes on you. And I still do. But Nathan and I—"

"Nathan and you are so much more."

I could feel the bile of anger beginning to surface. I had to keep it down. "How can you be so dense, Tim? I cannot believe you are so dense. Nathan is gay. You must know that."

Tim sputtered, causing a drop of scotch to trickle down his chin. "What the hell?"

"What the hell is right. Are you telling me you've known Nathan for six years, and all this time, you didn't know that he's gay?"

"But I thought..."

"Well, you thought wrong," I said. "Nathan has worked hard to keep his personal life under wraps. Gay rights may have come a long way since the Stonewall riots twenty years ago, but there hasn't been nearly enough time to change minds on Madison Avenue, not to mention the minds of middle America, where many of our clients sell the lion's share of their wares." I was referring to the Stonewall riots that had begun the night in the summer of 1969 when the New York police raided the Stonewall Inn, a gay nightclub in Greenwich Village. That raid set off a series of riots that began what the rioters and their neighbours hoped would be a renaissance in public opinion. That, however, was not quite what had happened.  I continued. "When I met Nathan at Harvard, we were both scholarship entrants and kind of stuck together. We bonded over feeling like the outsiders in a school full of well-heeled offspring of super-successful alumni. Nathan, the gay guy and me, the girl from the wrong side of the tracks. It made us fierce, I guess. Anyway, I cannot believe you didn't know."

Tim was quiet for a moment. "So, I guess that means…"

"Yes, it does. It means that you're the father."

Tim put his head in his hands and mumbled something. I caught only a few words. Can't be happening…just when I thought…how can I. Then his head jerked up. "Antonia, you told me you don't want any children. We talked about this. I didn't want any either, and we agreed. How could this have happened? Why didn't you tell me earlier?"

"I'll start with the last question first," I said. "I tried. I left messages for you to call me. It's not the kind of thing I wanted to leave in a phone message. You never returned my calls. I even flew to Nova Scotia to talk to you—to tell you. And we both know how that worked out." I could feel a tear almost beginning to form in my eye. I had to stop it from spilling out. I had to. "And what do I find? The man I thought I would be spending my life with entertaining a girl child while on a so-called research trip. How do you think that made me feel?"

"I really don't know, Antonia. You've always been so good at hiding your feelings. At least you've been good at hiding feelings other than anger and frustration. Did you do it on purpose?"

That was a low blow. "What? Get pregnant?" I could feel hysteria rising and knew I had to keep it at bay this time. "No, Tim, I did not do it on purpose. It was a week before you left. We had a fight, and then when we made up, I forgot my diaphragm."

Tim looked over at the open magazine I'd discarded on the couch beside me. It was still open to the page I'd been pretending to read when he arrived. The headline was "The Politics of Pregnancy." The line below the title read, "The recent Supreme Court ruling which cleared the way for new restrictions on abortion…evidence that the rights of women…are being ignored."

"You're reading about abortion. Why didn't you have one, Antonia? You must know all the reputable doctors who do them here in the city. You've mentioned more than once that friends had availed themselves of the services." I didn't say a word, so he continued. "You don't even like children."

I couldn't argue with that. I didn't. And I had little time for those women who went on and on about their kids. Who cares about someone's child's teething or walking or toilet training? It was undoubtedly true that I'd made my opinion on this clear throughout our relationship. I didn't want children. As I considered this fact at that moment, though, I realized an important distinction. I also didn't *not* want children, either. I was going to tell Tim I didn't have an abortion because I'd been too busy all summer and the time just slipped away. But that's not true because being pregnant isn't something you can just put out of your mind. I suddenly remembered a line from *Fear of Flying*—a line I'd highlighted. "Pregnancy seemed like a tremendous abdication of control. Something growing inside you which would eventually usurp your life." Erica Jong certainly had a way with words.

"Anyway, it's too late now," I said. I wasn't sure how we'd move on from here.

We sat there in silence for a few minutes as the sun began to set. The September sun had always made me happy because, as a child, it had meant I was finally back in school, the only place in the world where I felt I excelled. The only place in the world where I didn't have to think about the small apartment I shared with my mother and how hard she worked to pay the rent. For me, school would be my way out—and up—and I would get the top marks in my class if it killed me. And now, all these years later, here I was, a thirty-something single, pregnant woman. Although there were chasms between my circumstances and my mother's, it was hard not to see the similarities.

"So, what will you do, Tim?"

He looked at me, drained his glass and said, "I have no idea, Antonia. No idea at all." Tim stared into his empty glass. "I have to catch up at the office for a week or more, and then maybe I'll go see Mom for a few days."

And I thought about how that one moment of inattention to a little rubber object would have far-reaching consequences like the butterfly effect, except it would be through not only space but also time.

# 5

## Tim

### 1989

*When one is in love, one always begins by deceiving one's self, and one always ends by deceiving others. That is what the world calls a romance.*
~ Oscar Wilde, *The Picture of Dorian Gray*

DO YOU EVER RECOVER FROM NEWS SO SHOCKING and unexpected that life returns to normal? One minute you think you've finally figured out a few things about your life, and the next, you're shell-shocked, knowing with a reality so strong it hits with a physical force that your life is forever changed.

I lay on my back, my hands laced behind my head, staring up at the ceiling in the den. I could hear Antonia moving around in the bedroom—our bedroom—next door. I knew her ritual well and waited until I heard the door of the ensuite bathroom close behind her and pictured her sliding in between the 600-thread-count sheets she loved so much while I felt the scratchiness of the cheap sheets that adorned the Murphy bed where I had chosen to sleep.

After Antonia's various revelations, I was too shaken to think straight. Antonia asked me if I wanted to go to a hotel, and I might have done that, but I couldn't pull myself together. So, she suggested I sleep in the den. That seemed like a good idea at the time.

Now, I lay there, unable to sleep, the events of the past few months—and years, if I'm being honest—swirling around in my head like a tornado that never ends. And like a tornado, it swept up pieces of my life that I hadn't even considered were worth dredging up. When I arrived at the apartment earlier in the evening, I thought I had it all figured out. I had my life figured out. Stupid, eh? Who has his life figured out at age thirty-one? Who has it figured out at sixty-one? I was beginning to wonder if anyone ever truly figured out their lives.

I was thinking about the evening I'd left Manhattan behind me back in April. It wasn't my finest moment. I'd been thinking about escaping for a while. Escaping my clients. Escaping our friends. Escaping the city. And even escaping Antonia—the woman I loved and planned to spend my life with. That was then. I'd allowed myself to begin to think that every problem I perceived I had was someone else's fault. I had been working on a challenging ad campaign for an oil company and had decided this might make the perfect excuse for a road trip—ostensibly for research purposes, of course.  I chose Halifax, on Canada's east coast, because the CEO of Eastern Oil, my client, had a thing for Titanic memorabilia. I knew some of it was in Halifax, the final resting place of around one hundred and fifty of the disaster's victims. There was also another reason. My grandfather had been there during World War II, and ever since I was a child and saw grainy old pictures of him in his American naval uniform all those years before, I had felt a kind of tug. I wanted to get to know the place.

I'd been expecting to spend some quality time in my own company, with my own thoughts, without extraneous people and obligations sucking the life out of me. Then I met Meg—Megan McMaster. I had never met anyone like her. When we first met, she was aloof and guarded in a way that ought to have put me off, but it just made me want to get to know her more. She was the one who took me to see the Titanic gravesites, and her skepticism of American tourists and their interest in the macabre had even been alluring to me for some reason. Then we spent one amazing day together exploring the coastal towns and villages. With her untamed hair, fishermen-knit sweaters and well-worn jeans, Meg was the antithesis of Antonia's sleek hair, designer clothes and killer heels. Oh, then there was her fanatic love of whales and her doctoral research on the environmental impacts of the textile industry. Just that. Meg, the environmental activist and me, the Madison Avenue corporate sell-out working for an oil company. And I never told her, even though we were inseparable for weeks.

I sighed when I thought about Antonia's arrival at the cottage I'd finally decided to rent after a couple of expensive weeks in a hotel. At the time, I hadn't a clue what had motivated her to appear like that out of nowhere. Now I knew better. When Antonia and Meg encountered one another, I knew nothing good could come of it. I remembered feeling sheer, blind terror at the very idea. Antonia had told me she needed to talk to me. I just never paid attention to what was probably becoming a kind of desperation. I had dismissed her because I was smitten with Meg. Antonia had been right. She was young, very young. But I didn't care.

I had some crazy notion that I'd start painting again—that maybe I could be as successful as that smug Wyatt Lee, my art school classmate. I always made nice with him, and Antonia had made it clear she thought I was daft, but I envied him for pursuing his art. My so-called art was at the beck and call of any number of clients assigned to me by the agency. It was becoming increasingly common for these clients to be in businesses I couldn't stomach. I'd drawn the line at doing an ad campaign for a cigarette manufacturer, but the oil company hadn't seemed too far off the ethical mark. At least it hadn't until I met Meg. And no, I didn't tell her about my work. I never found a way into that conversation. It seemed I'd left that up to Antonia. And now, here I was.

My stomach started churning as I remembered that evening. After Antonia left, Meg had turned to me, anger flashing in her eyes.

"What was that mad woman going on about, Tim? Do you work for an oil company?"

"I was going to explain—" I had tried to say before she cut me off.

"Yes, or no?" I could still hear the hysteria creeping into Meg's voice. "Yes, or no?" she repeated.

"Yes," I had said sadly. I had begun to tell her how much her passion for the environment had opened my eyes, how getting to know her had been a pivotal moment in my life. But she refused to listen. Then she refused to take my calls.

I decided to stay on in Halifax for a while. I was still doing my work for our boss Ken and the agency remotely, but I could tell that Ken was becoming more impatient. Even his electronic messages sounded increasingly exasperated. And I hated talking to him on the phone, so I'd managed to avoid most of his calls because they always ended with Ken asking me when I was coming back to New York. It was easier to ignore that question when it was tagged onto the end of an electronic message.

I spent the next few weeks working on a watercolour portrait of Meg. I'd begun doing preliminary sketches for it the moment I met her, it seemed. If I couldn't have her in my life, at least I'd have her portrait. I thought about it now, sitting unfinished on the easel in the cottage's living room. As I lay there on the guest bed, the lights of Manhattan flickering below, I could picture the moonlight streaming in through the cottage windows, casting a soft glow across the portrait. Was that all I'd be left with? I was in love with Meg and had been planning to visit her grandmother, who had brought her up, to see if she could help me figure out how to win Meg back. I had to tell her grandmother that I was in love with Meg, that I knew we were meant to be together. But I hadn't been able to connect yet. But I wasn't giving up. When I got Antonia's message imploring me to return to New York, even for a brief time, I knew I couldn't avoid it forever.

When I thought about how rekindling my love of painting had made me feel, I realized it was probably time for me to give my notice to Ken and let him fill my position with someone who wanted to climb the corporate ladder on Madison Avenue, and I knew I'd have to do it in person. I knew I'd have to talk to Antonia about us and the apartment since we were co-owners. Then I'd have to make the final decision to leave—permanently. I'd win Meg back if it was the last thing I did. These were the thoughts whirling around in my brain as I boarded that flight back to New York.

As I sat there in my aisle seat, nursing a glass of scotch, I had found myself uneasy. It was almost as if a kind of existential dread had begun slowly descending on me—and that was before Antonia had dropped her bomb on me. I was in love with Meg—of that, I was sure. But what about Antonia? Despite all the times Antonia made me annoyed recently, there was still something that held us together. But I thought I had it all figured out. My excuse was I thought she had cheated on me with Nathan. I now knew I was the one who had been doing the cheating. And I was paralyzed with fear about the future. Now that I was back in New York, my dread had mushroomed, and I'd only been back a few hours.

The Manhattan sky was just beginning to brighten into day when I fell asleep with two thoughts: I'd try to delay the inevitable by not quitting my job just yet, and spend a week or two in the office, appeasing Ken. Then I'd visit my mother, as I'd told Antonia earlier, and then head back to Canada—a detail I hadn't mentioned to her.

~

Antonia had already left for work when I finally dragged myself into our sparkling white kitchen to see if I could find some coffee. Antonia had left a note on the counter.

I poured a cup of coffee from the remains in the coffee maker, then sat groggily at the breakfast bar, trying to focus my half-open eyes on the note.

*"Dear Tim.*

*It's been two years since you and I had a conversation about the future. We talked about the things we'd do and the places we'd visit. We always seemed to be on the same wavelength, at least until recently. I realized some time ago that you weren't happy with your work. That's one of the reasons I thought our new business venture with Nathan might help you to find your centre. Perhaps I misjudged. Anyway, do you remember teasing me about my love of Erica Jong's book Fear of Flying? Well, it turns out Erica has some insight I've been able to cling to for the past few months when I didn't know if I'd ever see you again. She once wrote, "Take your life in your own hands, and what happens? A terrible thing: no one to blame." I've taken my own life into my own hands and made a few decisions. I will never be able to blame anyone, especially not you, for how it turns out. I fully expect you to do the same. Whatever happens, Tim, remember that I love you and that I have never deceived you. I may have been deceiving myself for some time now, but that's my problem. We all must take our own lives into our own hands. Please don't leave without saying goodbye.*

*Love always, Antonia."*

I put the letter down on the counter and looked at my reflection in the window across the room. I was troubled by how much I disliked what I was seeing. I ran my hands through my hair, finished my coffee, took a shower and got dressed. I was finishing stuffing papers into my portfolio when I remembered that I should call my mother if I intended to visit her before returning to Halifax. When I called the house in Boston, the phone rang and rang. I tried the number a few times and then remembered that since Dad died five years earlier, Mom loved to spend the early fall in our family summer home in Maine, just outside Bar Harbor. I figured she must be there. I'd call her later, then figure out how to get to Maine. Then I called Ken's office.

"Hi Joannie," I said, "It's Mr. Sinclair."

I could hear what sounded like a gasp. "Mr. Sinclair! Are you back?"

I smiled, knowing very well the moment I hung up, she'd make a beeline for Lisa-Marie's desk to tell her I'd be in later. I'd known for a couple of years that Lisa-Maria, Antonia's ditzy secretary, had a massive crush on me. That much was obvious from how tongue-tied she seemed whenever I darkened Antonia's office door to discuss a project. I'd mentioned this lack of verbal skill to Antonia on more than one occasion. She always rolled her eyes and said, "Tim, you know very well that I'd never hire a secretary who lacked verbal skills. No, Tim, she only devolves into a pile of non-verbal mush when you're around." I smiled at the thought of more innocent times, then abruptly returned to the present moment.

"I am for the moment, Joannie, and I'd like to see Ken this morning. Could you let him know I'll be in?"

She said she would, then hung up, and I left to walk the half hour to the office. I had usually taxied to work with Antonia, but in the past, whenever I decided to walk, I always spent the entire time thinking about the day ahead. I thought about storyboards, client pitches, meetings, always meetings. Today was different. Today I was in the moment. I watched the people on the street—every single one of them had the appearance of someone with important places to be, important things to accomplish. It was written all over their faces—grim and determined. There wasn't a genuine smile among them. There wasn't a single person who seemed to be paying attention to the beauty of this sunshine-filled day. *I used to be like that*, I thought. *What's changed?* Then I thought about Meg and the little coastal cottage and knew the answer. I had changed.

I noticed the storefront displays. I paid attention to the feel of the breeze, which made wearing a tie on this beautiful day almost bearable. I wondered how long it had been since I'd worn a tie. I had surprised myself with how much I had enjoyed not wearing one.

When I arrived at the building that was home to Moffatt, Green, Berger and Partners, my employers for the past six or so years, I stopped to look up at where my office on the twentieth floor was. I could only hold my place for the briefest of moments, though, before being carried along in the sea of stampeding office workers who were making their way in through the revolving door to the elevators to be swallowed up for another day.

When I emerged from the elevator into the MGB lobby, the receptionist sitting behind the desk said, "May I help you, sir?"

Before I could introduce myself to this new hire, Lisa-Marie appeared from the hallway carrying an armload of files. The moment she saw me, she shrieked, "Mr. Sinclair! You're back!" then promptly dropped the file folders, which scattered their contents all over the shag rug.

I shrugged at the young woman behind the desk whose eyes were as big as saucers. Perhaps my reputation had preceded me. I smiled, placed my portfolio on the counter and bent down to help Lisa-Marie gather the errant files.

"I am indeed back, Lisa-Marie. Not sure for how long, but I'm back."

After she had composed herself, I nodded to the new girl and walked down the hall to my office. Along the way, the cubicle workers nodded, and some even smiled. I had a private office at the end of the hall. It was usually private, but it was also where the creatives in the agency came together to work on campaigns. No one was using it this morning, and for that, I was grateful.

I sat down at my desk and looked around. I felt like a fish out of water. I should feel at home, happy, content, settled. But I didn't. I felt the tension rising in my neck, and I wondered how I could return to this job, to this city. I finalized a few things related to the campaign I'd finally finished for Ken, the Berger in the Moffatt, Green, Berger name, and walked down the hall again toward his office.

Joannie must have been on a coffee break, no doubt discussing my reappearances with Lisa-Marie and the rest of the gossipy office staff.

I knocked on Ken's door, and he boomed, "Enter!" So, I did.

I thought I'd be tense as I approached my long-time boss, a man whose integrity and composure in a business that can be both disingenuous and frenzied had always impressed me. But I wasn't nervous. I felt detached. That's it—detached, almost disconnected from this place. Yet, I knew I had a long way to go before I felt at all settled with a decision as to what to do about Antonia's problem. Funny, isn't it? That's how I thought about it—Antonia's problem. Why didn't I think it was my problem? And why did I think I had to "do something" about it?

I didn't have time to ponder those questions because Ken stood up behind his desk and boomed, in that way he had, "Timothy Sinclair! The prodigal son has returned. Sit. I think we need to talk." He got up from behind his massive oak desk and sat in an oversized leather chair across from the equally oversized leather sofa, where he waved at me to sit. This was going well. If Ken wanted to give me a dressing down, maybe even fire me on the spot for working remotely for so long, he would have done it from behind his desk. That desk both protected him and lent him an air of power. I knew this because he had told me this once when we were sitting beside each other at a client lunch. It was one of the lessons he was trying to impart to me. I don't think I was listening as closely as I should have been.

So, we talked. First, I broke out the storyboards and the drawings for the campaign. I knew he'd be impressed. Ken was almost always impressed by my work when he saw it in its final form. Today was no different. Of course, my strategy was to remind him why he hired me in the first place. If I were going to leave the agency, I would do it in my own time, on my own terms, whatever they might be. I was a bit foggy on that detail.

Then I dropped my ask. I told Ken that I'd work in the office for the rest of the week, then I needed another few weeks away. I'd review the new client folio that he needed me to address, and then I'd get back to him with a plan in a few weeks. He reluctantly agreed.

I felt I'd accomplished something, at least. When I arrived back in my office, I closed the door and picked up the phone. I punched in Meg's number. Why I thought she might pick up today was beyond me. She had been ignoring my calls for so long, but I couldn't let this go. I held my breath as it rang once, twice, three times, as I composed my message that I'd leave on her answering machine yet again. I was about to speak when her voice cut in.

"Hello?"

I was so startled that I said nothing.

"Hello?" she said again. "Is anyone there?"

"Meg, it's me. Tim." I could hear an intake of breath. "Don't hang up. Please."

"I don't want to speak to you. Ever."

She said the words, but I could hear the falter in her voice. She missed me. I could tell. *This might be my one chance*, I thought.

"Meg, I know. I know you don't want to talk to me. But I want to talk to you. I need to talk to you. I know I don't deserve your forgiveness, but I hope we can start again. You have no idea how much you have profoundly affected me. Isn't that what you're hoping to do with your work? Change people's minds?

You've opened my eyes, and I think you'll open so many others' eyes with your work. I just need a chance to see you again."

"Where are you?" she said.

"I'm in New York—"

"New York! You've gone back to that…woman? I'm hanging up."

"Meg, please don't. Please let me explain what I'm doing here." Again, she hesitated, and I was in. "I'll be back in Halifax in a couple of weeks. I have some business here, and I want to spend a few days with my mother. Then I'll be back. Will you see me then?" I knew I was begging, but it was worth it.

"Okay," Meg said slowly. "I'll see you when you're here, but I won't promise anything."

That was enough for me.

# 6


*Perhaps it takes courage to raise children.*
~ John Steinbeck, *East of Eden*


STAYING TOGETHER IN THE APARTMENT WAS AWKWARD. It was also uncomfortable at the office because I could see the unspoken question in everyone's eyes. "Is he back to stay?" Finally, after about ten days, I figured I'd done all I could at the office to at least mollify Ken. Antonia and I weren't making any headway in our stilted conversations, so I figured now might be time to go to Maine to visit Mom.

I remembered the first time I'd taken Antonia to our family "cottage" near Bar Harbor in Maine. When we arrived, she was oddly furious. She asked me how I could have lied, but I didn't understand what she was talking about. I told her I hadn't lied. Then she informed me that a four-thousand square foot, three-story sea captain's house with five bedrooms and six bathrooms overlooking the Maine seacoast did not qualify as a cottage in her world. She had been expecting a cabin in the Maine woods. That was the difference between Antonia and me. She wanted everything, and I already had it.

Three days earlier, Antonia had asked me if I was still planning to go to see Mom.

"I suppose you'll talk to her about us," Antonia had said, sipping a club soda with her feet up on the coffee table while I sprawled in the chair across from her. "I know your mother has never liked me."

My eyebrows had shot up at that revelation. As far as I could figure out, Mom hardly knew Antonia. I had no idea how Antonia could have gotten into her head that Mom didn't like her.

Then Antonia had explained. "She wasn't impressed that I had to miss your father's funeral for that California trip."

This revelation made no sense. It had never once seemed to me that Mom had even noticed. She'd been so overwrought, and my relationship with Antonia had been so new then.

Then Antonia said, "I've always felt she thought I wasn't good enough for you. I suppose she'll be apoplectic when she thinks I'll be the mother of her grandchild. Well, tell her not to worry. She'll never have to be a part of this child's life."

I was stunned—on several counts. First, it was true that Mom had always thought our backgrounds were too divergent for our relationship to work in the long term. Still, it had never occurred to me that Mom, the vibrant, intelligent, generous Grace Sinclair, had ever thought we were better than Antonia. Second, I couldn't consider that my mother would sit still and not want to be part of her grandchild's life, regardless of the circumstances. For the first time since I'd known Antonia, I considered the possibility that she might not be quite as secure in herself as I'd always thought she was.

I was still thinking about this conversation as I signed the rental car agreement and decided to leave that day. It was less than eight hours door-to-door to our summer house in Maine, so if I left immediately, I could be there before dark.

I dropped back into the office briefly to pick up a few things and drop off a message for Antonia. Lisa-Marie took it and promised to get it to Antonia the moment she returned from her meeting. I realized leaving a folded note with Lisa-Marie might not have been a good idea (because she'd probably read it), but what did it matter?

I headed north on the I95 in my rental car—a big sedan of some kind. I did believe that my mother would want to be part of this child's life. I was ashamed when I wondered if I was the reluctant one. It did, however, seem clear that Antonia had no intention of sharing this with anyone. She seemed to want to keep this experience all for herself. I now wondered why I hadn't even asked her what she planned to do about her work. I wondered if she'd considered giving the baby up for adoption, a situation about which I would have expected to have a say. Maybe that's why she said Mom wouldn't ever be part of this child's life. The car swerved onto the shoulder the moment I considered that possibility. I pulled it back as quickly as I could respond. Could I let that happen? And what about Meg? I knew I'd have to tell her if I hoped for any future with her. I'd already lied to her once by omission. I couldn't risk doing it again. Either way, I looked at it, the situation was precarious.

I had left Manhattan at ten am and stopped twice—once just outside Boston and then outside Portsmouth, New Hampshire. I made good time on the highway, but the drive was still long, giving me far too much time alone with my thoughts—so it was just after six pm when I turned into Stonemill Road just before the village of Bar Harbor. The road snaked along the water, past a series of large properties, mostly summer homes owned by wealthy Bostonians and New Yorkers who escaped the city heat for a month or so each year. The houses were silent sentries along the rocky coastline the rest of the time, coming alive only occasionally for a family Thanksgiving or Christmas gathering. My parents had been the outliers. They had trotted us—my sister Kelly who was four years younger than I was, and me—out of the city for the entire summer every year. We loved it until we hit our young teenage years when we begged our parents to let us stay in the city for the summer. They adamantly refused but let us invite a friend to visit for a few weeks. Those weeks were golden. But a funny thing happened.

When I was about sixteen, I realized what a gift being away from the city in the summer could be. I spent the time boating with my dad and painting. Those last two summers before I went to college cemented my artistic dream. Now, whenever I visited the Maine house, I always felt like I could breathe again. And this time was no different.

As I pulled into the circular driveway behind the house (the front faced the north Atlantic), I automatically took a deep breath. I opened my window, smelled that first blast of sea air, and felt I was home. The first thing I noticed was that the formerly gravel driveway was now covered in paver stones laid in an artistic pattern that no doubt was my mother's design. Then I noticed new trees among the perennial beds that had always been there. The perennial border overflowed with late-bloomers—purple coneflowers, chrysanthemums and black-eyed Susans.

I turned off the engine and got out, stretching my back from the long drive. As I pulled my small suitcase from the back seat, my mother appeared on the porch. I smiled and wondered why I hadn't spent more time with her over the past few years. It wasn't that my mother particularly needed me. Mom still ran her interior design business in Boston, occasionally played tennis there and dined out with friends. I also knew my sister Kelly visited her twice a year from her current home in LA, where she ran a Pilates-yoga-ballet studio. I'd often wondered whether Mom ever dated. After all, a woman widowed at age forty-seven, still beautiful, must have to fend off any number of suitors. Maybe I'd get her to tell me about them.

I walked toward the porch and smiled to see her in what I'd often teased her was her uniform: white button-down shirt, flowing beige pants and two-toned (black and tan) Chanel ballet flats. I knew they were Chanel only because Antonia had noticed them and mentioned that fact to me on one of the odd occasions when we'd spent an evening with Mom in Boston.

Mom waited for me to walk up the steps before putting her arms out and pulling me into a hug without saying a single word. She might have said, "Why don't I see you more often? Or, "You never visit," or "Hello, stranger," but she said none of these. When she finally let go and held me at arm's length to look at me, she simply said, "Welcome home, honey." She had always called me honey, and I hadn't realized how much I had missed hearing it.

"Tim, honey," she said as we walked into the massive white kitchen with its beadboard cabinets and enormous marble island that accommodated six stools. "Let's get a glass of wine and take it out on the deck."

I loved that kitchen. It was my favourite place in the whole house. I could remember the many times I sat there with my sketch pad in front of me and a glass of lemonade at my elbow. When I turned seventeen, Dad had allowed me to switch that drink out for a beer once in a while, always telling me he wanted me to learn how to drink sensibly before I went to college and got in with a group of drinkers.

Mom had already prepared a tray of snacks—all my favourites. There was a round of soft brie cheese, several kinds of crackers, olives and a small bowl of potato chips. I smiled as I followed her out onto the deck with its eight Adirondack chairs facing the water. I was carrying the wine glasses and a bottle of chilled Sancerre, her favourite wine, which she directed me to in the refrigerator that was the size of one you'd find in a restaurant kitchen.

"So, tell me all about what you've been doing up there in Canada," Mom said once we were sitting comfortably, gazing out at the rocky shoreline and the small white caps beyond.

I started my story by telling her about the ad campaign I'd been working on and the Titanic research I needed to do in Halifax. She nodded and said little. I told her about how much I loved the area and how the cottage I'd been renting reminded me a bit of being here. At least I often had the same feeling, although admittedly, the cottage was a far cry from this "mansion," as Antonia had put it on more than one occasion.

We chatted about the times Mom and Dad had visited Canada, and I was surprised that Halifax had been among their destinations. I didn't know they'd ever been there. How had it never come up in conversation? Then Mom poured us a second glass of wine and said, "Tim, honey, what are you not telling me?"

"Quite a lot, as it turns out, Mom. Quite a lot."

She didn't press me just then. My mother was the master of the long game—she could wait out anyone. She had never been one to press for details—I think I'd always liked that. She almost made you feel that you would be missing out on something if you didn't cough up eventually. And so, as kids, Kelly and I had always ended up telling her the whole story no matter what it was. I'd seen her do this with her friends as well.

Mom picked up her wine glass and got up from her chair. "I'll just see how dinner is coming," she said, patting my arm as she went back into the kitchen, leaving me alone with the wind and the sea.

Mom had made clam chowder, my favourite. Dad had always liked to serve lobster whenever Kelly or I made it here for a summer visit, but I preferred chowder, and Mom knew it.

"Mom," I said as I finished the last drop of my chowder, "there are a few things I need to talk to you about."

"I know, honey." She got up to clear the dishes from the table. "And when you're ready, you'll tell me about them."

The following morning, Mom invited me to take a walk along the beach with her. It wasn't one of those wide beaches covered with fine sand. Littered with rocks and shells, it was a beach you could reach only by climbing down a set of steep wooden stairs. You could swim here if you walked out far enough, but the water was ice cold. Even now, in September, after an entire summer's worth of sunshine, the water was still only about fifty-six degrees Fahrenheit. It made me shiver to think that we used to run right in.

Mom was wearing a white sweater over her blouse with a white bucket hat that no one could carry off quite like my mother. The wind was slightly chilly as we set out. I started talking before we'd been gone three minutes.

I told Mom again how much I loved Halifax. Then she stopped and turned to me. "You've met someone there, haven't you? And now you don't know what to do about Antonia."

"Mom, I wish that was all. But yes, you're right. I have met someone." We continued along the beach. I bent down and picked up a flat stone which I tried to skip across the water. I was out of practice. "Her name's Meg. Megan McMaster."

Mom pulled her sweater tighter and kept walking.

I told her we'd met by chance at a museum on the Halifax waterfront and how aloof she'd been at first when she learned I was an American. Mom's eyebrows raised just slightly at that. Then I told her we'd spent time together and how much I'd grown to care for her—and I thought she cared for me. "I think I'm in love with her," I said, "but I've made kind of a mess of things, Mom, and I don't know what to do."

"Tim, I probably know you better than anyone in the world. And I certainly know when you're not telling me the whole story."

So, I told her that I'd neglected to tell Meg, the environmentalist, that I did work for an oil company and not just any oil company. My client was a company whose recent oil spill had threatened the habitat of the whales she was so passionate about.

"I know it was wrong to keep it from her," I said.

"Not only was it wrong but so very foolish," Mom said. She wasn't one to mince words. "Tim, you know these things always come out. What were you planning to do?" She walked on thoughtfully. "And where does Antonia fit into all this?"

"Yeah," I said, "about Antonia."

"You've just said you *think* you're 'in love' with this new woman, but you've always told me that you love Antonia. You've always been so vehement about it that I even came to accept that she might be the best thing for you despite your differences. Tim, honey, there's a big difference between being in love and truly loving someone. There's a difference between romance and love." We walked in silence for a few minutes, then Mom said, "The very essence of romance is uncertainty."

"Is that an original?"

Mom laughed. "No. I wish I could claim it, but no. It's Oscar Wilde. You know, Tim, that feeling of *uncertainty* is the essence of early romance, but *certainty* is the very essence of love. You've been so certain of Antonia for so long. How does that certainty dissolve so quickly?" She stopped and turned to me again. "Have you told all of this to Antonia?"

"Yeah, about Antonia," I said for at least the second time. "Yeah, there's something else." I took a deep breath and jammed my hands as deeply into my pockets as I could. "She's pregnant."

# 7



*Look with your understanding, find out what you
already know, and you'll see the way to fly.*
~ Richard Bach, *Jonathan Livingston Seagull*

MOM SAID NOTHING. SHE LOOKED AT ME, and I wondered for the briefest of seconds if I saw pity. Then, all she said was, "Let's head back," and we walked back along the pebbly sand, each of us lost in our own thoughts. When she was ready, I knew she'd tell me what she was thinking. I had to know. I was in deep trouble and needed my mother's help. Deep down, though, I knew she might very well just tell me I was an adult and I'd made my bed. Now I had to lie in it. And who could blame her?

For the next half hour, as we headed back along the beach, narrowly avoiding high tide, Mom said nothing. I could tell she was lost in her thoughts, but I knew that when she had sorted out her thoughts and feelings, she'd share them with me. She would never do it until she was ready. She'd always done this, and as a kid, I'd found it unnerving. Most of my friends' moms blew up the minute they were told about some crimes or misdemeanours perpetrated by their offspring, but my mother was different. She considered her reaction carefully and was well-armed when she finally addressed an issue. I did not doubt that she'd come at me head-on when she had gathered her ammunition. I knew this one was a biggie, but I still found the wait for her reaction excruciating.

We spent the rest of the afternoon wandering the Sunday farmer's market in the village, where Mom ran into at least three people who had been her clients. Over the years, Mom had designed interiors for so many Boston doyennes that she'd become something of an east coast design celebrity. After the first time she appeared on the morning show in Boston, she was inundated with requests for her services from people as far away as New York. New Yorkers (and Bostonians) who owned many of the houses in Maine had clamoured for her to decorate their gigantic "cottages."

"Grace, how lovely to see you! It's been ages!" One of Mom's clients was standing in front of creamy yellow and white cobs of fresh corn piled high on a table beneath a blue tent-like cover. I recognized her but couldn't put a name to the face.

"Miranda," Mom said. "It has been a while, hasn't it?"

"Too long, Grace. I hear you've been spending time at the club recently." Did she wink?

Mom looked decidedly uncomfortable. I knew because I'd seen this look before. Mom was about to hurry us away when Miranda reached out and put her hand on my arm. "My dear, this is Timothy! I haven't seen you since you were about sixteen years old, but I'd recognize you anywhere. Are you here to visit your mother?" That much seemed obvious. I stopped myself from rolling my eyes. She continued. "We should all get together for dinner while you're here."

"Just here a few days, I'm afraid," I said, still not completely remembering who this Miranda was. I had a vague memory, and it didn't conjure warm and fuzzy feelings.

"Lovely to run into you, Miranda. Must run." Mom tugged my arm, and we practically sprinted back to the car, forgetting about the corn-on-the-cob.

Once safely tucked into Mom's old Mercedes, I turned to her. "Okay, Mom. It seems that I may not be the only one with things going on in his life. You practically tore my arm off trying to get me away from Miranda, who, by the way, I have no memory of. What was that all about?"

Mom pulled the car out of the parking space and put her foot to the floor. "The old fool," Mom muttered. Then she addressed me. "That was Miranda Connaught. I'm sure you remember her."

"Connaught," I said, feeling a slight tickle at the back of my brain. The vague memory was coming into focus. "Is she—"

"Andrea Connaught's mother. Yes, she is."

I breathed in sharply. Andrea had been my "first." She'd been my first just about everything, up to and including…well, you get the picture. I felt the hair on the back of my neck begin to rise. I'd forgotten about that summer when I was sixteen. That was the summer Andrea told me she thought she might be pregnant. I remembered how mortified and scared shitless I'd been. I could see all my dreams and my entire future melting away before my eyes like ice cream on a hot summer day until it sat there in a sad puddle, never to return to its former glory. The relief I'd felt when she told me she'd been wrong was so all-consuming that I never saw her again as if I thought she might be a bad luck talisman. I had told my mother about this situation, but as far as I knew, Andrea had never told Miranda—at least, she hadn't back then. At the time, Andrea told me she wasn't planning to tell her mother about the scare. That was then. What they'd discussed in the intervening years, I had no idea.

As I sat in my mother's car all these years later, all I could think about was how it was happening again—and the stakes were just as high, or even higher. Or at least I thought they were.

"Oh my god, Mom. I haven't come very far, have I?"

"We'll see," she said as she focused on the road. "And by the way, although I haven't seen Miranda for some time, I did bump into Andrea at the liquor store a few weeks ago. It seems she's recently divorced. Make no mistake. Miranda was trying to put the two of you back together."

That sixteen-year-old feeling washed over me again, and I immediately considered fleeing the county. But I still had things to talk to Mom about. Then I remembered Miranda mentioning "the club."

"Mom, what was that Miranda—Mrs. Connaught— said about you spending a lot of time at the club?" I knew Miranda was referring to the yacht club where Mom and Dad had been members for years. It's where Dad kept his sailboat and where I learned to sail. It was also a social club with a well-regarded restaurant, a pool, tennis courts and a spa. I hadn't realized Mom was still interested in it. "I thought you gave up going to the club."

Mom shrugged.

"So, what made you start going back? You playing tennis there again?" Mom had been one of the club's champion tennis players for her age group before Dad died. He couldn't hit the broad side of a barn, as they say, but Mom was different. Although she still played occasionally in Boston, as far as I knew, tennis at the yacht club no longer interested her. At least, that's what she'd told me. She was hiding something from me now.

Mom pulled the car into the driveway and got out, going immediately to the trunk to retrieve the groceries we'd managed to buy before running into Miranda.

I joined her behind the car. "Spill, Mom," I said.

"You won't like it," she said, slamming the trunk closed and heading toward the porch with her grocery bags.

I was only a step behind her. "Try me," I said.

Mom unlocked the door and opened it. As she stepped inside, she turned back to me and said, "I've met someone." Then she disappeared into the kitchen beyond.

I followed her, wondering precisely what she meant by having met someone. I put the two bags I was carrying on the kitchen island. "Who exactly have you met?"

"You see," she said, getting herself a glass of water from the pitcher in the fridge. "You don't like it."

"I haven't said anything of the kind. Who have you met, and why won't I like it?"

"I've been seeing a man," Mom said, taking a long drink of water.

*That's interesting*, I thought as I sat on a stool adjacent to the island. *How do I feel about this?* "Well," I said finally, "I'm okay with the general concept. Now, who is it? Will I be as okay with who it is?"

Mom hesitated a moment. "It's Jack Lawrence."

I drew a blank. "Is he someone I know?"

"He is," Mom said as she unpacked the groceries. "Remember high school?"

"You're dating one of my old classmates?" I sounded almost as shrill as Antonia was whenever she heard something she could not believe. "You're old enough to be his...mother!" I was sputtering.

When I looked at Mom's face, she was trying not to split herself laughing. "Now, that is either the most flattering thing you've ever said to me or the most outrageous. I'm going with outrageous. No, not a student from your high school."

Then the penny dropped. "Mr. Lawrence?"

"Yes, Mr. Lawrence, but I suspect you can call him Jack these days. We ran into one another at a barbeque in June. I've been having dinner with him regularly ever since."

Mr. Lawrence—Jack—was my high school art teacher back in Boston. "Wait a minute. I didn't know he lived around here. Isn't he still in Boston?"

Mom explained that Jack had retired only a few weeks before she ran into him at the barbeque. He was renting a nearby house for the summer and had now decided he wanted to be here more permanently, so he took a long-term lease. According to Mom, Jack had stopped teaching to return to his first love—art. I remembered Jack as one of the good guys in high school—one of those teachers the kids loved. I know I did. He'd been the one who discovered my talent for watercolour painting and encouraged me to go to art school. I had often wondered if he'd have thought I sold out to work as a graphic artist for an ad agency. Maybe I'd get to find out.

I was kind of happy for Mom. I suppose some part of me thought she should still be loyal to Dad, but he'd been dead for five years. Surely, I could wish my own mother happiness in this next stage of her life. I decided I'd err on the side of happiness.

"And now, Timothy Sinclair, it's time we talked about your situation."

~

It was finally time. Mom poured the wine—a pinot noir this time—and we sat down again in the Adirondack chairs under the awning, watching storm clouds gather on the horizon as the sun set behind us.

"Before I tell you what I think, which, by the way, I fully intend to do, I need to ask you a few questions." Mom held her wine glass carefully by the stem, gently swirling the ruby-red nectar as she stared into it. Then she took a sip.

I nodded and steeled myself.

Mom put her glass down gently on the wide wooden arm of the Adirondack chair and said, "Do you want to be a father?"

No one had ever asked me this before. I thought about what Antonia said when I told her I thought she didn't want to be a mother. She had said, "I didn't *want* to have a child, but I didn't *not want* to have one, either." As Mom asked the question, I realized that it summed up my own feelings quite well, although I'd never needed to think about it before. I explained this to Mom.

"So, all these years, you and Antonia had always been on the same wavelength about children in your lives." I nodded, and she continued. "Okay. Now that you're going to be a father—at least biologically—I'll ask my question again. It's a simple one. Do you *want* to be a father?"

This question was not as simple as Mom might have thought. It had too many other questions hanging on it. I was having trouble answering, so Mom asked for the third time. "In this present moment, having all the information you have right now, do you want to be a father?"

"I think maybe I do." The answer surprised even me.

"Okay," she said as if checking off the questions on some unseen form. "Do you love Antonia?"

Another hard one—or so I thought. "Yes, but—"

Mom cut me off. "There are no buts in this. Do you love her?"

"I do, but—"

Mom's hand, held up in front of my face, silenced me.

I thought for a moment, trying to compare how I felt about Antonia with how I felt about Meg. What surprised m was how different the feelings were—too different to compare, but I had to be honest. "Yes, I still do." I listened to myself. "I still love Antonia."

As the words came out of my mouth, my mind began racing with all the other possibilities. I was in love with Meg and in love with the idea of fleeing Manhattan and the life Antonia and I had built there. I thought I'd decided I wanted to leave New York and spend my life in Halifax with Meg—if she'd have me. I suddenly had the crazy idea that since Antonia wasn't keen on being a mother, maybe Meg would adopt the baby and be with me. I could take the baby to Halifax. Mom's voice broke through my jumbled thoughts.

"Tim, you and Kelly don't know this, but I was pregnant when I married your father."

Not only did I not know this, I thought she must be lying to make a point.

"It's true. But what is also true is that your father was still in university and didn't want to give up his dreams. He agonized over what to do, and I almost gave up on him. In the end, he asked me to marry him because, on balance, he knew he loved me and had figured out that we'd be good together. And we were. We realized this even after I miscarried a month after the wedding. I'm not saying that your situation is the same, but you must know that I know what I'm talking about. If both you and Antonia are prepared to be parents, there is only one thing that needs to concern you. Your child. It's no longer all about you or all about Antonia, or even all about the two of you together. It is about this life you've created."

I was shaking as I put the wine glass I'd been clutching down on the broad arm of my chair and pulled the tartan blanket around my shoulders as the first big drops of rain began to plop on the deck in front of me just beyond the awning under which we were sitting. "But what about Meg?"

"Meg." Mom turned to me. "Someone once said that the most important thing a father can do for his children is to love their mother."

A tear escaped my eye as the first clap of thunder roared through the darkening sky, and the heavens opened.

# 8

# Antonia

## 1989

*Character—the willingness to accept responsibility for one's own life—is the source from which self-respect springs.* ~ Joan Didion

I DIDN'T HAVE THE ENERGY TO FACE TIM the morning after I shared my news. I had so much on my mind as it was with the three new clients I was pitching that week that I couldn't begin to try to fathom what he was thinking. And I wasn't ready to ask yet since he seemed to need time, something I'd already had. It also occurred to me that I might be tired because of the pregnancy, but that wasn't a trap I would let myself fall into. I'd seen enough pregnant friends to have observed how often they had used pregnancy as an excuse to get out of doing something. I had always rolled my eyes at what I considered a weakness. After all, hadn't women been having children for millennia and working in the fields or something throughout their entire pregnancies? I wasn't going to be one of those women who used pregnancy as an excuse. But Tim was a different story.

How had I expected him to respond to the news that he would be a father regardless of what role, if any, he would play in the child's life? I suppose it came as something of a shock to him. I at least had to allow that.

I was thinking about this as I slid into bed after we had decided Tim would take the Murphy bed in the den. As I lay in the dark, I suspected Tim was as stunned as I had been that day when my doctor's office called. It had been the day of that critical client pitch. It would never in my wildest dreams have crossed my mind that my puzzling fatigue was related to pregnancy, but it had been bugging me, so I had reluctantly called my doctor, and he'd insisted on several tests. I had hoped he might prescribe a magic pill to cure my lethargy, but that wasn't to be. And here I was.

On that first night after Tim had arrived back in New York when I had asked him what he would do, I hadn't expected him to tell me he'd eventually discuss the situation with his mother. I knew he'd been close to her at one time and that he'd been concerned he hadn't seen her very often in recent years since his father died. Our lives were so busy that he never seemed to find the time. I suppose I should have encouraged him to see her more often, even if he went without me, because I had always felt the sainted Grace Sinclair didn't like me. I couldn't even imagine what she would think when she heard the news that she was going to be a grandmother. I had never seen her angry, but I suspected this might be a bridge too far, even for someone as unflappable as she'd always appeared to me. In fact, I'd envied her. I wondered if perfect Grace Sinclair, with her perfectly well-curated life, would be able to help Tim. I certainly couldn't. I wondered when he planned to leave for Maine.

I'd never mastered the ability to maintain that steady, composed attitude toward situations where things didn't go as planned. I was a planner, and when plans went off the rails, I often found myself following right along behind them. I knew I had a reputation at the office for being somewhat explosive, but everyone knew I recovered quickly. Lisa-Marie had been the target of my wrath on more than one occasion, which was probably one of the main reasons she was more than a bit frightened of me. The truth is that my fury was perhaps more directed toward myself than anyone else. At least I had that much self-knowledge. This situation was probably the most egregious example of thwarted plans that I'd ever experienced in my life to date. Having a baby had not been on the agenda.

So, why hadn't I gone ahead and had an abortion? Why had I not taken matters into my own hands—as was my usual approach—early enough that I might not even have had to mention it to Tim? I had been too busy. My mind had been on other things. I hadn't gotten around to it. Who doesn't get around to having an abortion? Me. And as I lay there in bed that night, I couldn't give myself a good reason for that non-decision.

It wasn't that I was opposed to abortion in principle. I'd even helped a friend a few years earlier when she needed someone to be with when she had one. I had picked her up in a taxi and deposited her at the clinic. The nurse told me to return in a few hours, so I'd walked around a part of the city that I didn't frequent, thinking not about my friend who was at that moment undergoing a procedure or how she might be feeling after it was over. I was thinking about work. Of course I was since that's what consumed most of my twenties. But I also remember thinking how utterly stupid she'd been to have gotten herself into this situation. It was all so abstract—all right for someone else. How foolish we can be. And how arrogant. I suppose I'd never really considered the possibility that I might be in the same position someday. The prospect had never even crossed my mind. And now I was going to be a mother? All I could think about was that I had no business being a mother.

I got up early the morning after Tim arrived, so I was sure to be gone before he got up. I had a piece of toast and made a pot of coffee, leaving enough for him to have a stale cup at whatever time he found it. Then I took out a sheet of paper and wrote him a letter. I had to tell him that I'd remembered our dreams about the future—the places we'd wanted to go and the things we hoped to accomplish together. But I also needed him to know what I'd finally decided. Sometime during the night, I woke up, and one thing was crystal clear: I had to fall back onto the only way I knew how to live my life. I had to take my life into my own hands—and I'd have no one to blame but myself.

As I wrote the letter, focusing on how I was taking responsibility for my decisions, I couldn't resist a little dig. What can I say? It's who I am. I had to emphasize that I had never deceived him. If he chose to interpret that to mean I was pointing the finger of deception right at him, then that was his choice. I wasn't the one who had fallen for someone else. I wasn't the one who seemed torn. (I was reminded of that gaggingly stupid song from a singer called Mary MacGregor ten or more years earlier. It was called "Torn Between Two Lovers," and it had always made me snicker. I wasn't snickering now.)

I folded the note, put it on the kitchen island and left for the office.

~

Tim and I spent an awkward ten days together at the apartment. Our conversations were stilted, and we had made no progress in solving anything. I had expected some kind of reaction to my note, but he said nothing. It was infuriating, but I decided to keep my feelings to myself for a bit longer.

On the morning of the eleventh day, I got up to find Tim had left the apartment before me. I had an early meeting across town. When I finally arrived in my office, it was mid-morning. I dropped my briefcase on the desk and myself into my chair and then picked up the phone to call Nathan. Before I could say anything beyond, "Hi, Nathan," he jumped in.

"How are things going, Toni? How's Tim handling everything? What's going to happen now?"

"Oh, Nathan, I wish I knew all the answers. It's been so awkward being together in the apartment. I have no idea what's going on in Tim's head or what's going to happen now. All I know is that I've laid it all out for him, and now the ball's in his court. And the truth is, I'm not even sure how I want him to react. I suppose I just want some kind of reaction."

I could hear Nathan "hmmming" in the background as if he might be trying to figure out how to answer. Then he ignored the line of conversation anyway. He continued. "Are you feeling that maternal instinct yet?"

I had given Nathan chapter and verse on how I didn't think I was cut out to be a mother regardless of what happened. He had suggested I'd find that maternal instinct buried deep inside me if I could only get it out.

I laughed in that kind of ironic way people do when something sounds funny on one level, but in reality, it's deadly serious. "Sorry. I'm not sure I have any, Nathan."

"Let's have dinner tonight, Toni, unless you think under the circumstances you should avoid me and spend all your evenings with Tim."

I sighed. "I'm not sure Tim will even be there tonight. I'm not sure what his plans are. I only know that he plans to visit his mother in Maine at some point."

"Ah," Nathan said knowingly. "Time to run to Mommy. I cannot even imagine what the perfect Mrs. Sinclair will have to say about all of this." Nathan had met Grace twice. The first time he met her was when she visited New York on a buying trip to the fabric district, and we all got together for dinner at our apartment. That was back when Nathan was dragging his female friends out for dinner on every possible occasion in a vain attempt to ensure no one realized he was gay. I'd been one of them until I met Tim. By that time, he'd moved to second stringers. Thank god he'd stopped that nonsense.

"I'm sure Grace will have something sensible to say about it all after she gets over the shock of finding out I'm going to be the mother of her grandchild." I sighed again.

"Why don't I make a seven o'clock reservation at La Fresca, and if you can't make it, just call me by six."

"Is that so you can find someone to take my place?" I could almost hear Nathan thinking on the other end of the line. "Don't worry. You don't have to tell me about him. Not yet anyway," I said, knowing full well he'd tell me about any new relationship (presuming I was right and there was one) when he was ready and not before.

Nathan knew it would take something earth-shattering to keep me from dinner at La Fresca, my favourite place in the world. I could almost taste the *Risotto alla Milanese*, laden with butter, white wine, parmesan cheese and saffron!

At four-fifteen that afternoon, just as I was refiling the material from the client presentation I'd nailed, Lisa-Marie appeared in my doorway.

"Mr. Sinclair stopped by the office this morning while you were at that meeting." She stuck out her hand, which was holding a pink message slip, the kind she used when she took my phone messages. Unlike phone messages, though, this one was folded. "He left this note for you."

I turned from the filing cabinet and walked over to her since she hadn't moved. I took the note from her and opened it. "Why didn't you give it to me this morning when I got back from the meeting?"

Lisa-Marie shrugged. "I guess I forgot. Sorry."

I scanned the note, which was in Tim's handwriting, and then looked up at Lisa-Marie, who hadn't left her spot in the doorway. "I suppose you've taken the opportunity to read this?"

She shook her head wildly and turned on her heel. Of course, she had.

The note was short and simple—and in Tim's handwriting. "Have rented a car to drive to Maine. Decided to go immediately. I'll let you know when I'll be back. T." That was it. I'd be dining with Nathan this evening, after all.

# 9

## Tim

### 1989

*In any given moment, we have two options: to step
forward into growth or step back into safety.*
~ Abraham Maslow

AFTER MY REVELATION AND MOM'S THOUGHTFUL ADVICE (at least it seemed like advice to me, although I had no idea what to do with it), I spent two more days in Maine before heading back to New York. Since I already had my suitcase with me, I figured there was nothing to be gained by seeing Antonia again before I returned to Halifax to sort things out, so I dropped the rental car at JFK, bought a ticket to Halifax and hopped on a plane. I was still massively confused, but Meg had given me that tiny opening, and I wasn't going to blow the chance to see her again—and to explain myself. But I still had something gnawing at the back of my brain. Maybe it had something to do with Mom's final words as she shut my driver's side door and leaned in to kiss my cheek before I drove away.

"Tim, my darling boy," she said, leaning close to my ear as if to avoid being overheard. That was funny since there was no one else around. "Tim, your father and I always taught you that the only reward you get from taking the easy way out is that it's easy."

I remember them saying that to me on numerous occasions, especially when I was a teenager. This time, though, I didn't even have a clue what the easy way was.

~

It was after dark when I arrived back at my cottage on St. Margaret's Bay outside Halifax. I liked the darkness here. I had once loved the twinkling city lights and how New York truly was the city that never slept, but something had changed.

I dropped my small suitcase on the floor but didn't turn on the lights. I walked into the living room. There was no moon to give that warm, ethereal glow to the room that night, and I remembered something I'd learned when I was researching the Titanic disaster, ostensibly to provide more depth to my ad campaign for Eastern Oil—the same job that had triggered Meg's instinct to cut and run. I remembered several mentions from various survivor statements that it had been moonless the night the ship struck the iceberg in the North Atlantic. And I wondered why a disaster moment had settled itself in my brain.

I walked across the room to the window to stand beside my easel and look out into the darkness. I could hear the first drops of rain on the window and wondered if we were in for one of those nor'easters the eastern seaboard is so famous for. I leaned down toward the drafting table next to the easel and flicked on the task light. It gave the room just enough illumination to be eerie.

In the dim light, I could see the shape but not the details of the watercolour portrait I'd left on the easel. It was Meg. I remember thinking that if I never saw her again, this might be the only way I'd have to remember her. But now, she seemed at least willing to hear me out, whether I deserved it or not. I still felt a sense of dread when I pulled the covers up over myself half an hour later, hoping the light of a new day and a chance to talk to Meg would fix everything. Somehow, I knew it wouldn't.

~

I had arranged to meet Meg for coffee at a café near the waterfront in the city. Despite my rented cottage being only a ten-minute drive from Meg's house on the bay, she had insisted we go into town separately and meet there. She said something about having to meet with her dissertation supervisor, and I knew she had a lot of work left to do to finish her PhD work in time to graduate in the spring. So, I let it go and tried not to take it as a personal affront, although I couldn't have blamed her if she did mean it that way.

I arrived at the place fifteen minutes early. I needed time to collect my thoughts—as if I hadn't been trying to do just that for the forty minutes it took me to drive into town, find a parking space and walk two blocks. I ordered a pot of coffee and a muffin, but I couldn't eat a bite. My throat was dry, and the blueberry bran muffin, as moist as it was, tasted like sawdust in my mouth. I put it down and wished I had something stronger than coffee to drink. After narrowly avoiding choking, I went back to my contemplation.

Meg had sounded slightly yielding on the phone, a situation I didn't dare hope might be a reality. Perhaps she really did accept that I hadn't meant to deceive her. I just hadn't been able to find a way to tell her about my client—a client that flew in the face of everything she believed in so fiercely it was almost frightening. But Antonia's unexpected arrival had rectified that little omission with the sudden force of a tornado destroying everything in its path. I tried to feel once again the anger I'd felt toward Antonia at the time, but I couldn't seem to find the intensity that had been there before. Suddenly the jangling of the bell attached to the café's door drew my attention, and there she was.

It was raining again. I watched as Meg tried to fold up her umbrella without causing a torrent of water to cascade into the café. Then she stood up straight, pulled down the hood of her yellow rain slicker and shook out her wonderfully wild hair. Her cheeks were light pink, and her eyes were sparkling. I could feel myself falling into a bottomless abyss. I had no way of knowing if I'd find a way out. Then she saw me.

The smile she'd had only moments ago for the café's owner dissolved into a flat expression I could not read. I thought I might see displeasure, annoyance, even anger, although I'd hoped for happiness. I saw none of these emotions written on her face.

I stood up as Meg approached the table. We did that awkward dance of pecking one another on the cheek by way of greeting, avoided hugging and took up our places on opposite sides of the small wooden table. I poured her a cup of coffee from the pot the server had left on the table, and she shrugged off her wet raincoat. As inappropriate as it might have been, I couldn't help smiling at this beautiful, wild woman whose passion for the environment put the rest of us to shame.

"Meg, it's wonderful to see you," I began. "How are you? How's the dissertation work going? Do you want something to eat?" I couldn't seem to stop the stream of inane chatter.

Meg reached over and put her hand on mine as if to quiet me. "It's fine, Tim. I want to talk to you as much as you want to talk to me."

The server arrived at the table, and Meg ordered a croissant and jam, then took a sip of coffee. "Tim, I think I owe you an apology." She owed me an apology? I should have been on the floor grovelling for forgiveness. Meg continued. "I think I may have overreacted to the situation at your cottage that evening."

The situation. I suppose she really meant Antonia, but she couldn't bring herself to say her name. At least, that's how it seemed to me as I sat there listening like someone who deserved this kind of consideration—which I didn't.

"No, Meg. Your reaction was completely reasonable and understandable."

"No, Tim, it wasn't, and I see that now. How were you to know what was going to happen that evening? Maybe that was the moment you were going to tell me about your work, and if we'd been alone, I might have been able to think more clearly." Again, she couldn't seem to say Antonia's name. "Anyway, I had a chance to talk it out with my grandmother, and she helped me to see things more clearly."

I still hadn't had a chance to meet Meg's grandmother, Dr. Ellen McMaster. I had spoken with her on the phone once when I had answered it at Meg's place, and she seemed like quite a woman whose fierce love for her granddaughter, whom she had brought up after Meg's parents died in a car crash, was unshakeable. Dr. McMaster was a retired physician and someone I would have liked to get to know. I shuddered to think what she must think of me at this point. I had fences to mend.

"I should have told you from the very beginning, Meg. And I'm sorry."

The server put Meg's croissant in front of her. She started pulling little pieces off and popping them into her mouth. "I'm glad you didn't," she said. I must have looked puzzled. "If you'd told me about your New York work when we first met, I wouldn't have spoken another word to you. If that had happened, I wouldn't have gotten to know you as a person, and I wouldn't have had a chance to try to get you to see the world more the way I see it."

I was amazed. I had not been expecting this. "I don't know what to say, Meg."

"Just say we can start over." She stopped eating and tapped her mouth with a paper napkin.

There was nothing I wanted more in the world than to start over at that moment. But we weren't there yet.

"So, how was New York?" Meg didn't look at me as she asked the question—the question I'd been dreading.

I took a deep breath. "First, Meg," I said, taking her hand across the table, "there is nothing I'd like more than to start over." She smiled and let me hold it for a moment. Then I let it go and sat back, summoning all the nerve I could muster. "As for New York…it was…surprising."

"Surprising? In what way?" Meg sipped her coffee.

"Well, of course, I saw Antonia." I saw Meg stiffen, but she didn't react. "We share ownership of that apartment in Manhattan." I was stalling. "As it turns out, she's pregnant."

Finally, I had said it.

Meg's head jerked up from where she had begun to put globs of jam on what remained of her croissant. "She's what?" she said quietly. I had expected more of an eruption, but I found this stillness even more disturbing.

I swallowed. "Pregnant, but she doesn't—"

"Pregnant," Meg said quietly as she put her knife down on the plate, folded her hands on the table and looked directly at me. "You could have led with that, Tim."

"Meg, you don't understand. Antonia doesn't want to be a mother."

"Sad for the child," she said. "So, what now?"

Meg's intensity was rattling me. What now, indeed? I thought about that stupid fantasy I'd had of Meg saying, no problem. We could raise the child together. I thought of all the things I could say that would make her see that the two of us had a future together, but nothing came out of my mouth. My mother's words came back to me. "The most important thing a father can do for his children is to love their mother." Then I watched Meg as she slowly pushed her chair back from the table, put each arm into her raincoat, picked up her purse and umbrella and walked toward the door. She opened the door and walked back out into the rain without even a backward glance.

I was pinned to my seat as I watched her walk away. I didn't even say goodbye.

# 10

# Antonia

## 1989

*Love is everything it's cracked up to be. That's why
people are so cynical about it. It really is worth
fighting for, being brave for, risking everything for.
And the trouble is, if you don't risk anything, you
risk even more.*
~ Erica Jong, *Fear of Flying*

AFTER TIM LEFT FOR MAINE TO SEE HIS MOTHER, I didn't hear from him until more than a week later when he left me a message on our answering machine at home to tell me he'd be back in New York the next day. "Hi Antonia," he said, "I'll be back tomorrow. I'm driving from Halifax. See you when I get back."

Halifax? I only knew he'd rented a car and driven to Maine to talk to his mother—at least, that's what he said he was doing. Now he was in Halifax. I should have known he'd go back there. This couldn't be good. I had no idea what had happened or what to expect, but Tim and I had a history, and I needed to see this through.

It was early Sunday evening when I heard Tim's key in the lock. I was in the kitchen, toying with the idea of making pasta for a late dinner and thinking about the conversation Nathan and I had at dinner. Nathan had floated an idea about what I should do. It was crazy but interesting, nonetheless.

Nathan floated the idea that he and I and the baby should become a family.

"Why not?" he said. "You and I've been best friends for years, and we get along superbly. That's more than most straight couples these days seem to have. And you do know I love you, Toni. Maybe not the way Tim does, but it's love any way you look at it." Although all of that was true, and we both shared a love of order in our lives, I knew it would never work. We would both have other "friends" in our lives, and that might not bode well for a child. But I loved him for suggesting it. I came back to reality when Tim interrupted my thoughts.

"Hi, Antonia," Tim said, appearing in the doorway to the kitchen. "How are you?" He sounded tired.

"I'm fine, Tim."

Tim didn't say anything. Instead, he just slumped against the wall.

I walked past him into the living room. "Come on. We'll have a drink." I poured one for each of us—scotch for Tim and sparkling water for me since my doctor read me the riot act about drinking while pregnant—and we sat down in the living room.

"You look tired, Tim."

"Yeah," he said, sipping his drink. "I guess I am. Twelve hours of driving will do that to me."

"Then, why didn't you fly back and forth? The arrangements we have to make won't take that long."

"About that," he said. "I drove my Jeep back so I could bring all my things. I didn't want to ship my art materials." He said all this as if I understood his meaning. If I did, I chose to ignore my conclusions. I needed him to be clear about his intentions. But first—a Jeep?

"Your Jeep? When on earth did you acquire a Jeep? What happened to your Supra?" On that fateful night back at his cottage with Megan, he'd mentioned it was in the shop, as much as I'd rather hated that car, I expected him to get it back.

In my view, Tim's Supra had been his early-mid-life-crisis acquisition and one I never liked. I had always thought it was a bit déclassé—the kind of car men drove when they were trying to say, "Look at me," instead of, "Look how successful I am," the sentiment I thought he should trumpet. I had always pictured him in a BMW or even a Mercedes in due time. But a Jeep? At least he wasn't still driving that van.

"I sold it," he said. "The Supra never was very practical, right?"

"Since when had practicality ever entered into our vocabulary?" I corrected myself. "I mean, your vocabulary." I didn't want to assume there was any kind of "we" left. Tim just shrugged, and then his shoulders sagged as if in surrender. "How long are you staying?" I said.

Tim looked at me as if he didn't understand the question. "Here? You mean here in this apartment?"

I nodded. That was close enough.

"I guess until we decide it's not the best place to raise a baby."

And that was the moment when looming motherhood took on a whole new reality for me. I felt the first kick—a tiny life telling me she was there (or he maybe). A thumbs up? Maybe, but I wasn't so sure.

~

Tim returned to the office to much fanfare from Ken. At the first staff meeting a week later, Ken gushed over Tim and his work and how fortunate we were that he'd decided to continue to pursue his upwardly mobile career at Moffatt, Green, Berger and Partners. Then we moved to client updates, and it was almost like old times once more. Almost.

I had told Joannie I needed a half hour with Ken that afternoon. I couldn't wait any longer. In fact, I couldn't hide it any longer. I had to tell Ken about upcoming motherhood. As I sat in my office later that afternoon, just before my meeting with him, I felt sad. I knew I was grieving the lost opportunity for Nathan, Tim and me to form our own agency. Nathan and I had talked about this. He and I couldn't do it without Tim, who had lost interest (if his interest had ever been there at all), and now that I was having a baby, everything was changing. It wasn't that I was abandoning my climb to the top and through the glass ceiling. I just knew that the route might be different.

"Ken, thanks for seeing me," I said, taking a seat in his men's-club-like office. Every time I sat in this office, I looked around and considered how I'd redecorate it if I sat in that chair. The first thing to go would be the hideous leather furniture. Then I'd personally rip all the dark wood and wainscoting from the walls with a crowbar.

"I always have time for my staff, as you know, Antonia. What can I do for you today?"

I carefully arranged my red blazer over the black sheath dress. The dress had been an impulse buy at the Saks sale a year before. I couldn't resist the label (Karl Lagerfeld) or the price (half off), but it was too big for me. Right now, though, I was grateful for my lack of self-control. It just about fit around my waist at this point. I took a deep breath and came directly to the point. "Ken, I'm pregnant."

He sat there for a moment, looking like someone might look if his doctor had just told him he had lice. It looked like a cross between disbelief and horror.

"But you can't be, Antonia. I'm counting on you. And, of course, you're not married."

Ken was a bit of a prude about things like that. A pregnancy was proof-positive that one of his single employees wasn't as virginal as he thought.

"No, Ken, I'm not married," I said. "But it doesn't change the fact that I'm going to need a few weeks off. The baby is due on

December twenty-seventh. I can work right up until Christmas Eve, and I'll plan to be back in the office the third week in January. Will that work for you?" I wasn't even sure it would work for me.

Ken still looked shell-shocked. He was still back on the news of the pregnancy and hadn't yet moved on to the plan going forward. "But who's the father, Antonia? Are you telling me you and Tim are having a baby?"

Ken had long known that two of his employees were a couple. I remembered a stilted conversation we'd had at a Christmas party shortly after Tim and I moved in together. He was not a supporter of unmarried people living together. I suppose, at this point, he was considering how right he'd been to disapprove.

"Yes, Ken. We are. Now, what about my plan? Will that work for you?"

He asked me to tell him again, which I did. Then he shook his head and said, "That won't work, Antonia. You'll need more time off. And then, how much will you be available? We put in long days here."

I was slightly insulted. "I cannot imagine why you would say I'd need more time off or suggest that I don't know we put in long days. I can assure you, Ken, that I will be back in the office the third week in January, ready to work as I always have. Who knows? Maybe motherhood will make me even more determined." My head started to fill with images of bottles and cribs and nannies. I shivered slightly, realizing I had no idea what I was getting myself into. I knew I was probably in over my head, but I'd find a way to come up for air. I always did.

"Well, Antonia," he said, seeming to have recovered somewhat from this obviously distressing news, "you've never let me down yet. If you say you'll have it under control, I'll gladly give you a few weeks off to recover from this situation."

This situation. I almost laughed.

~

Tim settled back into work, and the two of us seemed to settle back into, if not bliss, at least a domestic truce. I had always been able to feel a depth in our relationship, and I wondered how we'd weather this most recent turbulence. Surely depth provided a bit of a foundation of stability.

We started out talking about banal, superficial topics at dinner every evening— the weather, the city, new restaurants, the office, of course. Then we progressed to gossip. You might think that gossip is superficial, but I assure you that when two people in a close relationship are talking about other people, they have moved to a deeper level of conversation than the weather. On Saturday afternoon, three weeks after we had settled back into our life in New York, Tim suggested we go to a movie.

"Let's see what everyone is talking about," he said.

And, so, we took in the three pm matinee of *Dead Poets Society*. As we walked home, Tim was pensive. He even took my arm as we walked the eight blocks back to our building through the fallen autumn leaves that had accumulated along the way.

Just as we reached the building entrance, he stopped under the canopy and turned to me. "I was thinking about that line in the movie—you know, that line Robin Williams's character said."

I had no idea which line he was talking about. John Keating, the teacher Robin Williams played, had delivered many lines worth pondering. I shook my head.

"Mr. Keating said, 'Just when you think you know something, you have to look at it in another way. Even though it may seem silly or wrong, you must try.' Remember that one?"

I did remember it.

"I think it's time I took that advice. It's time for me to look at something in another way. Antonia, we should get married."

And if that wasn't enough for me to consider, it wasn't the only thing Tim had decided to look at differently.

# 11

# Tim

## 1989

*You must strive to find your own voice because the longer you wait to begin, the less likely you are going to find it at all.*
~ Mr. Keating, *Dead Poets Society*

I COULDN'T GET HIM OUT OF MY HEAD. It was the first time in my life a movie had so moved me. A movie, for god's sake! There was something so compelling about Mr. Keating, the teacher, and his conviction that his students—in this case, well-off boys in an ultra-elite boarding school—could be so much more than they were. And that was really something for a group of over-privileged kids who already considered themselves better. He wanted them to see how they might be missing out on real life despite their apparent advantages. Was I one of those boys?

I'd been brought up with the proverbial silver spoon in my mouth. My parents might not have been the ultra-rich (there's always someone richer and someone poorer than you, my father always used to say), but my sister and I had so many advantages: good schools, music lessons, ballet lessons for Kelly, sailing lessons, a summer home, vacation to Europe and the Caribbean every year, and the list went on. I'd never done an inventory, but if I did, it would read like that. Yet, with all that and an enviable Madison Avenue job with a paycheque to match, I'd been carrying an undercurrent of discontent for years.

I guess I had blamed it on Antonia in recent memory, but I now knew it had nothing to do with her or our relationship. It was within me. When John Keating said, "*Carpe Diem*, seize the day, boys, make your lives extraordinary," I felt him talking directly to me. That was what was missing—something around which I could build an extraordinary life. And my extraordinary life began with the thrill of not knowing who this child would be but knowing that I had only a limited lifetime to get to know it. So, I told Antonia we should get married.

The truth is that I'd been thinking about this for a few days. That's why I'd found myself skulking around Tiffany two days earlier, emerging with one of their tiny turquoise boxes. I had my hand in my pocket, ready to pull it out at the right moment.

"Have you lost your mind, Tim?"

The first words out of her mouth were hardly the words an expectant suitor yearns to hear, but what did I expect? I'm sure my proposal had sounded just as off-putting to her as her words did to me. I decided to keep the box in my pocket for just a little while longer.

"I might have, Antonia. But the truth is we *have* loved each other for years. We're usually good together—if you can forgive me for the most recent transgressions. And we're about to become parents. It might not seem like the strongest basis for a marriage, but I'd wager it's more than many people have."

She glanced at the door where two of our neighbours were just on their way out. Judging by how they were dressed, it looked like they were probably off to a fancy restaurant. "Let's go up, Tim. I have to pee."

We rode the elevator silently, and I waited for her to finish whatever she was doing in the bathroom. She took much longer than usual, so I imagine she sat there alone, considering her options. I sat on the white sofa, propped up by white and cream cushions, looking around at the perfection of the white walls, cream hassocks, and cream shag rug, wondering what it would look like with a toddler running around. It was an image I didn't think I should share with Antonia, who loved the perfection of her décor. But it did make me consider the possibility that I hadn't thought very far ahead. So, we would get married and then the baby would arrive. Then what?

I needed to hear Antonia's answer to my proposal before I dared suggest the next step in my grand plan. And then there would be the awkwardness of telling my mother. I heard the door to the bathroom open and the click of the light going off.

"Well, Timothy Sinclair," Antonia said as she sank into the chair opposite me, "I must say you never cease to surprise me—"

"I know you've never liked surprises—"

Antonia held up her hand to silence me. "As I may have mentioned that fateful evening in your cottage in Nova Scotia, people change."

I was about to say that she didn't, but I thought it might be in my best interests to keep my mouth shut. I still hadn't gotten to the top of the abyss yet.

"Did you ever have to read Nietzsche in college, Tim?"

"I vaguely remember something long and unceasingly boring," I said, trying to remember anything specific about a long-dead philosopher. "I'm having trouble nailing down anything specific about him, though. Why?"

"I was a bit of a nerd back in my first couple of years in undergrad at Harvard—before business school. You know I couldn't afford to slack off. I wasn't one of those trust fund kids."

"Like me."

"I didn't say that, but you didn't have to rely on scholarships to pay your tuition. I did. You know this. Anyway, I fancied myself a bit of an intellectual back then before I realized that academics weren't going to get me up to and through any glass ceiling that would pay enough for me to be able to go to a class reunion someday and rub a few people's noses in it. But while I was still on that intellectual path, I read a lot of philosophy. I don't know if I truly understood it all back then, but Nietzsche's work resonated with me. I might even go so far as to say that it influenced the direction I took in moving into the advertising business."

I had no idea what she was talking about but thought better of saying anything. I was thinking about the old saying, "It is better to stay silent and be thought stupid than to open your mouth and remove all doubt." That's what I was going for anyway. I just nodded. She continued.

"The important thing about Nietzsche—at least to me—was that he advocated creating perfection in oneself by using our internal creative drive. I think that's what steered the last ten years of my life. But now, I'm no longer in complete control, and that freaks me out." Antonia picked up the red leather-bound book (that looked suspiciously like a diary) I hadn't noticed on the table and fanned the pages until she seemed to have found what she was looking for. "I remember the day I wrote this one down, Tim, but I didn't have any idea when it would come back to me. 'There is always some madness in love. But there is also always some reason in madness.' Timothy Sinclair, yes, I agree. We *should* get married."

My heart seemed to stop for a few beats as I realized my life was about to change. I slid the little turquoise box out of my pocket, opened it and lifted the ring from its black velvet cushion. I slipped the two-carat, pear-shaped solitaire on her finger and took a deep breath. I still had to tell her the rest of my plan. But perhaps that could wait a few days until the idea of getting married sank in for both of us.

~

"Have you told your mother yet that we're getting married, Tim?" Antonia said four days later as we sat in her office sharing sushi for a working lunch.

I expertly lifted a piece of sashimi with my chopsticks, dabbed it in the tiny cup of soy sauce and stuffed it in my mouth. "Not yet," I said rudely, speaking with my mouth full, hoping she might forget the question.

"What did you say? Did you tell her yet?"

I swallowed and wiped my mouth with a paper napkin. "Not yet."

"You know it's time, Tim. When are you planning to tell her? Should we visit her and tell her together?"

I'm sure Antonia couldn't miss the panicked look on my face. I could feel my eyes bulging, and I considered shouting but caught myself just in time. After all, we were in the office. I was about to say that doing it in person together was probably not the best idea. *Hmm*, I thought, *we are indeed in the office. That means that we're socially required to keep down the noise.* Maybe now was the best time to tell Antonia about my plan. She'd be forced to react quietly. Yes, now was the moment.

"Antonia, there's something I've been meaning to discuss with you."

Her head bobbed up from where she'd been eyeing the last piece of California roll.

"I'm leaving the agency."

She looked confused. "Leaving the agency? This agency?"

I nodded.

"You've had another offer?"

"Not exactly," I said, not daring to meet her penetrating gaze.

She put her chopsticks down on the napkin on the desk and sat up straight. "Well, what exactly do you mean, then?"

"I just mean I'm not going to work here anymore."

"So, you do have new employment."

I breathed in deeply and let it out before answering. "No, I don't. I'm just leaving." I thought for a moment. "To pursue other interests."

"To pursue other interests? Of course, you know that's what people say when they've been fired. Did Ken fire you? If he did, he can't do that. I'll speak to him—"

"No! Don't speak to him." I fiddled with my napkin. "I haven't told him yet. I wanted to discuss it with you first."

"So, your idea of a discussion is to tell me what decision you've already made?"

"I didn't mean it like that, Antonia. Your input does matter, but this is an important step for me, and I wanted you to be the first one to know."

She sat back, deflated. "I'm too tired and pregnant for this drama, Tim. Just spit it out. What the hell are you going to do with yourself if you leave this fantastic job without another even more fantastic one to go to?"

"I want to be an artist. I'm good, Antonia. I know I am."

"Have you been reading those art magazines featuring your old nemesis, Wyatt Lee? He's made an international name for himself in the art world, and you're jealous. Is that what this is all about?"

I allowed myself to be a bit insulted by this. "No, Antonia, it has nothing to do with Wyatt. But it is true that I think my work is just as good as his, and I want the chance to figure it out. I think this is what I'm supposed to do with my life."

She sat back with her hands folded over her baby bump. "And what about money? I make a decent wage, but we may have to make some changes to our living arrangements. And that will be expensive."

"About that. I don't think I ever mentioned the small trust fund my father arranged for me before he died. It's not enormous, but it does have enough money for us to buy a brownstone after we sell the apartment."

Antonia tapped the pencil she'd taken from a pencil holder cup. "That might work, but…"

I wasn't exactly sure what she was thinking about as she trailed off, but I had a pretty good idea. "I'll set up a studio at home and be a househusband. I can take care of our baby while you work toward that partnership you deserve here at the agency."

Antonia stopped tapping the pencil and began tapping her foot. That was a good sign. I'd seen her do it before at client pitches. She'd sit there listening to the client's idiotic questions about the pitch they'd just seen and figure out the best way to skewer them, then reel them in. I knew my best move here was to keep quiet until she'd had a chance to figure it out. I could almost see the wheels in her head turning as she considered all the permutations and combinations of what she was about to say. Finally, she looked up.

Antonia reached her hand across the desk to me. "Timothy Sinclair, we have a deal."

We shook hands and then laughed. I had just been promoted (at least that's the story I would tell myself).

# 12

# Antonia

## 1989

*Happy is the man who finds a true friend, and far*
*happier is he who finds that true friend in his wife.*
~ Franz Schubert

I WAS NEVER ONE OF THOSE LITTLE GIRLS who dreamed about her wedding. Growing up, I had friends who used to buy fat bridal magazines every month. On the weekends, we'd get together and cut out our favourites, pressing the magazine pages inside diaries. At least, that's what my friends did. I always feigned interest and pretended to cut out my favourites among the virginal, white frothy confections, but no one ever noticed that I didn't really ever do it. That's the thing about girls. They're so wrapped up in themselves that they don't notice anyone else. But if you had been able to talk to the group of us, you could have come away with the idea that we all truly cared about one another. Nothing could have been further from the truth. There is nothing so narcissistic as a teenage girl. Anyway, I never felt like I was part of the group, so I developed my aversion to spending time with women. And although I preferred the company of men, I had never felt that burning desire to be someone's wife.

I didn't see any particular value in attaching my future to some unknown quantity known as a husband. That's probably partly because my mother didn't have one. I grew up watching her claw her way through life, working so I could have the opportunities she didn't have. My father had left when I was a baby, so I never knew him, and I suppose the idea that a husband was useful never ignited in my brain. Then I met Tim.

That's not to say I ever really thought about marrying him. I guess I expected that we'd be a team—that our love would be the foundation and structure to support our business and home life. But that never included me being anyone's wife. So, when Tim said, "Antonia, we should get married," I thought, "Yes, we probably should." And the fact that he didn't say, "Antonia, will you marry me?" was what did it.

You see, I never thought about what a marriage proposal should look like, either. Asking someone to marry you is a bit fraught. You're putting yourself out there on a limb, risking that the person on the receiving end of the proposal might just take out an axe and chop that limb off. But putting it out there that marriage is something that we, as a team, should do under the current circumstances was so much better. That being said, though, I needed to think about the situation a bit more before agreeing that we *should* get married. So, I sat on the toilet for a bit longer than necessary, ruminating. I suppose to some degree, in the back of my mind, I was ready for that possibility to raise its head, but I wasn't prepared for Tim's next volley.

"I'm leaving the agency."

I was sure I'd heard him wrong. "Leaving the agency? This agency?" *Of course*, I thought, he's *had another offer. He's good, and other agencies know it. Maybe this could be a good opportunity for us to stretch out as a team. I could stay at Moffatt, Green, Berger and Partners (and finally get to be one of those partners eventually) while Tim makes his mark in another agency.* "So, you've had an offer then?"

"Not exactly," Tim said, totally avoiding looking me in the eye.

I knew something was up, so I stopped eating and asked him to be specific. I could see his hesitation. Whatever it was, he wasn't comfortable sharing. But he had to. We were a team.

That's when he dropped the bomb—a bomb that, in my view, was even bigger than me telling him I was pregnant. He simply told me he was not going to work here anymore. And no, he had no future employment plans. He was going to be an artist. An artist! Who, in their right mind, would be an artist these days?

Yes, I knew all about his old friend Wyatt, the internationally recognized artistic genius. Still, we also knew other people in the city who were eking out a living as artists of one sort or another. There was Nathan's old friend Barry, the actor who had one Broadway credit and now waited tables in a bistro in Greenwich Village. Then there was Annalise, an old friend of Tim's sister, Kelly. Annalise had been a ballet school classmate of Kelly's when she was fourteen or so. Tim had told me the story of how Kelly had spectacularly fallen during the end-of-year performance, which ended her ballet dancing dreams. But Annalise eventually graduated and was now a dancer with the New York City Ballet. Regardless of how internationally recognized the company was, Annalise herself seemed to live from hand to mouth. (Of course, she wasn't a star. Who could say, though? Maybe she would be one day, but she sure wasn't then. The sad truth is that there isn't room for many stars in the arts business.) The bottom line was the bottom line. If Tim wanted to play artist, I'd be the sole breadwinner. I realized I had grave misgivings about moving in this direction. Then he mentioned the trust fund.

My ears perked up the minute I heard that it just might be possible for us to buy something bigger and more practical than the apartment we currently owned. We'd make some money selling it, but the brownstones we loved would still be out of reach without a cash infusion. My mind was racing with thoughts of picking up a brownstone needing renovation, doing the work to turn it into something special, then turning a tidy profit at some point. Oh, and it would be a better place to bring up a child. But Tim, a househusband? Honestly, I wasn't sure about that part of the plan. But I kept that to myself, and we made an agreement. Now, I'd have to learn to live with it.

~

Tim finally broke the news to his mother—the marriage news. He'd fortified himself with a small glass of scotch one evening not long after we'd made our agreement, then picked up the phone. I left him alone and went into the bedroom so he wouldn't think I was eavesdropping which, naturally, I was. I could hear every word from the other side of the bedroom door.

"Hi, Mom," he began. "I have news."

There was a pause. I supposed Grace was speculating on what kind of news it could be. Or maybe she was ignoring him and telling him how wonderful it was to hear from him. Blah-blah-blah. After a long pause on Tim's end, I heard him say, "No, not that, Mom. No promotion at work." Another pause while Grace filled in. "Actually," Tim said, "the truth is, what I wanted to say…"

I rolled my eyes. *Just spit it out, Tim,* I thought. *Just tell her.* Finally, he did. Then, all I could hear was silence.

Finally, Tim said, "Of course, it's Antonia." What in the world? She didn't suppose he was running off to Canada to marry young Megan, did she? Tim continued. "No, not yet. I'll let you know." Pause. "Of course, yes. I love you too." And he hung up.

"You can come back in now," Tim said as I peeked around the corner.

"That seemed to go well," I said. "So, you told your mother about your employment plans as well?" I knew he had not.

"Geezus, Antonia. One thing at a time."

"So, what are you going to have to let her know about?" He looked at me sideways. I answered his unspoken question. "Yes, of course, I was listening."

"Oh, just when the wedding is going to be," he said, getting up quickly to go into the kitchen, leaving me alone.

"When the *wedding* is going to be? Timothy Sinclair," I said. He didn't answer. "She doesn't think there's an actual wedding for her to attend, does she?"

He appeared at the kitchen door, looking just slightly sheepish. "What was I supposed to tell my mother, Antonia? That she couldn't come to her only son's wedding?"

I put my two hands on my bump and said, "Tim, she knows I'm pregnant, and I'm pretty sure she knows how pregnant I am. This is not a good look for a bride. I thought we'd just do it quietly at city hall."

Tim just shrugged, poured himself another glass of scotch, and then sank into the couch beside me, causing me to topple over toward him.

"Come on, Antonia," he said. "It might be fun to have a bit of a party. We're celebrating, aren't we?"

I thought about it for a moment and decided to let it go for now. "What do you suppose she'll say when you tell her you're going to use your inheritance to buy a house where you can be a househusband and make art?"

"You know what, Antonia? I don't have any idea how Mom will react to that one. She's always been supportive of my art, but I suspect the fatherhood thing will only highlight the need for a level of responsibility. Mom's always been big on responsibility."

Maybe Grace Sinclair and I could find some common ground after all.

~

The following day I had back-to-back meetings. I had just returned from an outside meeting when Ken tapped on my open door.

"May I come in?"

"Of course, Ken. I'm just getting reorganized after that meeting with the charity we're considering representing." Ironically, it was an arts organization.

"I won't keep you long," he said as he approached the desk. "I just wanted to be the first one in the office to give you my congratulations." Ken was beaming, and it was clear that Tim had told him our wedding news.

I was standing beside my desk, where I had been unloading my briefcase. Before I knew what was happening, Ken came around my desk and threw his arms around me.

"Antonia, my dear. You're like a daughter to me, and I couldn't be happier that you're going to be married before your little bundle of joy arrives."

Little bundle of joy? Dear god. What decade did Ken inhabit? Well, I should have expected this kind of outpouring of—what was it exactly? Bliss? Joy? Maybe, but I think I also detected a soupçon of relief there. One of his best and brightest wasn't going to be an unwed mother. I suppressed a snicker.

"Well, then," he said, stepping back and straightening his tie. "I'll look forward to my wedding invitation. My wife adores weddings. I take it that it will happen soon?" Was he peering at my midsection?

I nodded. Tim had clearly neglected to tell him the rest of his news. But as Tim had said, one thing at a time. As Ken left, I looked down at my phone and noticed the message light was blinking. I picked up the receiver and punched the "play messages" button.

"Antonia? Kelly here. I just heard the news from Mom. I was hoping to find you in your office so we could have a bit of girl talk about the wedding. I don't want you to be sucked into the jet engine that Grace Sinclair can become when plans are afoot. You and I don't know each other that well, but that's all about to change. I'm finally going to have the sister I never had. I'm thrilled, by the way. Anyway, call me when you get a chance, and we can head Mom off at the pass! Don't worry about the time difference. I'll take your call whenever, and Greg and I'll plan to be in New York for a few days before the big day. Love and kisses to all of you. Oh, by the way, I think it's totally awesome that I'm going to be an aunt!"

As I listened to Kelly's voice all the way from California, I smiled in spite of myself. She'd picked up that awful habit of saying everything was awesome after that stupid movie from a few years earlier (something about Ridgemount High?) and sounded like a total Valley girl. I wondered if she'd taken up surfing along with her yoga-Pilates-ballet teaching. And who was this Greg person she mentioned? Then, as I reached down to erase the message, I started to get a bit short of breath as Kelly's words about the big day sank in. *Oh, my god*, I thought. *This is really happening.*

~

There wasn't a moment to waste. If I wanted to be able to move at all during the wedding and not just sit there behind a wedding cake looking like Jabba the Hutt, the festivities had to happen soon. I began by enlisting Nathan to contact his wedding planner friend, Jacob, to see if he could squeeze in a very small, last-minute wedding. The term very small is interesting, isn't it? It means different things to different people.

Very small to me meant fewer than a dozen people for a brief ceremony and dinner at a nice restaurant. Very small to Jacob, however, meant fifty people in a small ballroom in the Plaza Hotel, with bespoke floral arrangements for every one of the eight tables for six, including an over-the-top concoction of towering autumn flowers for the head table (bride and groom), a Veuve Clicquot champagne fountain (damn it, I still wasn't allowed to drink), neon green signature drinks made from that awful Midori liqueur (why would I care? Again, still no drinking), chicken Française in lemon butter accompanied by an arugula salad with raspberry vinaigrette after appetizers of mini quiches, followed by tiramisu for dessert. According to Jacob, that last one was because no one actually ate the wedding cake. So, I told him I wanted a carrot cake that people *could* actually eat under all that frothy white frosting. He nearly collapsed, but in the end, I got my way.

~

We'd had four weeks to plan the wedding scheduled for Friday, the twenty-seventh of October. I would still have two months to go until the baby was due. I let Nathan and Jacob plan everything after I noticed how well they seemed to be getting along—and the fact that I didn't have the energy to do it.

Once we settled on the date, I remembered all those Saturday afternoons in someone's bedroom, paging through bridal magazines, and I wondered if those magazines still existed. The minute the thought came into my mind, I scolded myself for slipping farther down the slippery slope of the wedding business. A wedding planner, was one thing, but a frothy wedding dress was quite another. But still.

The truth was that I had to find something to wear—something that would fit elegantly over my increasingly large bump. Three weeks before the wedding, I still hadn't decided what I'd wear. Kelly had fallen into the habit of calling me every other day to check on wedding preparations. I liked Kelly and felt we were making progress in developing, if nothing else, a long-distance relationship, but the whole situation was starting to wear on me. Whenever she called, her first question was, "Have you found the dress yet?" I hadn't.

Two weeks before the big day, I finally walked into Saks Fifth Avenue for the first time since I'd started to show, as they say so politely. Until that moment, I didn't have the heart to browse the rails of clothes I could only dream about wearing. I'd already started considering a personal trainer to help me get back into shape after the childbirth thing. As I stepped onto the escalator to the second floor, I noticed a display I'd missed when I walked in. When I got to the top of the escalator, I turned around, took the down escalator, and made my way over to the display. I stood in front of it, examining it carefully.

It was a wedding display awash in wedding paraphernalia. There was a wedding table set with beautiful (expensive) china and cutlery, a massive floral arrangement of autumn flowers mixed with orange bird-of-paradise and greenery, and stunning sparkly gold candles. But none of that was what caught my eye. Standing beside the table was (presumably) the bride—or at least a headless, stylized mannequin—wearing the dress.

It was *the* dress. It was the perfect dress. It was my dress.

It took me some time to convince a sales clerk (or whatever they had started calling them recently) to dismantle the display sufficiently for me to see the size of the dress since I was told it was the only one in the store.

The young woman, clad in a sleek, black suit with a pencil skirt, looked disapprovingly at me. "I'm not sure this is right for you, Ma'am," she said as she hesitantly approached the display with a small step stool.

I gave her my most withering look and said, "I'll be the judge of that."

Her eyes widened as she placed the stool next to the mannequin and stepped up. She began fiddling with the zipper at the back of the dress while I contemplated it.

It was full-length. (Of course, it was. A bride must wear a full-length dress, mustn't she?) It had a plain, wide neckline that plunged slightly at the front and a bit further in the back. It had those leg-o-mutton sleeves that were puffed above the elbow and came into a long cuff that extended from the wrist to just below the elbow. The cuffs were fastened with a row of tiny white buttons—very bridal-like. But most importantly, the dress had a raised empire waist with gentle gathers. Those soft gathers would fall from just above my bump, gracefully camouflaging it. I could feel tears bubbling up from somewhere within me. I had to have this dress. If I couldn't get this young woman to help me buy it, I thought I might actually strangle her.

"Ma'am, it's a Laura Ashley. And it's a size ten, but her pieces are made quite small. I don't think it will work for you."

At that moment, I did not doubt that her only reason for saying that was because if I decided I wanted to try the dress, she would have to dismantle the mannequin and wrestle the dress off it. That might be too much work for her.

"Well," I said stiffly, "since I usually wear a size eight, I believe it might do very well. Please get it off the mannequin for me. I'll be looking at earrings over there and will try on the dress when you let me know it's in a fitting room." Yes, the bitch in me had returned. I sighed a deep contented sigh.

Twenty minutes later, I was standing in a spacious fitting room in Saks, peering at myself in the three-way mirror. Somewhere deep beneath my veneer of efficiency and practicality, a tiny seed of melancholy raised its head. And for a moment, I could see that gaggle of teenage girls devouring the bridal magazines as I looked on. Maybe I hadn't been as immune to it as I thought.

~

Kelly and her boyfriend Greg (Gregory Elliott-Murray II, to be exact) had arrived as promised three days before the festivities. Although the two of them were staying in a hotel (not the Plaza—not their style, or so she said, although I realized I didn't know her well enough yet to know what her style was), Kelly had spent every waking moment with me in our apartment—with me at lunch, with me at dinner, with me at the spa for a manicure. Well, you get the picture. She and I had become besties. It seemed strange to me since we had almost nothing in common except Tim and a certain skepticism about her mother, Grace and her agendas. Then there were the pearls.

Grace had insisted on giving me pearls that had been in her family for several generations. I wasn't a pearl-wearing kind of woman—and I suspect Kelly and I had that in common, which was probably why Grace gave them to me and not to her daughter. But I had to admit that they were beautiful.

She presented them to me the evening before the wedding while we were all at Sardi's—Kelly's choice—for dinner. As the desserts were being handed around, Grace slid a distinctly Tiffany turquoise box from her purse across the table toward me and said, "Welcome to the family, Antonia. I know you and I have not always seen eye-to-eye in the past, but today we move into a new era."

What did she mean? We didn't see eye-to-eye? I couldn't remember ever having a conversation with her deep enough for us to disagree on anything despite my belief she didn't really like me. I looked down at the box.

"Open it," she said, smiling.

When I opened the box, I found myself staring at a double strand of creamy white pearls.

"They belonged to my grandmother, who survived the Titanic disaster, "Grace said. "She had them aboard that doomed vessel. The family lore is that her mother was wearing them that night, so I suspect they are filled with good luck if you believe that kind of thing."

"I didn't know that, Mom," Tim said. "Why didn't you ever mention your grandmother had been on the Titanic?"

"I suppose it never came up. I was going to mention it when you said you were doing some Titanic research for an ad campaign, but I suppose other matters took precedence, darling. Why don't you do the honours for your soon-to-be-wife?" Grace gestured toward the pearls.

Tim got up, picked up the necklace and stood behind my chair. As he placed them around my neck, the pearls settled warmly onto my collarbones. My hand immediately went to my neck to feel them there, and I realized that I'd seen so many people do that on television and in the movies. The almost reflexive gesture seemed to be a real thing. I got myself up as gracefully as possible and went to the other side of the table to embrace my future mother-in-law. "They're lovely, Grace," I said. "I will cherish them as much as you have through the years." I had no idea if she had cherished them or not, but I could do no less.

The server then began to pour the coffee.

Kelly, who was sitting directly across from me beside her mother, sat up straight and put her napkin on the table. "Well," she said so everyone at the table could hear her, "Greg and I have news as well."

I saw a look of horror pass over Grace's face. She looked at me, and I suspect we were having a shared moment for the first time. Surely Kelly wasn't going to announce a pregnancy as well? Grace sat stiffly, waiting for her daughter's news.

"Greg and I are moving!"

"Leaving California?" Tim said. "I thought you loved the vibe there."

"We do, but sometimes opportunities are too hard to pass up."

"Are you moving to New York, dear?" Grace said. I suspect she was hoping that it wouldn't be Boston. I have no idea what made me think that, but I seemed to be sensing something in the air around Grace when it came to her daughter. If I had to guess, I would conclude that Tim was her favourite. Perhaps it was all that California-earth-mother-yoga-granola feel Kelly oozed. It was sort of wholesome, but it wasn't something I could understand. I was a New Yorker at heart and everywhere else.

"No, not New York," Kelly said, shaking her head. Her blonde ponytail swung back and forth. "We're moving to Canada!"

Tim, a coffee cup poised between lips that had just sipped and the table where he was placing it, coughed. I didn't look, but from the corner of my eye, I could see a drop of coffee dribble from the side of his mouth. *Canada*, I thought. *Not this again.*

Tim managed to put his cup down without spilling any. "Canada, you say, Kel? Canada's a big country. Where in Canada?"

I sat there benignly, feeling like the Mona Lisa. My hands were folded lightly in my lap, and I breathed slowly. *Well, this is interesting.*

Gregory Elliott-Murray II, who, as far as I could figure out to this point, couldn't even speak, said, "Toronto. We're moving to Toronto. I'll be directing a film there."

Did I see Grace roll her eyes? Even if she didn't roll hers, I can tell you I rolled mine. Kelly had told me Greg was a director, but I'd never heard of anything he'd ever directed.

"But why move there?" Tim said. "I would expect that the film is a one-off, and when it's over, the opportunities back in California would be much more than in Toronto."

"You'd be surprised, Tim. You'd be very surprised. There's a lot going on in Canada, and Kelly has a line on a yoga studio looking for a new partner," Greg said.

Kelly smiled and then asked a passing server for another spoon so she could share Greg's chocolate mousse.

~

It was unseasonably warm that Friday afternoon in New York City. The sun was shining as we made our way to the Plaza for the five pm ceremony, followed by cocktails and hors d'oeuvres, then dinner.

At five pm sharp, the justice of the peace walked into our private ballroom at The Plaza and fifteen minutes later pronounced us husband and wife in front of forty-eight of our nearest and dearest, who stood holding champagne glasses, ready to toast the minute the deed was done. Nathan and Kelly were the best man and maid of honour.

"Now, ladies and gentlemen, I present Mr. and Mrs. Timothy Sinclair," the JP said as we turned toward our friends. Applause and clinking glasses ensued, and I stood there with a smile plastered on my face, thinking, Mrs. Timothy Sinclair? Who is that?

# 13

# Tim

## 1989

*Every father should remember one day his son will*
*follow his example, not his advice.*
~ Charles Kettering


REFLECTING ON MY LIFE, I REALIZE I've never had great timing. The moment the justice of the peace said those words, "I now pronounce you husband and wife," was the first time it occurred to me that I was taking on a new role—husband. And a feeling of dread began creeping up my spine. What did I know about being a husband? Poor timing, wasn't it? Maybe I should have asked myself that question before broaching the marriage subject with Antonia. Because we all know I wasn't even so great as a boyfriend—which is why later, as I sat beside Antonia in the little ballroom while our friends and family enjoyed their dinner, I realized that there was a great big elephant in the room. It was an elephant that would likely reside with us for a long time if we didn't confront it. And we probably should have faced it before the husband-and-wife pronouncement thing. That elephant was Meg, or more precisely, my lapse. Would Antonia be able to trust me? After Antonia and I decided to get married, the subject never arose again, and it probably should have.

The Meg thing hung over me like a ghostly spectre during the weeks that followed. On a Thursday evening less than two weeks later, we were slumped in front of the TV screen, watching in amazement as events unfolded in Berlin. We should have felt like we were witnessing a pivotal moment in history—because we were. The Berlin wall was crashing down right there in front of the eyes of the world, and it meant a whole lot more than a dismantled wall. But we didn't feel it. There were too many more imminent things hanging over our heads. That's the moment when Antonia asked, "Tim, do you still think about Megan?"

What was I supposed to say? If I'd said no, I'd be lying. I mean, who completely forgets something like that? Wipes it out of his brain? So, the honest answer would have been yes. But if I said yes, Antonia was likely to misinterpret it. I did think about Meg from time to time, but never in a way that suggested I regretted my decision. I suspected, though, that Antonia's preference would be for me to say no, never.

Before I could answer, Antonia said, "Do you ever wonder what she's doing? Who she's seeing?"

I did, but even I, with my inability to get the timing right on just about anything, knew this was not the moment to say so. So, I said, "Antonia, you and I are a team. I've never looked back." Which was technically true. I never looked. And then there was the other issue hanging over our heads.

We'd put our apartment on the market and had started looking for a new house almost immediately after we decided to get married, but everything we saw was either too small, too big, too poorly located, too dirty or too something. We hadn't walked into a single house where we felt at home. On the upside, though, our realtor had just that day handed us an offer on our apartment. And it was an offer too good to pass up. Our gloominess that evening stemmed directly from the realization that we'd be homeless if we didn't find a new abode soon. And then there was the timing issue. Again.

Could we really move out of our apartment in the middle of December—the buyers' preferred closing date—only days before Antonia was due to give birth?

"We can't do it, Tim. We can't sell this apartment without knowing where we're going to live."

"I know," I said miserably. But the offer was so good.

~

"Hi, Ken," I said, tapping on Ken's office door the following day. "Got a minute?"

"Sure, Tim. I'll just finish my call here, and we can talk." He gestured for me to take a seat. Then he mumbled a few inaudible words into the telephone receiver before putting it down.

I suppose he was speaking normally, but to me, it just sounded like a buzzing noise, as if I had a wasp's nest in my head. There was a good reason for the buzzing. I was about to tell him that I was leaving the agency. I was guessing he wouldn't be too pleased.

After a few pleasantries—how were the newlyweds doing and all that—I decided the best approach was to make quick work of it and just get it out. That's why I could have slapped myself up the side of the head for allowing myself to be sidetracked into a discussion about one of our new clients. But who was I kidding? I was procrastinating. Finally, there was an opening.

"Ken, you know how much I've loved working for you these past years." So much for just getting it out.

"Of course I do, Tim. And I've enjoyed working with you." He narrowed his eyes. "What's this all about?"

"It's about the job. My future—"

Ken held up his hand. "Just stop right there, Tim. If this is about your salary, I completely understand that your expenses are about to soar. Children are extraordinarily expensive. I should know; I have three." He laughed. "That's why I was going to tell you next week that I've approved a raise for you. I think you'll be more than pleased when you see it." He sat back, looking immensely pleased with himself. This was going to be even harder than I thought.

Ken wrote something on a small notepad and tore off the top sheet. He then turned the slip of paper around and slid it across his desk toward me. My eyes almost bugged out of my head when I saw the figure he had written down.

"What did I tell you, Tim, my man, a good raise?"

I swallowed hard. There was no doubt about it. The figure was a good one. That, along with Antonia's salary, would put us into a very nice tax bracket. And we did have the baby coming. I was starting to lose my resolve about my future. But if I changed my plans, who would look after the newest member of the Sinclair family? It wasn't just about me.

"Ken, it's just that I do like it here, but I think—"

"Dear heavens," he said, looking slightly alarmed. "You've been headhunted. You want to leave. What will it take to get you to stay?"

I stared at him from the other side of the desk, not knowing my next move. Then he lobbed a grenade in my direction. "Tim, what if I made you Executive Creative Director." That one was a bit puzzling since the agency didn't have such a position as far as I knew. "I've been thinking about it, and we need someone like you in a new position. The creative side is the heart and soul of the ad business." I still didn't know what to say, and if I thought that was a grenade I had to hold for a moment, he sent another even more powerful bomb in my direction. "And I think it's time we made Antonia a partner in the agency."

That was it. How could I not let Antonia achieve her dream of taking another giant step up the ladder to the top? What if accepting the new position was the price I had to pay for Antonia's promotion? And what if I said no? She'd never forgive me, but of course, I wouldn't have to tell her, would I? *Geezus, Tim*, I said to myself, *not again. You're not going to deceive her again?* No, I couldn't do that. If she ever found out—it was too gruesome to consider. But if the only reason I wouldn't do it was the fear of getting caught, I sure wasn't a very good candidate for fatherhood.

"Actually, Ken, it's not that. I haven't been headhunted." Ken looked slightly relieved. "The truth is I've decided to move my career in a different direction. I've decided I want to pursue my art."

The lines across Ken's forehead deepened as he tried to get his head around my statement. "But Tim, that's what you do here."

I shook my head. I was becoming more and more sure of myself as the conversation progressed. "Ken, you know the kind of artwork I did before I started into this advertising business. You must remember the portfolio of work I'd done before you hired me—the one I brought to that first interview. You said my art was inspired. I always wanted to be a fine artist, but I also like money. I'm used to it, I guess. So, I settled."

Ken sat back in his chair and steepled his fingers in contemplation for a moment. "You know, Tim, the day I hired you, I went home and told my wife I'd probably just done a terrible thing. I told her I'd just hired someone into an advertising job who had no business being here—that I'd robbed the world of a potentially great artistic talent. We also made a bet that day, and I think I might just have won it. I bet her you'd leave within ten years to pursue your art. She said you'd turn into a family man and stay for the paycheque. So, you see, I've won, but so has the world."

I hesitated before responding just to be sure I understood. "So, you're saying that you're okay with this?"

"Okay with it? From the agency's perspective? Not at all. But do I have a choice?"

That was when I realized that we all had choices. Ken had chosen to accept my choice to move on. But there was still something bothering me.

"I hate to ask you this, Ken, but what about Antonia?"

"Will I still put Antonia forward for a partnership?" He stopped and looked down at something on his desk before continuing gravely. "As it happens, Tim, I had planned all along to make sure she's a partner sooner than later. It was going to be my Christmas present to her."

I was so elated that I thought I might kiss him—but I held myself back.

"You know what Sartre said about choices, Tim?" I didn't, but I thought I probably should. I shook my head, and Ken continued. "He said we are our choices."

Sartre had the last word on that one. And I had one more person who needed to know about my choice.

~

The moment I walked back into my office and sat in my chair, I picked up my phone and punched in Mom's number. I still hadn't told her about my career plans. We started with small talk about the baby.

Antonia and I were expecting the baby to arrive two days after Christmas, on the twenty-seventh of December. At least, Antonia expected it to arrive on time and on budget, as she always said when it came to agency projects. When I told Mom that Antonia fully expected the baby to make an appearance on the precise arrival date and that she expected to return to work after a three-week Christmas-New Year's break, Mom laughed uncontrollably.

"You know what they say, Tim. If you want to make god laugh—"

"Tell her your plans." I'd heard that one so many times as I grew up. I think it was Mom's mantra for family life. At least we were on the same page about that one—Antonia certainly wasn't. Now that I had Mom softened up, it was time.

"Mom," I said, "I have some work-related news."

"I'm listening, Tim."

I told her I planned to leave the agency to work on my art and be a househusband, then waited for her response. There was silence on the other end of the phone. "Mom, are you still there?"

"I am," she said slowly. "I'm thinking. I'm thinking about that wonderful watercolour painting of our sailboat that you did for your father when you were in college. Do you know how often we had guests offer to buy it?" I didn't. This news came as a complete surprise to me. "I always thought you were wasted in that advertising agency. In fact, if you want to know the truth, Timothy, I blamed Antonia. I always thought it was her influence that kept you there, chained to a desk, attending meeting after mindless meeting, feigning interest in obnoxious clients. So, if you expect me to be horrified about your decision, I'm not. I am only concerned about your family life as it will unfold over the next few years."

"Not to worry, Mom. Antonia, as it turns out, is getting that partnership she's been working toward, and since we can't seem to find a house we want, I won't even have to dip into that trust Dad left to me." I heard a swift intake of breath. I hadn't told her about that part of the plan. It turned out that my plan to use the trust fund money on a house wasn't the thing that was making her gasp.

"You don't mean to tell me that you plan to bring that new baby home to that white-on-white apartment with its glass tables and marble floors? It's a death trap for a child. No, my dear, that won't do." She stopped for a moment, and I could hear papers rustling. "As it happens, I have a client in New York whose house I did up a few years back. She's been contemplating either updating a few things or selling. I think it's time she sold. If I suggest it's time to sell, she'll listen to me. And you two will love it. I promise you that. And I'll broker it."

Mom had made up her mind. I went along for the ride. In the end, after Antonia balked at buying something my mother had decorated, we walked into the three-story brownstone on a tree-lined street on the upper west side of Manhattan, and we knew we were home.

We negotiated a few extra weeks on the offer to sell our apartment and bought the brownstone. We were supposed to move in on Christmas Eve.

~

What did I know about being a father? Where are the courses? The teachers? The guidance? Then I thought about it. I did know how to be a father. Dad had taught me so many things without even trying. That's what I was thinking as I looked in the basinet on Christmas Day. My son, less than twenty-four hours old, was snuggly bundled in a white flannel blanket with blue stripes. He had come three days early, and just looking at that angelic face framed by a shockingly full head of dark hair made me forget that the movers had, the day before, Christmas Eve, dumped box after box after box in our new living room alongside new furniture pieces in various states of disassembly or packaging. He made me forget about the great leap of faith I was taking on so many fronts. He made me forget about everything else except that I was his dad, and I didn't have a sweet clue.

"What shall we name him?" Antonia asked from her perch on the side of her hospital bed.

I was surprised we hadn't come to any decision about a name yet, although, to be truthful, we had expected this little guy to be a little girl. Her name was going to be Emily. But here he was.

"What about William?" I said. "That was my grandfather's name. We could call him Will for short."

"Hmm," Antonia looked pensively at our little guy. "William? Won't people think we named him after Lady Di's seven-year-old?" I hadn't thought about that. It was a current thing. "And if we call him Will, the kids at school will call him Willy, and we all know where that leads." My wife was very astute. "Your father's name was Douglas," she said.

"Yeah, but I don't like that name. And everyone would probably start calling him Doogie after that strange character on that new TV show." Antonia looked at me as if she had no idea what I was talking about. "Doogie Howser?" I said. She shrugged. I continued. "Anyway, this little guy doesn't look like a Douglas to me."

"Well, what *does* he look like?" She was starting to sound a bit exasperated. "Homer?"

I was appalled. "You want to name our baby after an obnoxious cartoon character?" A new cartoon show for adults called *The Simpsons* was the latest craze. Only the week before, we had tuned into the debut episode but made it fifteen minutes into the show before switching it off and deciding it wasn't for us. The thought of naming him Homer was horrifying. Antonia was laughing.

"Let's call him Nicholas," I said.

"As in St. Nicholas? Because he was born on Christmas Eve?"

I just shrugged. Perhaps it wasn't original, but I liked it.

"I like it," Antonia said. She turned toward the baby. "Welcome to the world, Nicholas Timothy Sinclair."

*Nick Sinclair*, I thought. *That's a strong name for a guy's guy. Maybe he'll play hockey or even football. I think I could learn to like this dad stuff.*

# 14

# Grace

## 1989

*It's come at last…the time when you can no longer
stand between your children and heartache.*
~ Betty Smith, *A Tree Grows in Brooklyn*

I KNEW TIM HAD SOMETHING SERIOUS TO TELL ME the day he called and said he was driving up to Bar Harbor from New York. I hadn't seen him in months, although we spoke on the phone regularly. But driving almost nine hours in a rental car to visit your mother right out of the blue? At age fifty-three, I'd learned a thing or two and one thing I knew for sure. My son did not drive nine hours to see me unless there was something serious going on.

I heard the car drive into the circular drive at the back of the house. I used to call it the front of the house since it faced the road, but Douglas, the sailor, always said the front of the house was the side that faced the water. Since he'd died five years ago, I, too, had started calling it the back. It was a kind of tribute to him. I popped the collar of my white shirt up and glanced in the mirror to check my lipstick. I always thought there was no point in having your son think you've let yourself go. Then I checked the tray of snacks I'd prepared—all Tim's favourite things, including brie cheese (which he'd loved since he was five years old) and the inevitable potato chips. I'd had to search those out specifically since they weren't something I ever kept in the house.

I watched Tim get out of the car and reach for what looked like an overnight bag in the back seat. I waited on the porch, and when he made his way to the top of the steps, I drew him into a bear hug. I suppose some mothers might have said, "Hi, stranger," but that's a loaded greeting, isn't it? I may not see my son often, but I never think of him as a stranger. He had his own life, and I have mine. I was just happy to hold him in my arms for a moment. Even at thirty-one years old, a son is still your child.

Once we had settled into the Adirondack chairs on the front porch facing the choppy Atlantic waves with a glass of wine, I eased into the conversation by asking him about the recent trip I knew he'd made to Canada for work. I remembered the two or three visits Douglas and I had made to Nova Scotia over the years long before we bought this Maine house. I remembered taking a whale-watching trip and eating lobster. Of course, there was lots of lobster in Maine, but I'd always felt there was something special about the Nova Scotia variety.

As we talked about Nova Scotia and, in particular, the city of Halifax, I sensed there was more to the story of Tim's research trip than he was saying. Finally, I asked him what he was not telling me, then poured some more wine to let him talk in his own time as I'd always done with both Tim and Kelly when they were children. I could play the long game, and I wasn't surprised that the story he wanted to tell me didn't come out until the following day when we were walking along the rocky beach.

Tim talked some more about Halifax, and I suddenly knew. He didn't even have to say it because I could hear it in his voice. He'd met someone, and Antonia, the woman I always thought he'd marry, seemed to be an afterthought. I'd only met Antonia a few times over the past five years, and I recognized that they were from very different worlds. Despite these differences, I sensed she was good for Tim. He was a bit of a dreamer as a child—always dreaming of being an artist. And Antonia was pragmatic, much like I'd been at her age. In fact, I saw a lot of myself in her. And now, he seemed to think he was in love with someone else.

Tim's eyes shone as he told me the story of how he met Megan McMaster in Halifax. Then he told me about her work as an environmentalist. I'm sure my eyebrows raised as I put his work with the oil companies over the past few years together with this revelation. It was almost inevitable that Megan would have taken the moral high ground on this one. Then he told me the whole story. How he'd neglected to tell her the truth about his work. That he'd messed it up. Then he told me the real news—Antonia was pregnant.

~

How is a mother supposed to react to such news? First, my son has had what can only be described as an affair and thinks he is "in love" with a young woman he hardly knows and with whom he has not been honest. Then he discovers his long-time girlfriend is expecting his baby. What exactly was he expecting from me? How could I tell him I thought he was being an idiot—that his fling was just that: a fling? Because that *is* how I felt. Of course, adult children might ask you what they should do, but we all know they are unlikely to do as we suggest. I've always found it more tranquil to keep my mouth shut and let them find their own way. But this was a big one. It involved more than just Antonia and Tim (or even Antonia, Tim and Megan, for that matter). There was a baby. And that changed everything.

I convinced Tim to come into town with me to the farmer's market. It was Sunday afternoon, and the sun had finally appeared from behind the fluffy clouds. As we meandered between the stalls, picking up apples, pears and squash, I was thinking about the little bit of news I'd been planning to tell both Tim and Kelly about for a few months. Perhaps, though, today, we would just stick to Tim's issue. Then I spied her.

That vile Miranda Connaught—an old client and neighbour—whose daughter Andrea was recently divorced and spending the fall with her mother, was standing beside the pile of corn I wanted to approach. I tried to duck, but it was too late. She'd seen me.

I remembered that summer Tim had dated Andrea, and Andrea had announced at some point she was pregnant. I had always thought it was a ploy to trap my son, but she had eventually backed down and said she was wrong. I had always suspected she was lying anyway. Tim had been only sixteen years old at the time, and I cannot imagine what Andrea thought we would permit him to do under the circumstances. I knew without a shadow of a doubt that Andrea had never mentioned any of this to her mother. Anyway, here was Miranda, smiling with that toothy smile of hers, gold bangles jangling from both wrists, brandishing a corn cob.

I'm not sure if it was the suggestion that we all get together for dinner that did it or the absurd wink she added to her statement that she'd noticed I'd been spending a lot of time at the Club (the yacht club, to be precise) lately that sent me packing. But I immediately told her we had to run, and run we did. Tim was positively breathless when we ducked into my old Mercedes, which was parked on a side street two blocks down.

As we drove the short distance back to the house, Tim asked me why I was spending time at the club. He thought I'd given that up when Douglas died. I knew it was time to tell him my little bit of news. I just wasn't sure how he'd feel about me dating anyone, much less his old high school art teacher. But as far as I was concerned, Jack Lawrence was much more than a retired art teacher. He was the best friend I'd ever had outside of Douglas, and he was an artist of increasing repute. So, I told Tim about our budding romance, and he was happy for me.

What I didn't tell him was that a gallery owner from Montreal had noticed Jack's dark oil-on-canvas paintings of the wild north Atlantic. I could have told him that, but he would have asked for specifics. That would have led to more questions than answers. I felt it might not be the best time to tell him that the Montreal gallery owner had a branch in Halifax, Nova Scotia and that he wanted Jack to consider selling some of his pieces on consignment to the Halifax gallery. He said the customers buying from the Halifax gallery were always looking for north Atlantic scenes regardless of the artist's home base. I suppose I could have told him that, but then it would have led to me having to tell him the next part. Jack and I were going to Halifax in three weeks. Under the circumstances, it just seemed awkward, so I kept it to myself.

~

"What do you suppose he'll do?" Jack was helping me set the table the evening after Tim left. We were barbequing chicken, but the sky was threatening rain, so we planned to eat at the big kitchen table where we could look out at the darkening sky and the white caps in the distance.

"I can't be certain," I said. "People think they know their children, but we don't know them any better than they know us. All I know is that he mentioned going to Halifax, and he may be there as we speak, and anything could happen."

"Does seem a bit dangerous, doesn't it?" Jack picked up the open bottle of Sancerre that was chilling in an ice bucket. "Ready for a glass?"

I nodded. "Please." I took the glass from him gratefully and sat down at the table, staring out the window. "You know, Jack, I'm thinking about calling Antonia."

"Are you sure that's a good idea?"

"No. Not at all, but under the circumstance that she's about to give birth to my first grandchild, I thought that might be reason enough. Perhaps we could forge a relationship, but I don't think she likes me."

"What? Who wouldn't like you?"

"Hard to believe, I know," I said as I took the first sip of my favourite wine. We both laughed.

"Be right back." Jack put his wine glass down and went outside to the deck to retrieve the chicken from the barbeque, placing it on a large platter I'd prepared. He returned and served us each a piece alongside the tri-colour pasta salad that was Jack's favourite. Then we ate.

"On another matter," Jack said after savouring his first few bites, "I've plotted our route to Halifax to visit that gallery. You don't suppose Tim could give us any restaurant recommendations?"

I looked at Jack, thinking that was an odd question, but saw the wink and a tiny smirk. He was, of course, teasing me. Neither of us would be asking Tim for any Nova Scotia recommendations any time soon. Frankly, the less said about that interlude in my son's life, the better. I had my fingers crossed that he'd do the right thing regarding Antonia and his child. It would have been what his father would have expected. As I drained my wine glass, I could only think about something Sigmund Freud once wrote: "I cannot think of any need in children as strong as the need for a father's protection." I hoped my faith in my son wasn't misplaced.

~

It was a cool, crisp fall morning a couple of weeks later when Jack and I pulled out of my driveway in the little BMW he'd bought for himself as a retirement present when he left his teaching position earlier in the year. We were headed to Nova Scotia. The drive would take us north toward Bangor, then along what we called the Airline Route, a twisting and turning secondary highway to the border where we'd cross into Canada. Then we'd drive through the province of New Brunswick and eventually into Nova Scotia. It would take us eight or nine hours to get there, so we had a full day ahead.

As Jack pulled the car onto the road, he popped a cassette into the deck, and Frank Sinatra's soothing voice quietly filled the car. I was thinking about Tim and his fondness for old-fashioned swing music and wondered if Antonia had grown to love it as much as he did. The day after I mentioned it to Jack, I had tried to call Antonia to tell her I would be here for her and the baby, but I hadn't been able to connect. I left her a message that I hoped she would interpret as cautiously supportive, but I had no way of knowing what she'd think. She didn't return my call, but I hadn't expected her to, nor had I asked her to do so. I knew she was very busy with her job, and I could imagine how comforting it would be to have that for daily stability, at least. Then much had happened the ensuing weeks, some of which I hadn't had a chance to tell Jack. However, I knew we'd be trapped together in a car for eight hours, so I had saved a few things to discuss en route. He broached the subject of my news before I got to it.

"So, what's this news you've been wanting to tell me?" Jack said as he maneuvered the car onto Route 179, heading toward Aurora.

"How would you like to take a trip to New York in a few weeks?" I could see Jack's eyebrows jump.

"New York City, you say. Aren't there a lot of art galleries there?" He was teasing again. He knew exactly what I meant.

"And perhaps a wedding, as well."

"Well, then, my dear, we'll go to New York. As long as we can squeeze in a visit to the Museum of Modern Art, you will have a willing plus-one." I knew I could count on him.

Then we settled down to muse about what kind of wedding could be planned in less than a month and what I'd give the newlyweds as a wedding present.

"I was thinking I could offer to babysit for a week later in the spring so they could take a delayed honeymoon. I might even offer to pay for the honeymoon," I said, thinking this through a bit further.

Jack's eyebrows raised yet again. "You sure you want to have a baby for an entire week—day and night? And especially night."

I wasn't sure at all. I'd have to think about it a bit more.

It was a long drive. We stopped twice along the way and finally found ourselves pulling into the hotel in Halifax in the dark. I always found it disappointing not to be able to see much of an unfamiliar city upon arrival, but then the next day was such a treat. This time was no exception.

The following morning, when I opened the drapes, I was greeted by a deep blue autumn sky as I gazed down from our sixth-floor window to the Halifax Commons, a wide-open space covered with grass and baseball diamonds. As I gazed around, I could see trees sporting their fall colours lining the surrounding streets, but the Commons itself was devoid of trees. We were too far from the harbour for any water view, but I was looking forward to seeing it. It wasn't long before I had my wish.

After breakfast, we decided to walk down to the waterfront. Jack had an appointment with the gallery owner at eleven o'clock, and the gallery was located on Water Street, which ran along near the water, so we'd be able to explore a bit before we had to be there.

I was impressed by the restoration of the historic buildings on the waterfront. Although I'd visited the city on several previous occasions with Douglas, I had bought a new guidebook to the city to remind me about it. I had spent a few evenings the week before reading about the history. I knew that Halifax was among the oldest cities in Canada, settled in the eighteenth century. The restored waterfront buildings dated to that time, but a portion of Halifax's history was of even more interest to me.

During the second world war, Halifax was a lifeline to the Allied forces in Europe, assembling convoys laden with supplies in the part of the harbour known as the Bedford Basin. I remembered Douglas showing me grainy photographs of Halifax back then because his father, William Sinclair, had been here during the war as a young American naval officer. I had always thought that a story set here during the war would have been worth considering if I had been a writer.

As Jack and I toured the waterfront buildings, we noted an especially interesting one that housed three restaurants: The Upper Deck, The Middle Deck and The Lower Deck. As you moved down the decks, the prices went from high to low, so Jack and I decided we'd come back and have lunch at the middle deck. I was looking forward to getting inside this old stone building.

At eleven o'clock, I stood beside Jack outside the Kaufman Gallery on Water Street, taking in the artwork displayed in the windows that flanked the door. I was especially captivated by the sculpture to the left of the door. It was what looked like that dress Marilyn Munro wore the night she sang Happy Birthday to JFK. The dress, cream-coloured and covered with a million rhinestones, stood on its own, lit from within. I marvelled at how it seemed to be caressing a body, but there was no body beneath. And there was no head or arms—just a dress in all its splendour. I was picturing it in the corner of my living room in Boston. *It's probably dreadfully expensive,* I thought. *But it never hurts to inquire.* We opened the door and walked in.

Jack introduced himself to the young woman sitting behind a small, blonde wood reception desk. She said she would fetch Mr. Kaufman immediately, then disappeared into a back room.

"I'll just browse while you have your meeting, Jack," I said, eyeing a few pieces I thought I'd like to see up close.

I left Jack just as the gallery's proprietor, Nigel Kaufmann, swept into the room because sweep he did. I had seen his picture in the gallery catalogue Jack's Montreal contact had sent to him, and he looked exactly like the art world *bon vivant* I had expected, with his tartan scarf flung jauntily around his neck. It was blue with the greenish-yellow and black lines I recognized as Nova Scotia Tartan. He practically bowed to Jack as he offered his hand. They nodded toward me. I smiled and continued to peruse the artwork on offer.

I made my way back toward the entrance to take a closer look at the sculpture from behind and found a little card beside it affixed to the wall. The piece was indeed called "Marilyn," and the artist's name was "Ellen McMaster." McMaster, I thought. *Where have I heard that name recently?* I looked at it again and racked my brain, but nothing came. As I turned away, I suddenly remembered. Tim had mentioned that Megan's surname was McMaster, and for the briefest second, I wondered, *Is it possible they're related?* I immediately put it out of my mind. The world wasn't that small, after all.

Then I wandered toward a group of watercolour paintings. I stood in front of one particularly captivating one of the Halifax Harbour and thought this would be a wonderful souvenir of my visit. I looked at the card on the wall next to this one. The scene was called "First Impressions," and the artist's name was…What? *That can't be right*, I thought. I looked at the painting to see if I could see the artist's signature. There it was, and it was as familiar to me as if I'd written it myself. The artist was Timothy Sinclair. I would have recognized the signature anywhere. How? I wondered. How was it possible that one of Tim's pieces was displayed in this gallery? Although, perhaps I shouldn't have been so shocked. After all, Tim had been here in Halifax for several months this year, but I hadn't realized that he had returned to painting. With all the other issues at the top of his mind, he seemed to have neglected to mention this. Had his artwork once again taken a more prominent role in his life? I hoped it had. I'd have to ask Mr. Kaufman before we left.

After twenty minutes, it seemed Jack and Mr. Kaufman had successfully concluded their business. I assumed it was successful since they were both beaming and shaking hands. I made my way over to them, and Jack introduced us.

"I am so delighted to meet you, Mrs. Lawrence!"

I laughed. "Actually, it's Sinclair," I said. Nigel Kaufman nodded enthusiastically. "As in Timothy Sinclair."

"I am so sorry," Mr. Kaufman said. "I don't think I'm following."

"How long have you been offering watercolours by Timothy Sinclair?"

His face once again broke into a wide smile. "Oh, my word! Isn't he marvellous? He was in a while back and left these on consignment." His face fell a bit. "I'm not certain if I'll get more. Are you interested?"

"Oh, yes, I'm certainly interested," I said. "Timothy Sinclair is my son."

Mr. Kaufmann clapped his hands in what appeared to be glee. "How utterly marvellous!" He said. "The artist's mother. I must take a photograph of you beside the piece." He then ran toward the counter and rooted beneath, pulling out a large, ungainly camera.

I had no choice, it seemed, so I posed for a photograph. When we had finished, I said, "Mr. Kaufman, what can you tell me about the sculpture in the window?"

He was once again delighted to tell me about his artwork. He first explained the nature of the sculpture. The artist fabricated the dresses herself at her sewing machine—she had done many—from chiffon silk and then treated them with a proprietary substance that allowed her to sculpt them into the shape they would be worn on the body. Then she lit them from within with a stunning, ethereal effect.

"And what about the artist?" I said. "Is she local?"

"But of course! Ellen McMaster—well, I'll let you in on a little secret. It's actually Dr. Ellen McMaster and she is a Halifax star. But make no mistake, Mrs. Sinclair, she is world-renowned. World-renowned! She has always been a sculptor, but in recent years since she retired from her medical practice, she has been a full-time artist, much to my absolute delight!"

"Does she still live in Halifax?" I said.

"She does, indeed," he said.

"That is so nice," I said, trying my best to be nonchalant. "It must be wonderful to be able to pursue such a talent after retirement." Jack started to give me that look as if to say, where is this going? I was getting there. My intuition hairs were all standing at attention. "I suppose her family must be so proud." I hoped I wasn't batting my eyelashes as I said this.

Mr. Kaufman's face fell. "Alas, it's just Ellen and her granddaughter now."

My ears perked up. "Oh, how lovely that she has a granddaughter. Is she an artist as well?"

"Megan?"

I almost swallowed my tongue. I kept quiet and hoped he would continue.

"Oh no. Megan is a scientist."

~

"Why the sudden interest in artists from Halifax, Nova Scotia? Do you know this McMaster woman?"

Jack and I were hurrying away from the gallery back down toward the Middle Deck restaurant as we had planned. Dark clouds were now covering the sun, and I felt a raindrop splotch on my cheek just as we reached the restaurant door.

"Not exactly," I said. "Truly, not at all. But I think I may have uncovered a connection." Jack looked confused. "Let's get seated and get a glass of wine, and I'll tell you."

Once we were settled, had ordered fish and chips, which seemed to be the house specialty, and I had a glass of sauvignon blanc in a large glass—tumbler size—sitting in front of me, I said, "You remember me telling you about Tim's fling and his apparent dilemma?"

Jack nodded. "Go on."

"What I didn't tell you was the name of his dilemma. It was Megan McMaster."

Jack stopped with his wine glass halfway to his lips. "Do you mean…?"

"I do mean," I said triumphantly. I felt like Sherlock Holmes just uncovering a clue.

"But surely you don't think Nigel's Megan is the same Megan Tim dated while he was here?" Jack was so kind to use such a benign word. Dated. I just stared at him. "Come now, Grace, I suspect if I went over there," he nodded toward the payphone on the wall just outside the restroom doors, "and picked up the phone book, I'd probably find a hundred McMasters here in this city. If I'm not mistaken, it's a common name here—as common as Sullivan in Boston."

I shrugged. "Possibly. But the possibility is tantalizing."

"Grace Sinclair! You aren't planning on doing any more sleuthing, are you? That cannot come to any good, and I suspect you know that. It's pure, unadulterated snooping."

Jack was right. He was so right. Nevertheless, after Nigel Kaufman mentioned that Megan was a scientist (Tim's Megan was an environmentalist specifically, he had told me), I had gently pressed him for a few more tidbits. Nigel proudly divulged that Megan McMaster was almost finished her PhD at Dalhousie University here in Halifax in a department called Environmental Science. I almost fainted at how the world is, indeed, so much smaller than we think.

"It's just so interesting, Jack," I said sweetly.

# 15

*The beginning is always today.*
~ Mary Wollstonecraft Shelley

A FEW WEEKS LATER, ON THE TWENTY-SEVENTH OF OCTOBER, Jack and I found ourselves in New York at the Plaza Hotel, watching a justice of the peace marry Tim and Antonia. What does a mother think about at her child's wedding? That she's lost him? That she won't be as important to him any longer? Perhaps, in a way, but not in any way that truly matters. I was thinking about the moment Tim told me he and Antonia were going to make their relationship permanent and what that might mean to him.

When Tim called to tell us about the wedding, I expected it to be in a small private dining room for a dozen people at a New York restaurant. The small Plaza Hotel ballroom filled with at least fifty people among the masses of flowers (and that champagne fountain!) was remarkable given how little time they'd had to prepare. Holding a glass of champagne, I stood beside Jack with the rest of the guests, watching my son as he said he promised to "keep myself only unto thee until death do us part" and sincerely wondered if he would be able to do that. I mentally slapped myself for even thinking that.

I was trying to get a better look at Antonia's dress—carefully chosen to disguise the bump—when Jack leaned down and whispered directly in my ear, "Have you ever thought about getting married again, Mrs. Sinclair?"

I turned abruptly, changing my focus from Antonia's dress to Jack. I contemplated him for a moment, then leaned in to whisper directly in his ear, "If that is a proposal, Mr. Lawrence, you're going to have to do better than that." I then turned my head back toward the action where the JP was now proclaiming Tim and Antonia husband and wife, but in my peripheral vision, I could see Jack's lop-sided grin.

I looked to my other side, where Kelly, my free-spirited daughter, was standing hand-in-hand with her latest man, Gregory Elliott-Murray II, who, as far as I could determine at this stage, having met him only last evening, might be from a family of means. It was hard to tell, though, with these Californians. The usual trappings of wealth were often buried beneath a veneer of blasé casualness, but the Patek-Phillippe watch adorning his left wrist hadn't passed me by. Douglas and I had never been wealthy enough to be a part of that rarefied echelon, but many of them were among my clients. We may not have been in that wealthy stratum, but we had done very well. I realized I probably had more respect for those who embraced their wealth than those who affected a kind of nonchalance about it—as if it meant nothing to them when usually it meant everything. So, I considered my daughter.

At last evening's family dinner, when she mentioned she had news, I thought my heart would stop right there and then. I didn't think I could take any more news of grandchildren. Thankfully, it was only that she was moving to Toronto. The only fly in that ointment was that she was moving with Gregory, who didn't seem as free-spirited a man as I had always thought Kelly would choose. But I've said it before: we really don't know our children. Perhaps that was a good thing anyway. For if Antonia were going to help to ground Tim, Greg might do the same for Kelly—and the fact that he appeared to have money would benefit a young woman with champagne taste and a beer budget. I had always worried about her—at least since her dream of a career in ballet had been dashed. So, if she now had someone else to worry about her, perhaps I was off the hook.  If both of my children were finally moving into real adulthood, perhaps I was free. Maybe I would marry Jack, after all.

As I brought my mind back to the present moment, I looked around and had to admit that the wedding was fun. I cannot remember ever saying those words before. Throughout my life, I'd always gritted my teeth whenever a wedding invitation arrived. And the closer I was to the main protagonists in the wedding production, the gritting became grinding. Has there ever been a wedding in history during which there was no drama? After all, a wedding is nothing if not a piece of theatre. I had expected this one to be no different, but it was. Everyone seemed to have a good time. There was no speech extolling embarrassing events in the bride's life. There were no clashing in-law antics. There was no child running by granny and snatching her wig. There were no tears because the wedding cake topper was all wrong. There was no screaming match between mother and daughter. I have seen all these and more at weddings, and the older I get, the longer the list becomes. This one was different.

The wedding planner, Jacob, who I had the pleasure of meeting after the ceremony, had done a stellar job. He was one I'd recommend to anyone who asks in the future. He had created in that ballroom the ambience of a country garden in the evening, filled with autumn flowers and candles everywhere. There were cream and gold candles on every table, pillars in niches, and large candles on two free-standing candelabras flanking the table where Tim and Antonia sat. In my view, candlelight can overcome so many deficiencies in both a room and one's appearance. I always felt I looked better in candlelight. Then there was the food. It was, in a word, divine, and the carrot cake/wedding cake for dessert was beyond belief. Antonia had made a good choice with that one. And the Veuve Clicquot fountain I mentioned? It is my favourite champagne, after all. I believe Antonia and I might have found common ground.

~

Tim's next phone call came three weeks before Christmas —and before the baby was due—while I was baking Christmas cookies in my city kitchen, as I liked to call it. I had moved back into my house in Boston from the Bar Harbor house the week after Jack and I returned from the wedding. He had helped me pack and would join me in another week.

Tim began by telling me he had work-related news. Of course, I expected him to tell me that he had been elevated to Vice-President, Creative at the agency. That would be wonderful for Tim since a raise in salary would be welcome at this point. He had told me Antonia expected to be off work for only a few weeks, but I expected she'd find that this wouldn't be long enough for her and agree to take a more extended maternity leave. But I was wrong.

"I'm leaving the agency," he said. "I'm going to focus on my art and stay home to look after the baby." None of this was sinking in, I'm afraid. "Mom, are you still there?"

I was, but I was thinking. My mind was replaying the tape of Tim's life as a child and young adult. His art had always been such an essential part of who he was—until he met Antonia, which is when he found a way to use his talents in a new direction. I knew it was her influence that had pushed him toward advertising. But I also knew that it had never made him truly happy. I thought about the watercolour he'd done for us when he was a student and was now hanging in my living room. I told him guests often asked if they could buy it from us. This surprised him.

Then I thought about his work hanging in that gallery in Halifax and realized why it was there. This was his life. This was what Tim was supposed to do with his life. How could I discourage him?

Then he told me about their real estate dilemma. He and Antonia had a great offer on the apartment, and as far as I could tell, it was too good to pass up. Then I remembered I had a former client with a brownstone in New York. She'd contacted me a month earlier to ask if I could help her decide if it was worth renovating—again. As far as I could see, the house was still beautiful, as I had re-designed it for her five years earlier. When she called me about her idea to redecorate, I perceived she was hoping for a push in that direction anyway. I could suggest to her that it might be better to sell and let me have a go at a new space. So, I'd offer to broker the deal, and Tim and Antonia could probably move in around Christmas since Judith, my client, spent most of the winter at her house in Arizona. I quickly considered the difficulties of a move so close to the baby's due date but felt like this might be the best option under the circumstances. I suggested it to Tim.

"At least take Antonia to see the house," I said. "I'll set it up for tomorrow, and if you can manage to get an extension on that offer you have on your apartment, it might all work out."

And so it did. I thought Antonia might balk at living in a house Tim's mother—her new mother-in-law—had decorated, but I was sure once they'd moved in, she'd change as much as possible as quickly as possible. It turned out I was wrong. She actually *did* plan to go back to work within three weeks, and decorating was the furthest thing from her mind.

~

As I mentioned, Jack and I had decided we'd spend the Christmas season in Boston. I figured it would be simpler to get to New York from here if and when I was invited to meet a new baby. This year would be our first Christmas together and the first Christmas I'd had a man in my life since Douglas died five years earlier.

I was in my living room in Boston on Christmas Eve, gazing at the heaping plates of Christmas cookies I'd made in Maine and brought home in old cookie cans adorning the coffee table. I was draping the final glittering silver garland around my silver and red-themed Christmas tree, with Jack, standing on a small stepladder behind it, when the phone rang. I forgot to let go of the garland, nearly toppling him and the tree that had taken hours to decorate. I ran for the phone, leaving Jack holding the garland and shaking his head.

"It's a boy, Mom," Tim said breathlessly without even a hello. "You have a grandson!"

And suddenly, it hit me: I'm a grandmother. *What in the world do I know about being a grandmother?* That was my first thought. My second one was: *I'm too young to be a grandmother*. And there you have it. My cognitive dissonance was starting. I could never have known that grandmothering and that dissonance would haunt me for many years.

~

I finally met my new grandson on New Year's Eve. Tim and Antonia had decided to invite the whole family to celebrate the beginning of a new decade with them in their new home. Jack and I were flying from Boston, and Kelly and Greg were coming from California. Their move to Toronto was on hold until the spring.

Jack and I checked into what was becoming our favourite New York hotel, The Algonquin, and settled into our room. We loved that it was one of those New York City icons of the past that remained steadfast in its commitment to its guests even into the 1980s, and I hoped beyond. Its location on West 44th Street, not far from Times Square, made it ideal for the kind of walking Jack and I had learned we both liked to do. I was also slightly tickled at the knowledge that it shared a block with other icons: the Harvard and the Yale Clubs. I also loved the tuxedoed servers, who seemed to like nothing better than to make me feel like royalty. It had been doing its thing since 1902, and I hoped that by 2002, its hundredth birthday and the year I would turn sixty-six, I could still visit. Perhaps I'd even plan that.

We checked in at two in the afternoon on New Year's Eve but weren't expected at Tim's until six-thirty. That allowed us to take a walk in Central Park and enjoy the season's first snowfall. As much as I disliked those nor'easters in Maine, I loved this kind of snowfall. The flakes fell as if in slow motion from a carpet of fluffy white clouds in the sky. Since it was the first snow event of the season, there were no piles of slush on the street corners, no ice underfoot. There was just that hush that descends when snow falls, even in the Big Apple.

Jack and I walked in companionable silence as we made our way into the centre of the park. I had always marvelled at this oasis of calm in the middle of the most exciting city in the world. It was so astonishing and so necessary. We traversed the snow-covered walkways that snaked toward the lake at the centre.

I tried to take in all the elements of this beautiful day—the thin coating of white that was slowly enveloping the bare limbs of the trees, bringing them to life the only way possible in a long winter, the dogs frolicking in the snow-covered grass just off the walkways, the sound of the breeze as it moved past my ears (I'd forgotten my hat). I could feel snow settling on my hair, and I didn't even care that I'd look like a wreck by the time we got to the end of our walk. We spent a lovely hour in the park that afternoon, and it didn't matter in the least what my hair looked like when we arrived back at the hotel— because things had changed in a way I had never expected.

By the time we arrived at Tim and Antonia's brownstone several hours later, and I was taking my new grandson into my arms, holding him close to me so I could smell that baby smell, I knew I'd have to tell them. But I'd give it an hour or two so that we could all fuss over the new life that had joined this crazy family.

Nicholas was finally tucked into his crib, and the grownups had settled into the living room with drinks while the caterer Antonia had insisted on hiring, set the New Year's dinner on the dining room table so we could serve ourselves whenever we were ready. I sat on the sofa next to Kelly, who was telling a funny story about her yoga class. Tim was on my other side in a massive armchair. He was holding a drink and looking far more relaxed than any new father had a right to look. Antonia was fussing around, making sure the caterer, who seemed to me to know her business quite well without Antonia's continual oversight, did everything correctly. This dish had to be here, that one over there, and on and on. I wondered if Antonia was getting back into the bossy groove in preparation for returning to work in a couple of weeks. Yes, she was really going to leave Tim with the full-time care of a newborn. I knew she had bought Tim a truckload of parenting books because Tim had told me during our last telephone conversation.

*What to Expect When You're Expecting* had become Antonia's go-to reference book for all things related to pregnancy and childbirth. According to Tim, she had been delighted when the author came out with her new book *What to Expect the First Year* mere months before Nicholas was due. Of course, she had presented this to Tim, telling him it was a sign. He was to follow the advice scrupulously—never mind that its target audience was mothers. According to what Tim had told me, Antonia's obsession focused on decoding Nicholas's crying, as per the author's instructions. So, the fact Tim looked relaxed suggested to me that he'd pitched it in the fireplace when Antonia wasn't looking.

Kelly's Greg was knocking back what I counted to be his fourth Pernod and orange juice and looking a bit bemused by another family gathering. I only hoped he'd pass out before he got sick. That eventuality would put a serious damper on what I knew Jack and I had to do—although I was still a bit reticent to make myself the centre of attention when a new baby had just been presented. But I looked over at Jack, who winked at me and nodded almost imperceptibly. I was the only one who would have noticed.

I nodded to him and raised my champagne glass which I had just refilled (for the first time). He stood up and walked toward the fireplace, where a lovely fire crackled expensively. He cleared his throat.

"Well, everyone, before we ring in this new decade, I thought I'd like to say a few words." Even Kelly stopped talking and turned her attention to Jack. As a former teacher, he had a way about him that made "students" pay attention. When Tim was in high school, he had told me more than once how enthralling Mr. Lawrence's stories were. I could see Tim put his glass down and turn as if he were still one of Jack's students.

Jack continued. "I know I take a risk here, being something of an outsider in this small family group." Tim started to interject, but Jack nodded to him, and he settled back down. "But I've felt like an honourary member ever since Tim sent me that card when he graduated from high school." I frowned. I hadn't heard anything about a card, but Jack must have cherished it to bring it up now. "Tim, you'll remember this, I'm sure. I could tell you'd picked out the card very carefully." Tim half-smiled and nodded. "Inside was a quote from Ralph Waldo Emerson, who once said, 'In art, the hand can never execute anything higher than the heart can imagine.' You know, Tim, I kept that card inside one of my favourite art books on my coffee table for all these years. Now I think I really understand what it means. I believe that an artist's best work comes from a heart full of the highest things he can ever imagine if he will only let his heart—rather than his head—do the imagining. I've seen some of your recent work, Tim, and I know your heart is full. We have something in common. This evening my heart is fuller than it has ever been." He raised his glass. "I'd like to propose a toast." Everyone raised a glass, and he continued. "This is to the new decade ahead—a decade that I know will be the happiest of my life because Grace Sinclair, the most remarkable and beautiful woman I have ever met in my long life, has agreed to marry me. And you're all invited to celebrate with us in February in Antigua."

# 16

# Antonia

## 1989



*Reality is divinely indifferent.*  ~ Richard Bach

I HAD READ EVERY BOOK I COULD GET MY HANDS ON and even took copious notes. My parenthood research quest began the day after I told Tim I was pregnant. By that time, I was already six months pregnant and well into an intense study of how to be pregnant. But at that point, I had not begun looking for parenting material. When I started looking, my first discovery was a parenting book by a psychologist called Dr. Thomas Gordon. I remember discovering it at a bookstore in Greenwich Village one Saturday morning. It was called *Parent Effectiveness Training*, which seemed to speak to my corporate vision of what parenthood could be if done correctly. Since I was an accidental mother, I planned to make the best of it and was determined to get this child right. I pulled the book from the shelf and flipped to the table of contents. When I saw chapter one's title, I knew this would be a winner. It was "Parents are Blamed, but not Trained." When I saw that, I felt a slight tremor of emotion—so not like me. The idea resonated with me more than anything I had ever read or heard about being a parent. And I didn't want to be blamed—for anything.

I devoured that book. It was mostly about how to communicate with kids as they grew up, but I found the section on how to change unacceptable behaviour especially interesting. In fact, it occurred to me that some of the techniques could easily be used with my staff at work, and since I was being made partner in the agency, those skills would be increasingly essential. Changing a few people's behaviours would be the first order of business when I returned to the office after the baby's birth. In any case, the notes I made on that book were the beginning of my binder system.

I created three separate binders for different aspects of parenting. The notes from Dr. Gordon's book formed the foundation for my binder on communication. I colour-coded the section markers and created a section for each of the developmental stages of this child: infancy, early childhood, middle childhood and the teenage years. I also added notes from a book called *The Six Stages of Parenthood*, which I thought complemented the childhood stages very well. I felt strongly that the section on dealing with teenagers would be handy at the office.

While I was pregnant, I had relied on the book *What to Expect When You're Expecting* (my go-to pregnancy primer—everyone needs one), so I pounced upon *What to Expect in the First Year* when I saw it was from the same author. This inspired binder number two, which I would devote strictly to babies. I would soon find out how to decode those different baby cries. How different could it be from differentiating dogs' barks?

*The Second Shift* was the final book that inspired a binder. This one was a definite keeper. It actually put a dollar figure on the time a mother—the regular kind—spends on childcare and housework, then added that figure to her paid work salary, finding that a working mother put in more than a month more work than a father every year. That was interesting, although Tim and I were dividing things up differently. I expected to spend much more time working than Tim would ever do at home while caring for this child. However, I realized that I couldn't leave it all to him and that we'd need to figure out a way to divide the expected activities. I called this binder "Roles."

Although when I started them, I thought the binders were just for me, when Tim decided he'd be the househusband, I knew I'd have to ensure that Tim was familiar with the material. Was I a bit compulsive about those binders? Yes, but that's who I have always been. I put the final touches on my binders three days before Christmas. Since the baby was due two days after Christmas, I felt like I was ahead of the game, as was my usual approach to a new project. I planned to brief Tim on the binders on Boxing Day since we were scheduled to move into our new house on Christmas Eve, and Christmas Day was usually otherwise occupied. I didn't see how this could be a problem, although I'd had a recent telephone conversation with Grace, who sounded skeptical about my timeline. She didn't put that thought into words, but I could hear it in her voice. I reassured her.

As far as I was concerned, we had ample time to organize the new abode before I went back to work. Three weeks would be more than enough. Then Tim would take over parenting duties full-time. Grama-to-be Grace needn't worry. It was all under control.

On the twenty-third of December, at precisely 3:07 pm, I felt the first twinge. *Dear god*, I thought, squirming in my orthopedic office chair, *I still have one more meeting before I can take off for the Christmas break. Anyway, this cannot possibly be related to labour since the child isn't due for four more days.* So, I picked up my portfolio and headed to the boardroom, where a potential client awaited my team's pitch. I swept into the room and noted with pride that my two other team members had already set up the whiteboard, the flip chart and the slide projector. All was well. Then I felt another one.

To this day, I have no idea how I made it through that forty-five-minute meeting while being so distracted. By the time I arrived back in my office after bidding the client (we had managed to reel him in) goodbye and spending ten minutes on a debrief with my two team members, the best I could do was drop into my chair. Lisa-Marie appeared in my doorway, a worried frown on her face.

"Antonia, are you okay? Did the meeting go well? Can I get you anything?"

At least Lisa-Marie and I had come to a kind of professional truce since Tim and I had married. She no longer carried a torch for him, so it was easier to navigate our relationship. I had recently begun to think she was happy for us. Although, I suspected she was secretly giddy with delight to be able to watch me turn into a beached whale. Well, when I returned to the office after only three weeks off to give birth, I'd be wearing my green knit sheath dress with its matching wide green leather belt and those power shoulders I loved so much. I looked forward to seeing the look on Lisa-Marie's face.

I was about to ask her if she could get me a cup of tea and tell her she could then go home to begin her week-long holiday when another wave practically knocked me over. I checked my watch. It had been precisely fifteen minutes since the last wave, which had been fifteen minutes after the one before.

"Are you all right?" Lisa-Marie said, coming toward me with a look of increasing alarm.

"You know," I said as calmly as I could while keeping my hand planted firmly over my mid-section, "I believe I might be in labour."

Even beneath her full face of foundation (which someone as young and pretty as she was did not need) and that bright fuchsia-pink blush she wore high up on her cheekbones and into her hairline, I could see the colour drain from her face.

"Oh. My. God!" Lisa-Marie said, reaching toward my telephone. "I'm calling an ambulance. Right now!"

I managed to slam my hand over hers. "No need. No ambulance. Just call Tim. He's at home with the packers. He'll know what to do."

And he did. Tim arrived within the half hour, just as another contraction assailed my professional demeanour. He had taken a taxi, and it was waiting outside for us. I had expected him to be frantic, but Tim was calm, collected, unruffled—generally far more tranquil than he should be under the circumstances. But I suppose that's how I managed to get to the hospital with my packed bag, which he had remembered to bring so that I could experience twelve more hours of excruciating pain.

They say you immediately forget the pain of childbirth, but they—whoever they are—are men who have never given birth. I will grant them this, though. When the nurse placed that baby boy on my chest, and I looked down at the mass of dark matted hair, my heart melted a little. I felt a wave of love that took me entirely by surprise. Maybe I could do this mother thing after all.

~

At four o'clock in the afternoon the next day—Christmas Eve—the nursing assistant wheeled the baby's bassinet into my room and handed me a bottle so I could feed him. By that point, she knew better than to broach the breastfeeding subject. She had already been subjected to the stare of death when she'd come in to discuss this with me earlier. I had made up my mind about the subject months ago.

I took my baby boy into my arms and settled in to feed him. He was a charmer, to be sure, and I was surprised at how much I liked the feeling of taking care of a little human being. I was a bit troubled, though, by the fact that he didn't yet have a name. We had expected the baby boy to be a baby girl. I had no idea why, but that's how it was. I felt strongly that he should have a name and soon.

I had just put him back in the bassinet, and he was sleeping soundly when Tim walked in. He told me about the moving going on without me. I suspected he was leaving out the gory details so I wouldn't worry, but he shouldn't have been concerned. Tim was more than competent. I would never have considered leaving him in charge of a tiny life if he hadn't been. I was surprised at how protective I'd begun to feel. Then we broached the subject of a name.

Tim suggested William, his grandfather's name. I thought it was a good, strong name, but when Tim mentioned that we could call him Will, all I could think about was the bullies in the schoolyard who would inevitably call him Willy, which could lead nowhere good. I suggested Douglas after Tim's father, but he didn't like the name. So, exasperated, I suggested we call him Homer and be done with it. Of course, I wasn't referring to Homer of Ancient Greek fame. I was referring to Homer of *The Simpsons*, a puerile, moronic adult cartoon thing that had recently aired its first show. I fully expected it to be cancelled immediately. Anyway, Tim was horrified, as well he should have been. We settled on Nicholas. I suppose I should have told him that I'd recently discovered that my father, whom I had never known, was called Nick. But I'd save that for another time. After St. Nicholas, it was.

~

I must have been completely distracted when, late on Christmas Day, as Tim and I sat in my hospital room eating hospital-cafeteria-style turkey—at least something that passes for a Christmas dinner in a hospital—he suggested a New Year's Eve party.

"It's just a week away, but I think everyone would make the trip to meet Nick—and it is the start of a new decade, after all."

I vaguely remember mumbling something. When I think back, I can only think that I was trying to say, "Bad idea," but it came out more like, "Mm-hm," or something like that. In any case, whatever I mumbled, Tim interpreted to mean I was delighted. It was my own fault for not being clear. I wasn't exactly delighted.

For all my adult life, I'd been effecting a kind of persona that could only be described as competent. I had a horror of being thought incompetent. Of course, like all other young adults, there were things I wasn't completely competent in, although even if someone put a gun to my head, I wouldn't be able to state what that might be. No, I was one of the competent ones. I was the one who got things done. At the office, they all knew they could count on me, so Ken often asked me to go the extra mile. It might even be said that my colleagues expected nothing less of me. I suppose I could have said no, but I knew it would not be in my best interests in the long run. And, as it turned out, I was right. I had no doubt that this was how I managed to be offered this new partnership. So, when it came to the home front, I realized this burden of competence was going to weigh on me there, too. How could I tell Tim I was tired? How could I tell him that his competent wife just wanted to go home and chill? How could I say I didn't feel up to hosting a party in a week, new decade or no new decade? I had put myself in that box for most of my life and wasn't prepared to come out. So, we were having a party.

Two days later, when I walked into our new house, Tim was carrying Nicholas over the threshold. Shouldn't it have been me? Oh well, nothing about this situation was normal. I supposed I might as well get used to it.

To his credit, Tim had done a remarkable job of getting almost everything unpacked and settled. As I looked around, I was grateful, although it was clear I'd have to go around and fix things. The three paintings he'd hung in the living room were in the wrong places. The cushions on the sofa were the wrong ones—although that hardly mattered since I was sure we'd have to replace the white sofa before long, and that would mean new cushions. I would have to rearrange the bedroom furniture, and the baby's room needed a rethink. But, other than that, I was proud of Tim.

"Have you had time to set up your studio yet?" I said, sitting down gratefully on the sofa while I unwound my scarf.

"My studio?" Tim looked perplexed.

"Of course. The attic space? Remember we talked about that being a terrific place for your art studio?"

"Of course, I remember," Tim said as he placed Nicholas on the sofa beside me and began removing his heavy blanket. "But it's only been a few days." He looked around. "To tell you the truth, it was all I could do to get the house to where it is. And, by the way, you're welcome!"

"Oh god, Tim. Thank you! I appreciate it more than you could imagine." I tried not to look at the wrongly placed paintings in my eye line. "I just thought you might want to get started."

"We're not all like you, Antonia." Tim sounded slightly irritated. Tim's exasperation was not on my agenda for today. I'd have to change the subject. So, we talked about our upcoming New Year's Eve party.

"Mom and Jack are driving from Boston," Tim said, "and I think Kelly is bringing Greg with her from California, although she wasn't very clear about that. I think she plans to fly on the morning of New Year's Eve. I hope you don't mind that I told her they could stay here."

I shrugged. "And what about Grace?"

"Oh, Mom and Jack want to stay at The Algonquin Hotel. They were quite adamant about that."

Well, at least that was good news. Over the next few days, I managed to find a caterer willing to do some last-minute cooking so we'd at least have trays of food, and Tim arranged a delivery from a local liquor shop, for which I was very grateful, not having imbibed anything at all for the past few months.

Those days between Christmas and New Year's Eve were among the most peculiar ones in my life. I felt like a fish out of water in so many ways. Because I wasn't going back into the office for a couple of weeks, I didn't have that touchstone to ground me. I was a mother, and I was a wife, and I didn't know how to be good at either of those roles.

I tried to feel at home in this new house, but nothing seemed comfortable or familiar. The furniture was recognizable, but it seemed to represent a life that was now gone. The day before New Year's Eve, I was sitting in my new kitchen, gazing out the back onto a small deck where snow had accumulated. This was not an experience we ever had on the forty-first floor; it felt strange. I lifted the glass of wine on the counter in front of me and took a sip. As the glass reached my lips, I realized what was wrong with me. I was grieving.

I was grieving for a life lost. Life as I had known it for a decade—the life I had created—was gone. I would never again be that single-minded career woman, never be one half of a New York power couple. Those plans had crumbled. I now had responsibility for another human life, and for the first time in my adult life, I admitted to myself that I felt incompetent. I hated that feeling and desperately needed to hide that from the world. So, I made myself a promise never to let them know the truth.

~

Kelly and Greg rolled into the house at three o'clock on the afternoon of New Year's Eve. They had been up long before the crack of dawn in LA to get on a plane headed east. Now they were here.

Kelly and I still didn't really know one another well, and it was clear we had little in common, although I found her endlessly entertaining. Although she was only four years younger than Tim, Kelly always seemed many years younger the way she bounced into every room. She had been living in California for the past three years and in Boston before that, so I hardly knew her. I knew she had dreamed of becoming a ballerina, but an injury had put a stop to any notion of a professional career, although she still taught ballet to kids and yoga and Pilates to adults. Yoga. What was that all about? I guess it was part of the California thing, something I could never comprehend.

Kelly had long blonde hair—although Tim had informed me it was from a bottle—just like you'd expect of a California girl. And she had that west-coast tan. Greg, her current beau, looked the part of the matching surfer boy. I couldn't be sure, but I suspected that beneath that expensive, carefully curated exterior meant to trick you into thinking he was just one of the guys lurked a shrewd, calculating young man who did nothing without a good reason. He must have had a good reason for being here with Kelly's wacky family on New Year's Eve when surely he and Kelly could have had their pick of parties to ring in the new decade. Maybe he did love her, but I doubted it.

The moment she walked in the front door and dropped her suitcase on the floor, Kelly began looking around.

"Where is he? Where are you two hiding him?" She peeled off her knee-high boots (where in California did one buy winter boots, I wondered) and started ranging around the living room and then the kitchen. "Is he upstairs? Of course," she said, heading for the staircase, "he's in his room. I'm going up!"

Kelly's enthusiasm for babies seemed to know no bounds. Who would have guessed? Once she found Nicholas, it seemed clear that I needn't worry about spending time with my baby over the next few days. He would be otherwise occupied.

Once we had Kelly and Nicholas settled, and Kelly and Greg organized in the guest room, we all sat down in the living room where I'd managed to arrange enough flowers—potted poinsettias and red and white roses mainly—and candles, so the place looked somewhat festive. Tim poured Greg a Pernod and orange juice (how could he drink that? I felt a headache coming on just thinking about it), then put another log on the fire in the massive fireplace that was the focal point of the living room. We sat chatting about their upcoming move to Toronto as we waited for Grace and Jack to arrive.

At precisely six-thirty, the doorbell rang. My mother-in-law had arrived. I followed Tim into the foyer, where he was welcoming Grace and Jack in from the cold. As Tim helped Grace off with her coat, I noticed how Jack looked at her. There was no doubt that the two of them were in love. I suddenly realized that the previously unknown feeling that suddenly started to descend on me was envy. I knew Tim loved me, but I hadn't seen that look in years. I was startled when I realized when I'd last seen that look. I was in Tim's Nova Scotia cottage, and it was the one I'd seen on Megan's face when she looked at Tim. I wondered if Tim ever thought about her.

I shook off the creeping melancholy that threatened to overtake me if I let it and turned my attention to our newest guests. Of course, the only thing Grace was interested in was her grandson. When Kelly heard the doorbell, she asked if she could go upstairs and bring Nicholas down to meet his grandmother. Now, Kelly was coming down the stairs with the little bundle in her arms. When she got to the bottom of the stairs, Grace was waiting.

"Meet Nicholas Sinclair. Nick, my gorgeous nephew, meet your grandmother. You can call her…" Kelly looked at Grace. "What will your grandchildren call you, Mom? Surely not granny."

Grace took Nicholas into her arms and held him close as if she were trying to take in every little thing about him—how he felt, how he smelled, how he looked. "I suppose he can call me Grace."

Kelly wrinkled her nose and tossed her blonde ponytail. "Geezus, Mom. He can't call you Grace. I don't even call you Grace."

"Do you want to call me Grace?"

Kelly looked alarmed. "No. Who calls their mother by their first name?"

I didn't say a word. For my entire life, *my* mother had been Marilyn to me. I might have called her mommy when I was very young, but I have no memory of that. She was always Marilyn until the day she died. We were two equals. However, I thought I'd keep that to myself. There was no advantage in starting the New Year's celebration with oversharing.

After everyone had a chance to fuss over Nicholas, I finally took him upstairs and tucked him in so we could get on with dinner. I was more tired than I was willing to admit, but I knew I'd have to play the hostess. So many roles, and yet the only one I seemed to be looking forward to was being a partner at Moffatt, Green, Berger and Partners. I wondered how long I'd have to be hidden beneath the "partners" moniker. Moffatt, Green, Berger and St. John sounded better. St. John and Partners would be even better—all in due time. I was deep in thought as I sat in a chair by the fire, sipping a glass of champagne, when I noticed Jack seemed to have taken charge. What was he saying? Everyone was raising a glass. What had I missed? I had no idea, but I raised my glass anyway and tried to stay with the conversation to catch up.

"I've never been to Antigua," Kelly was saying. *Who's going to Antigua?* I thought. Then she continued. "I can help you find a dress, Mom. This is so exciting!"

"So, when did you two decide this?" Tim said. He didn't seem nearly as excited about whatever this was as his sister.

"While we were in Central Park earlier today," Grace said as I still tried to catch up.

"I decided months ago," Jack said. "I just had to find the right moment to convince your mother."

Were they getting married? Dear god. Another wedding. Well, at least that would keep Grace busy. I'd had nightmares about having to fend her off once the baby was born. This seemed like good news. I raised my glass once again. "To the happy couple," I said. Tim glared.

~

We ate and drank the new year and new decade into existence, then called it a night. I fell into bed and had been there no more than half an hour when Nicholas started crying. I crept out of bed and slid into his room next door to ours, grabbing him to me tightly. "Come on, little guy," I said softly. "Let's go get something to eat."

I took him with me downstairs while I prepped his bottle. We went back upstairs, and I sat in the glider rocker in Nick's room while he sucked contentedly. After he had finished, I walked around with him on my shoulder, taking a few minutes to stare out the window at the snowflakes illuminated in the streetlights as they swirled to the ground that was covered once again with a fresh blanket. "I wonder where we'll be ten years from this night, Nicholas? What do you think?" But his tiny eyes had closed tightly. I put him back to bed.

Tim turned as I slid back into bed, his face illuminated by the eerie red light of the numbers on the clock radio on his bedside table. "What do you think about Mom and Jack getting married?" he said.

"More to the point—what do *you* think?" I didn't think he really cared what I thought.

Tim pushed his pillows up behind him and sat up against them. "To tell you the truth, Antonia, I'm more negative about it than I thought I'd be."

"Any idea why?"

"I'm not sure. I like Jack. I really do. I've known him since I was in high school, and he was a great teacher. I think he and Mom are good together. And I don't begrudge Mom her happiness. She's not that old and should have someone in her life. But I can't help but feel…" He trailed off as if he didn't want to say the words out loud. I knew all about that feeling. "I can't help but feel like this means Dad is truly gone. I don't think I'd feel this way if I hadn't just become a father myself. What if I died? How would Nick feel?"

"Well, Tim, my darling, we don't know that little kid yet. Give him a few years, and maybe we can figure that out."

"Yeah, about that," Tim said. "Any predictions for the future?'

"You mean, like, where will we be in ten years at the start of the new millennium?" I thought about it for a moment. "I suppose we'll all be where we're supposed to be." And at that moment, I truly believed it.

# 17

## Tim

### 1990–1993

*Good decisions come from experience. Experience
comes from making bad decisions.*
~ Mark Twain

EVERYTHING SEEMS LIKE SUCH A GOOD IDEA at the time, doesn't it? I mean, you come up with these schemes and plans and then when it comes time to execute them, you start to question the wisdom of your decisions. It wasn't that I regretted making the decision to be a househusband. It's just that as the reality set in, I began to wonder if I'd bitten off more than I could chew, as the saying goes. I hoped I hadn't made a bad decision.

True to her word, and I'm sure much to the surprise of everyone at the office, Antonia returned to the agency three weeks after Nick's birth as she had planned. I watched her that morning as she dressed even more carefully than usual. By the time she was ready, I could only marvel at her ability to pull off a sweater dress cinched tight in the waist merely weeks after giving birth. When I mentioned this to her, she said, "This is what new motherhood looks like, Tim." I shrugged. I guess it did if you had a husband who was willing to stay home while you climbed to the top, fighting the corporate battles all the way. I wondered how she'd manage to get her coat on over those power shoulders. But after all, on the corporate battlefield, you do need strong shoulders.

Antonia kissed Nick on the forehead and pecked my cheek as she picked up her briefcase while the taxi idled out front. "I'm not sure what time I'll manage to get away on my first day back, so don't wait for me for dinner." Then she hurried down the steps to the cab without a backward glance.

From everything I'd read in those books Antonia had given me, I concluded that Antonia was something of an oddity among mothers. First, you need to understand that the books targeted moms, not dads, and the authors chose the content carefully to resonate with new mothers. I mean, when a book covers everything from burping, breathing and farting to how to deal with touchy-feely strangers, I have to think that these are the subjects that interest new mothers. But they didn't interest Antonia. And it wasn't that she didn't want to spend time with Nick. Even over the past week, after a courier delivered a box of files she had to review before returning to the office, she kept Nick with her as she read through them, even feeding him while she worked. But as for the other things—burping, breathing etc.—Antonia wasn't the slightest bit interested. I guess she figured I'd deal with it all. I only hoped I didn't begin to feel like the hired help with my own son.

The first few weeks Nick and I were alone all day went by in a blur. I finally settled us both into some kind of eating, sleeping and playing routine. I had decided to take advantage of this opportunity to teach Nick about all the things that interested me, even from this early age. He'd learn about art, 1940s swing music, and NHL hockey (I had played hockey—not well—as a teenager and still loved to take in a game in Boston whenever I was home visiting Mom). The winter weather kept us indoors for long swaths of time, but every day, I managed to get us both bundled up and out the door for a while.

I learned the best streets with the widest sidewalks for pushing a baby carriage and the ones where the sidewalks weren't cleared of snow and ice. I observed what appeared to be other mothers (maybe they were nannies?) doing the same thing and wondered if I'd ever meet anyone in the neighbourhood. That had never been something I'd been concerned about before in my entire life. But things had changed—and dramatically. So, you might reasonably ask: did I ever miss going into the office?

That's hard to answer with a simple yes or no because I wasn't always sure what it was that I missed or didn't miss. I didn't miss the endless meetings or being told by idiot clients what direction my art had to take. I honestly didn't really miss the people at work, although I secretly feared I might. But what I did miss was the actual work itself.

I'd always loved the part of my job where I got to sit alone at my drafting table and create a visual storyboard for a campaign. I didn't always agree with the story's direction that someone on Antonia's staff had created, but that's how it was done in the early years. Later on, I had more creative control. I missed those creative moments. And that brings me to the attic studio.

The space was on the third floor of our brownstone. You could reach it only via a very narrow, steep staircase that I didn't relish climbing with a baby in my arms. It was a real attic space with a peaked roof, a small oval window overlooking the street below and two skylights. It seems the former owner had fancied herself a bit of an artist, according to Mom, who had decorated the place, but Mom's client had never used it. So, the natural light wasn't bad. Still, I had done nothing about getting back to my painting when, somewhere around the second week in February, Mom called to ask me about her upcoming wedding in the Caribbean.

"Tim, darling boy. How are you and that handsome grandson of mine?" she said. I mumbled something about us getting on well and getting into a routine when she came to the real point of her call. "Have you and Antonia booked your flights yet for the wedding?"

*Oh god*, I thought, *something else I'm supposed to be doing. What's wrong with my brain?* "Geez, Mom, sorry. Not yet, but we're getting right onto it."

"You really should, you know Tim, since it's around that March break time, although the resort we've chosen is more likely to have Brits with their children on half-term. Exciting, isn't it?"

Mom sounded like a young girl, and I was happy for her. But the prospect of a week on a Caribbean island—as nice as it would be to get away from the continual snow this winter—with a wife whose head would be back in her office and a baby whose demands would fall on my shoulders, wasn't nearly as wonderful as it sounded. It wasn't nearly as enticing as it would have been a few years earlier. That being said, I couldn't miss Mom's wedding.

Nick was fast asleep, and I was pouring over copious notes when Antonia walked in at seven that evening. She poured herself a glass of wine, picked at the plate I'd left in the oven for her and hovered over me where I was sitting at the kitchen counter.

"What's all this?" she said after we'd finished with the update on her day at the office and my usual report on Nick. She was leafing through my notes.

"I spent some time this afternoon on the phone with Alan. Now I have to figure all this out before I get back to her."

"Alan? Alan, our travel agent?" I nodded. "Why do we need a travel agent? With a new baby and all…"

"We're going to Antigua. Remember?"

Antonia wrinkled her brow, suggesting she was both confused and alarmed. It was clear she had no idea what I was talking about. I reminded her.

"Tim, there is no way I can get away next month. You must know that. You must remember what it was like."

"Antonia, we've known about this since New Year's. Didn't you tell anyone at the office that you had to be away?"

She had not. And now she was adamant she couldn't go. She did, however, have a contingency plan, as any good businesswoman might. She told me I should go alone and enjoy a vacation. She said I needed it. She would stay home with Nick.

I was panicked at my physical reaction to her suggestion. My head started buzzing, and I could feel a churning in my stomach. All I could think about was that Nick couldn't be left alone in New York with Antonia. And the fact this thought even tickled the edges of my consciousness, let alone fell on my head like a ton of bricks, took me by surprise. Was I really thinking I couldn't leave my infant son at home alone with his loving mother? I was terrified that I had to consider this. I took a deep breath and realized something. I was the problem here, not Antonia. I was becoming so attached to Nick that I was completely paralyzed. I hadn't even set up my studio yet. I hadn't lifted a paintbrush. I had let my responsibilities for a baby blot out me. As much as I hated to admit it, Antonia was right. I needed this. So, I went.

~

Mom and Jack were getting married at The St. James's Club on the island of Antigua. The resort consisted of a hotel-like portion, oceanfront suites and several layers of villas situated on a gentle hill that curved down to a pool and the cove where the resort offered paddle boats, ocean kayaks and wind-surfing. Mom and Jack had booked a two-bedroom villa surrounded by fragrant bougainvillea and palm trees and offered me the second bedroom. Kelly and Greg, who were scheduled to arrive the day before the wedding, were booked into an ocean-front suite. And Mom had been right about the resort: it catered to an almost-entirely British clientele.

I had to admit that it was so much better than those resorts catering to American families. On the first day, sitting by the resort pool, I marvelled at how the British parents seemed to have actual control over their children. When the children jumped into the pool, splashing other guests, the parents immediately admonished them, and they complied. When the children spoke loudly enough to annoy their neighbours, a parent would take the child by the hand and tell them, in no uncertain terms, to use their indoor voice. I could learn a lot about parenting just sitting here with a drink in hand, taking in the Caribbean sun. I began to feel better—I was doing research.

One of the best parts of being at a resort catering mainly to British guests is that fourth meal served every afternoon at 3:30 at St. James. I refer, of course, to that fundamentally British tradition: afternoon tea. I loved it.

The afternoon before the wedding, while Mom and Kelly (who had finally arrived earlier that morning on an overnight flight—why she couldn't have come a day earlier was beyond my comprehension) went to a spa, Jack was off doing some sketching and Greg was probably at the bar, I sat myself down at a table on the patio. I ordered Irish breakfast tea, scones with marmalade, lemon curd and clotted cream (who even knew about that excellent stuff?) and finger sandwiches. I wouldn't need to eat again until dinner.

As I waited for my tea, I pulled out a paperback copy of *Bonfire of the Vanities*, the Tom Wolfe bestseller. I'd been meaning to read it since it was published a couple of years ago, and I finally had time. I had taken it with me to Halifax but had never found the time or inclination to read it then. I was thinking about how much had happened in less than a year—it would be a year next month since I'd left New York in search of...of what? I wasn't sure anymore. Anyway, the book was supposed to be the definitive take on late twentieth-century New York City, and since I was no longer a real part of that life (being a stay-at-home dad hardly put you in that rarefied circle), I thought I should keep up.

I had just cracked the cover and begun reading the prologue when a shadow fell over the page. I looked up. My heart stopped for a split second. I would have recognized that mop of unruly dark hair anywhere. And that smile. Then she put her hand on the back of the chair next to me and said, "May I join you?"

Megan—except, of course, it wasn't. The accent was wrong. Not American, but not Canadian, either.

"If you'd rather I didn't," she said, looking around at the patio tables, which were all full. The only empty seat was at my table. "If you'd rather read alone, I quite understand."

I quickly got a hold of my manners and closed the book, sitting up straight. "No, of course not. Please join me."

She seemed to hesitate for a moment. "Oh," she said. "You're an American."

A jot of lightning coursed up my spine. Those were the very first words Megan had said to me last year when I first met her at that museum on the Halifax waterfront. We hadn't gotten off to a very good start. What was it about Canadians and Brits when they met Americans? Were we that off-putting?

"Yes," I said, "guilty as charged."

At that, the beautiful young woman with the wild dark hair gathered her sarong around her, pulled out the chair across from me and plopped herself down. She took a pair of humongous sunglasses from the straw bag she'd laid on the table and arranged them on her face, practically covering it. "Isn't it brilliant here? The rain was tipping down when we flew out last week. This is glorious." She looked as if she had closed her eyes as she tilted her head toward the sky. I couldn't be sure, though, since the sunglasses obscured her eyes. "Oh, I am so sorry," she said quickly. "Where are my manners? I'm Tilly."

"Tim," I said. "Tim Sinclair."

"It is lovely to meet you, Tim Sinclair. Pardon me for being so forward, but I do love to observe people, and I noticed that you've been by yourself a lot over the past two days." Dear god, was she a stalker? How would I get out of this? "Are you here alone?"

"No, no, no," I said. "I'm here with my mother. What I mean to say is that my mother is here. I mean, she's here, but…"

"Oh, I am so sorry once again," Tilly said, removing her sunglasses so that I could now see her ice-blue eyes. "I suppose that might have sounded slightly creepy. I'm not coming on to you if that's what you think."

I mumbled something to the effect that, of course, I didn't think so when clearly I did.

Tilly held up her left hand and waved it at me. Then she pointed to her finger. "Married. As a matter of fact, just married." She looked around and then put her sunglasses back on just as the server asked her for her order. "Earl Grey," she said, "with milk and whatever else he's having." She turned back to me. "I'm on my honeymoon." I started to say something, but Tilly interrupted me. "Of course, your question is: where is my husband? Where, indeed?" She sighed.

"No, it's none of my business."

"You are sweet for an American," she said. "I believe he's playing golf this afternoon. Golf! Who plays golf?"

I shrugged. It had never been anything that I was interested in. I remembered a few years earlier when Antonia had taken a notion that it would be good for business if we—she, Nathan and I—took up golf. She said that many business decisions were made on golf courses. I couldn't have cared less. I hated it. It had reminded me of that Mark Twain line. He's often been quoted as having said that golf is a good walk spoiled.

We sat in silence for a few minutes, with the palm trees swaying high above us, enjoying the Caribbean afternoon. After the server delivered our tea and accoutrements and we had inhaled much of it, Tilly said, "I've told you why I'm here. Now it's your turn. You may have mentioned something about your mother." She smiled sweetly.

I have no idea why, but I told this complete stranger my whole story. I worked backwards from Nick to my wedding to my dilemma and finally to Megan. She sat there rapt. When I had finished, Tilly said, "Oh my, Tim. I should have told you I'm a writer. That would make such a good story." Not exactly what I'd been expecting. "I believe we have to live in the now—the present. What happened to us before and what decisions we made—good or bad—might have led us to where we are now, but they're not the now. You know what I mean?"

I did. I think.

"Do you think everything happens for a reason, Tim?" Tilly bit into a scone, then took a deep breath as if in rapture.

"To tell you the truth, I haven't given that much thought, Tilly."

"Well, think about it for a moment," she said, wiping her mouth with the linen napkin on her lap. "Wouldn't it be lovely to think that the bad things that happen to us are there to guide us toward our right path? And wouldn't it be nice to think that if a stranger sits down to have tea with you, there might be a reason for it?"

I laughed. "Yes, it would be nice."

"Then, Tim Sinclair, I offer you this. *"Never close your lips to those whom you have already opened your heart."* She sipped her tea daintily. "Charles Dickens, of course."

~

Mom and Jack were married at sunset the following day. We stood in a small circle at the water's edge as the waves lapped at our toes. We were all barefoot, and the thought of Grace Sinclair getting married in bare feet almost made me laugh out loud. When the officiant whom the resort had provided arrived, the short service began. I could see people gathering to watch yet keeping their distance. Out of the corner of my eye, I spotted

Tilley holding the arm of a tall, good-looking young man with a smile plastered across her face. I smiled and nodded toward the honeymooners, then turned my attention back to the ceremony.

Antonia and I had been married now for a mere four months, but it felt like so much longer. After all, we'd been together for almost six years, and I suppose I'd come to believe it was forever—at least until last April when I met Megan. But I couldn't think about that now. It was behind me. I had to focus on the future, and right now, my mother's future was supposed to be the most important thing on my mind.

As my thoughts returned to the present moment, I heard the officiant pronouncing Mom and Jack husband and wife, and I thought, *I know you're happy for them, Dad. I am, too.*

Suddenly, Kelly was there in front of me, holding out a champagne flute. "Where the hell is Antonia, Tim?"

"Home with Nick," I said, taking the offered glass.

Kelly's long blonde locks moved around her shoulders as she shook her head. I thought this must be the first time I'd seen her without a ponytail since she was a teenager. "She should be here, Tim. You could have brought the baby with you. Mom would have loved that."

"It's not that easy to travel with a baby, Kel." I felt just a bit defensive, which was odd because her view on the subject probably echoed what I felt. Antonia and Nick could have come, except for the Antonia-work thing.

Kelly shrugged. "Oh well, you're here. By the way, Greg and I have found a house in Toronto., We're moving next month. Will you come to visit us?"

"Sure," I said. "Let's just wait until Nick is a bit older, okay?"

"Whatever," she said, turning away from me and returning to Greg's side. "Toronto's an awesome city, Tim. Just saying."

~

As winter turned into a New York spring, Nick and I ventured farther out into the city, finding playgrounds populated by kids, moms and nannies—lots of nannies. By May, we'd settled on a playground a fifteen-minute walk from the brownstone where the mothers (and some of the nannies) began to chat. They seemed to find me endlessly fascinating when they discovered I was a househusband. They couldn't get their heads around the fact that I was "willing" to "let my wife" work while I stayed home. Let my wife? I didn't bother relating that to Antonia because I knew what her response would be: what century do they think this is? I have to admit, I agreed with that sentiment. But I did find the moms a veritable font of baby and child-related information.

They told me about the best baby gear stores, where to buy books for kids, and how to find a well-vetted evening babysitter—I wrote that telephone number down as quickly as I could. As the months wore on and Nick started to crawl and then walk, the moms started a new conversation. It was all about where they planned to send their kids to pre-school. Of course, in the next breath would be the question: where are you going to send Nick? Nick wasn't even a year old. The thought had never entered my mind, but according to them, it should have.

The popular choice for preschool among this well-heeled group was a nearby Montessori school. As far as I could tell, it seemed to be the flavour of the month. When I mentioned this to Antonia one evening, she immediately pounced on the idea. She seemed a bit rattled that she hadn't thought of this herself, so she gave me strict instructions to conduct thorough research on the school and report back. I almost saluted.

I knew nothing about Montessori pre-schools. Let's be honest here: I knew nothing about pre-schools in general. Who did before a little guy came into his life? Anyway, as far as I could figure out, Montessori was a method of teaching young children created by a woman in the early twentieth century whose name was—you guessed it—Montessori, Maria Montessori, to be precise. It seemed harmless enough. From what I read about it from a book I borrowed from the library, they seemed to emphasize independent learning. I had no idea what that might mean for a kid as young as two or three. In fact, I worried that it might be a bit *too* loose. This aspect of the method made me wonder if Antonia really knew what we might be getting into. After all, she was about as regimented as they came. Anyway, she had her mind set on Nick going to Montessori school and eventually, he did. It would be a few years yet before Antonia got into a screaming match with a Montessori teacher about their so-called non-traditional grading system and their loose approach to curriculum. Loose and non-traditional were not words in Antonia's vocabulary. But I'm getting ahead of myself.

It was summer by the time I realized I should get going on my artwork. Antonia had begun asking about it more and more frequently, and every time I talked to my mother, she seemed to be on the same wavelength. So, in early July, I dragged my supplies, drafting table and easel—which had been languishing in a corner of the basement—up those narrow stairs and began to set up a space I thought might nurture creativity. I had deliberately left my old work in a large black leather portfolio, which I tucked away beside my drafting table. In my mind, it was from a different life—a different me. Then, one morning in August, while Nick was sleeping downstairs and I was working on a preliminary sketch of the playground we frequented, I dropped a charcoal pencil.

As I bent down to pick it up, my eyes rested on the portfolio, leaning against the leg of the drafting table where I had tucked it a month earlier. I sat up and considered it for a moment. I realized I was hiding something away, so I pulled it out, laid it on the drafting table, and began pulling paintings out.

The first ones that came out were the watercolour paintings of the cemetery and the grave markers for the Titanic victims. I considered them, and it occurred to me that they were pretty good. The next one was of the Halifax harbour. It was even better. The third one was Meg. It was the watercolour portrait I'd worked on after Antonia had appeared at the cottage, and Meg refused to speak to me. At the time, I'd thought it would be my only remembrance of her. And, as it turned out, I'd been right. I clipped it up on the wall and stood back to consider how it made me feel.

As I gazed at Meg's likeness, I felt sad. But I wasn't sure what made me sad. Was it that I'd lost her? Or was it that I'd found her at the wrong time? And, once again, I was reminded that timing wasn't one of my strong points.

I slid the painting back into the portfolio and tied it up. Then I slid the portfolio back into its spot behind the drafting table. I wondered if I'd ever take it out again.

~

As far as I could tell, Antonia was relishing her new partnership and the perks it offered. Chief among them was the large corner office she now enjoyed, in addition to not one but two assistants. Lisa-Marie, who had recently married, was still with her, but Antonia had also hired a young man whose name I could never seem to remember. She regaled me with stories of the office, and I felt further and further removed from that life. Over time, the fact that I hadn't had any success with my art made me feel increasingly removed from life in general. If I had realized this might go on for several years, I might have made a different decision. Maybe.

Antonia seemed to go from strength to strength at work. The day she called me from the office to tell me they were adding her name to the firm's name, I could hear the elation in her voice. She had finally accomplished this major goal—she was smashing the glass ceiling she and all the other women I'd worked with talked about. Then the invitations started trickling in. Within a year, they were gushing.

The invitations were sometimes to speak to mixed groups about the Madison Avenue approach to marketing and advertising. More and more frequently, though, women's business organizations asked her to talk about women making it to the top of male-dominated fields. And as far as I could figure out, the number of organizations for businesswomen was mushrooming. Antonia spent at least three days each month flying to Chicago, LA, Denver, London and even Toronto. I was proud of her, and she seemed to be flourishing. Only once did the topic of having another child ever come up. Antonia put a stop to it as quickly as possible. "You can work one child into your life," she said. "But having two children makes you a professional parent." That was the end of the conversation. I never brought it up again. With only one child, I could probably get more work done anyway, but even one child was always a going concern. There was always something new to consider.

By the time Nick was three years old, Antonia had decreed it was time he began his music education.

"Don't you think three is a bit young?" I said the Saturday afternoon when the topic came up for serious discussion—at least Antonia was serious about it. "I mean, does anyone even teach kids as young as three?" I was more than supportive of a child having a music education, but this seemed premature.

"The Suzuki people," she said. "That's who teaches kids that young."

And I was off again to research another flavour-of-the-month—at least, that's what it seemed to me. I found a Suzuki teacher, a quarter-size violin (who knew they made them that small?) and embarked on violin lessons with a three-year-old.

At first, Nick seemed excited about the lessons. He was becoming a very active child, always running up and down the stairs, a ball of electric energy. I wasn't sure he could sit still for long enough to learn to play the violin at such a young age. And who had the patience to play only one song for a whole year? Yes, that's right—one piece for a whole year. The child had to play it, and the parent had to listen to it. I soon realized that for the rest of my life, I'd go screaming in the opposite direction if anyone even hummed "Twinkle, Twinkle Little Star." And that wasn't all.

Have you ever heard someone learning to play the violin? All that squeaking and squawking was enough to drive even the sanest parent nuts—and by that point, I'm not so sure I was the most rational of parents. But the thing that drove me over the edge wasn't those weekly private lessons I had to attend with Nick and his teacher. It was the mandatory weekly group sessions where ten or so kids and their parents sat in a circle while the children all played varying versions of "Twinkle, Twinkle, Little Star" until I thought that at any minute, I'd go mad. Antonia might have had her day of reckoning with a Montessori teacher, but mine came during one of those group sessions when Nick decided he'd had enough, put his violin on the floor and proceeded to run back and forth between the other children.

"Don't worry," the teacher whispered to me. "Whatever he wants to do is just fine."

"No," I said, finally finding my voice, "no, nothing is fine. If he doesn't want to play, he shouldn't be here."

The teacher shot me a look that I interpreted as meaning I was an idiot and then said, "Mr. Sinclair, we must persevere."

*No*, I thought, *we must not persevere. We must know when to hold them and when to fold them, when to walk away and when to run,* and this was my moment to run. Nick and I never went back to Suzuki school.

~

Mom and Jack had now been happily married for three years. Mom sold her house in Boston, and they moved into the Bar Harbor house full time. They made the trip to Nova Scotia to visit the Kaufman Gallery two or three times a year, and every time I talked to her, I could tell that they were becoming increasingly enamoured of Halifax. I even worried that they might pull up stakes and move there. I would have to disabuse them of this notion as subtly as possible. It became my pet project. Every time Mom called to tell me about their most recent trip, I always had something negative to say about Nova Scotia—rain, drizzle and fog, the lack of airline connection to major cities—basically, anything I could think of and not all of them were well-conceived or perhaps even true. When I reflect on my behaviour, I'm not proud, but I could not let them move there. They might want me to come and visit, and that would be out of the question. Jack was fast becoming a fixture of the art scene there, and I was only a tad jealous. But the day she called and told me they were considering real estate in Halifax, I felt my heart beat faster—and not in a good way.

"You're not seriously considering buying property there, are you, Mom"

"I suppose we are, Tim. I know you have baggage, but you're a big boy and will have to get over it. Anyway, we're not moving there. We're just looking at a small house in the city where we can stay whenever Jack has to be there. He and Nigel are moving toward a more permanent relationship."

Nigel had offered Jack a partnership in the gallery. I was happy for Jack, but I wondered why it had to be in that city. I also had the unkind notion that Jack was a tad old to be starting a new venture. Then Jack called me one afternoon while I was getting ready to pick Nick up at preschool.

"Tim, my boy. I have a proposition for you."

This sounded interesting.

"You know those paintings you showed me when your mom and I were last over to dinner?" he said.

I did remember. Jack, who had always been one of my art cheerleaders, had asked to see what I was working on. It was a natural curiosity, given our past relationship as art teacher and student. So, I had taken him up the back stairs and given him a private showing—of two pieces.

"Well, Tim, I'd like to have a showing of your work in the Halifax gallery. I think the local art lovers would lap them up in a heartbeat."

My heart began racing. I could actually feel the pulse in my neck throbbing. This was an offer too good to pass up, but I had to. I simply could not go to Halifax.

# 18

# Antonia

## 1990-1993

*Two roads diverged in a yellow wood,*
*And sorry I could not travel both*
*And be one traveller, long I stood*
*And looked down one as far as I could…Then took*
*the other… ~ Robert Frost*

I REMEMBER WHEN I WAS A LITTLE GIRL, and my mother worked late, leaving me home alone after school. I'd unlock the front door of our bungalow and make my way to the kitchen. I was a latch-key kid before anyone had ever heard the term. She always left me a snack. Sometimes it was a peanut butter sandwich, but some days, when she felt very happy (a situation that happened less and less frequently as I got older), she'd leave me a bag of potato chips and a book. Mom used to pick up used books whenever she had a chance. Whatever else I might have thought about my mother, I had always been grateful that she had encouraged the reader in me.

One memorable day when I was twelve, I came home to find a bag of chips and a book. The book was usually a dogeared soft-cover book, but that day, it was different. It was a hardcover book that looked like it had hardly been touched. I opened the front cover. There was a note in my mother's printing—she printed everything because she said her handwriting was illegible. The note said, "I know you're probably too old for this book, but I thought you might enjoy some of the stories." It was *Aesop's Fables*.

I sat down and began devouring the book along with the bag of potato chips. It took me two days to get through all the fables, and when I'd finished, I sat down and wrote about my impressions in my diary. One story had made my hair stand on end, and I could not figure out why it affected me this way. It would be many years later before I would truly understand the moral of the story.

It was one you've probably heard many times. In its original form, the moral said this: *Be careful what you wish for, lest it come true.* Aesop may have written that morality tale many years BCE, but it wasn't until about three years after Nicholas was born that I truly began to feel its meaning. And once I felt it, I couldn't unfeel it.

Tim and Nathan had always been right about me. Over the years, when we worked together at the agency, each one of them, in their own way, had occasion to mention that I seemed to be driven. I had an internal engine that pushed me forward toward an often unknown target. Sometimes, when I could figure out what the target was, that determination within me excited me even more. What I wished for most back then was to be successful. And not just a successful woman—a successful person. Those were not the same at all in the 1990s. I wanted people not to have to talk about me as if I were successful "for a woman." I didn't want to be differentiated from the men. I wanted to be their main competition. And the day Ken had told me he and the other partners wanted to elevate me in the agency, I felt I might be getting there. But it only made me feel that I needed another goal and then another.

The timing, however, wasn't perfect. But when Tim told me he would take over child and housecare duties, I knew I had it made. I worked long hours and took on more responsibility. I was richly rewarded for these decisions—at least at work. Eventually, outside organizations began inviting me to speak at bigger and bigger gatherings—to be a mentor for young women in business. I discovered that I loved being in the spotlight and cultivated my persona to fit the organizations' wishes and demands. I was good at it, and eventually, I could command greater fees. There was only one snag in all this, and it was a big one. The more successful I became, the more I had to hide myself. I could never tell Tim (and especially not his mother, the sainted Grace Sinclair) the truth. I was jealous.

I was jealous of Tim and his relationship with Nicholas. I could see their bond growing stronger daily, and it sucked a tiny piece from my heart every time I noticed it. The only thing I could do was double down on the work-related responsibilities to prove, at least, that I could be a success on Madison Avenue.

I remember coming home from work one evening, tired as usual, when Tim began telling me about the latest mommy discussion at the park or at a play date or whatever. At first, I bristled at the image of Tim in the park with the New York yummy mummy brigade, but I put that aside as he spoke.

"It seems we should be thinking about where Nicholas will go to preschool," he said as we sat in the living room with a glass of wine.

I sipped my wine as I considered this, and the wisdom of such a consideration didn't escape me. "Oh my god, Tim, how could we have let this get away from us? Of course, we need to think about this. We should have started already. He needs to be on lists before they're all filled."

Tim shrugged. "The girls say we should be considering the Montessori School over on Wyatt Avenue."

Montessori—now there was a word I'd read about in one of those parenting books I'd reviewed. I immediately pounced on it. "Yes, they're probably right," I said, mentally berating myself for not thinking of it myself. "Tim, why don't we gather as much information on the school as we can." By "we," I naturally meant him. I was busy, after all.

Tim did as I asked, gathered the research, applied, and eventually took Nicholas for an interview (who interviews toddlers?), and in due course, he was accepted. We prepared for his first day of preschool. That day, Tim was on parental duty because I was busy with an important client pitch that first September morning, but I finally managed to get away early one afternoon a few weeks later. So, I presented myself at the school, requesting to observe my son's class.

The headmistress looked at me disdainfully. "Mrs. Sinclair," she began.

"It's Ms. St. John," I said, correcting her.

"Yes, of course, it is," she said. Already, I didn't like the direction of this conversation. "Nicholas is busy with his cohort at the moment," she said, fiddling with a folder on her desk. She was sitting at her desk while I stood in front. "I'm sure you understand."

I didn't understand at all. I continued to insist, and she finally got tired of me standing there, so she agreed to let me have fifteen minutes. I was told, in no uncertain terms, not to interfere.

To say I was perplexed by what I saw that day would be an understatement. There were what I could only describe as stations where each child wandered whenever the notion struck. No one seemed to be in charge of this group of preschoolers. Were they expected to police themselves? Was this what their brochure called independent learning? When I asked later about structure for three-year-old children, I was told that structure was over-rated. I disagreed but kept my opinion to myself—for the moment.

Eight months later, when I noticed that Nicholas could never keep still and didn't seem to know how to focus on anything, I had it out with the headmistress again. It was not my finest moment, but one thing I had noticed about my little son—despite spending less time with him than I would have wanted—was that he was energetic. I was frightened that if he didn't either have a preschool experience where he could learn his social boundaries or find an outlet for all that energy—or preferably both—he would have problems in school. There was a lot of recent chatter in the news and in the magazines I occasionally had time to read about something called hyperactivity. As far as I was concerned, no one would label my child. I would find a way to deal with this before it became a problem. In the end, the problem took care of itself as they so often do in life. Suffice it to say that there was a shouting match pitting me against the headmistress. I may have even called her a bogus granola airhead—or something like that—and eventually told her to "bite me" when she told me I was an over-weaning absent mother with a severe guilt complex. But, then, who can really remember what is said in the heat of the moment?

I pulled Nicholas from the school immediately. Interestingly, Tim wasn't the slightest bit perturbed about it. He even snickered when I later related the details of the argument to him. It turned out that he had noticed the same issues but had followed through with this Montessori thing because he thought it was what I wanted. What I wanted was to have a well-adjusted child. No, what I really wanted was to spend more time with my son, but that didn't seem to be in the cards.

~

Sometime before Nicholas's fourth birthday, Kelly called us from Toronto, where she had been living for two years, running her new yoga-pilates-ballet studio, and asked if she could stay with us when she visited New York in a few weeks. Of course, we agreed. She was attending a conference for yoga teachers. What she didn't tell us was that she and Greg had gone their separate ways. When she arrived, she was a mess, both literally and figuratively.

I had never seen Kelly so dishevelled. I hoped it didn't have anything to do with the yoga lifestyle thing, which I didn't get at all. But more than that, she seemed genuinely devastated by her breakup. She had just celebrated her thirty-first birthday and had desperately wanted a child. One evening while she was visiting, she got drunk. Well, I think we all did a little.

After her fifth glass of wine, she turned to me and said, "What's wrong with you, Antonia? Why don't you love your son?"

I began to get up off the sofa, ready to slap her up the side of the head, when Tim caught my arm.

"If you loved your son, you'd spend more time with him." Kelly seemed to be on a roll.

"How would you know what a mother should or shouldn't do?" I said, a red tide of anger rising up my spine.

As soon as the words were out of my mouth, Kelly began sobbing. This was not pretty sobbing. It was wracking, snivelling sobs with tears pouring from her eyes. "I'm so sorry, Antonia. It's just that I had a miscarriage last year, and I don't think I'll ever be able to have children." She had never told us.

Wasn't it ironic? The woman who so wanted a baby couldn't have one, while the one focused on her career didn't seem to have a choice.

The following day, Kelly seemed to have forgotten entirely about her outburst. I still bristled when I thought about it, but I was willing to let it go. She bounced down the stairs for dinner, holding Nicholas's hand. "Oh, my actual god, Antonia! Nick and I were just upstairs dancing."

I looked at Nicholas and saw his rosy cheeks and the widest smile I'd ever seen.

"I danced with Auntie Kelly, Mommy. We had music."

"We did have music, Antonia, and I'm going to take Nick with me tomorrow when I have lunch with my old friend, Annalise. I'm going to show Nick some real dancers."

Then I remembered that Annalise was an old friend of Kelly's from back when she was an aspiring dancer. Annalise now danced with the New York City Ballet. Good god. She was going to show him ballet dancers. I was sure that could come to no good.

# 19

# Grace

## 1990–1993

*When your mother asks, "Do you want a piece of
advice?" it's a mere formality. It doesn't matter if
you answer yes or no. You're going to get it
anyway.* ~ Erma Bombeck

JACK AND I SETTLED EASILY INTO MARRIAGE—in fact, more easily
than I could have predicted. Douglas and I had enjoyed a strong
bond for many years, but after he died, I learned to like my own
company. I liked the life I had between Boston and Bar Harbor. I
liked my homes, my work and my life. When Jack and I started
having dinner regularly at the yacht club, it just seemed to add to
my enjoyment of life, but I wasn't looking for anyone to rescue
me from widowhood. I didn't need rescuing—I was no damsel in
distress—because I had come to terms with being a widow, and
life didn't frighten me. I was surprised at how much I enjoyed
this man's company—someone I'd known only slightly when
Tim was in high school. Then our relationship developed into so
much more, and I realized I had room in my life for another
relationship—another adventure. The day I married Jack on that
beach in Antigua was truly one of the happiest of my life, and the
next few years did not disappoint.

First, together we made the decision that we would settle
into a seaside life in Bar Harbor, so I sold my house in Boston,
and Jack sold his. Then I set up a trust fund for Nicholas. Of

course, I didn't tell Tim and Antonia about it, but it would be there when needed. Although I had great faith in Antonia and her career, I have to admit, feminism notwithstanding, I had always thought she might come to regret her decision to be so removed from the day-to-day aspects of little Nicholas's life.

I remember the moment I first began to think that my concerns about Antonia might have been justified when I noticed what looked like jealousy of Tim's relationship with Nicholas. It was an odd feeling because although I had considered the possibility that my daughter-in-law might regret—at least a little bit—her decision to be the sole breadwinner for her family in the long term, I didn't want to be right. I say this not because I doubted my son's talent as an artist but because I had always been aware of the vagaries of the artistic life. Jack and I often talked about his own teaching career. He had chosen to see it not so much as his second choice but as his first step toward a career as a fine artist. Like me, he was a pragmatist at heart. The fact that this second step began when he was sixty-five was irrelevant. The point was that he had begun. But Antonia was a different matter.

Antonia was always a woman on a mission. Ever since Tim had begun dating her, I knew she was hell-bent on making it to the top. She seemed to go from strength to strength, at least as Tim told it, but Antonia and I never had a single conversation about her career. I got the impression from her that it was a subject she preferred not to talk about with her mother-in-law. That was fine with me. I was more interested in my grandson, anyway. But by the time Tim and Antonia began talking about sending Nicholas to preschool, I could see the cracks in her armour. She seemed almost desperate.

We were having Thanksgiving dinner in New York with Antonia, Tim and Nicholas. Nicholas was not yet a year old. While we were all savouring the first bites of our turkey dinner, Antonia began expounding on the great benefits of Montessori schools. I wasn't certain if she was giving a lecture on the method or desperately seeking validation of a decision she had clearly already made. I knew only a bit about the approach, but it occurred to me that perhaps it was a bit early in my grandson's life to be considering a school of any kind. I made the mistake of voicing my opinion. Reaction was swift and, dare I say, testy.

"Well, Grace, I don't suppose you know what it's like to have children these days. It is, after all, the 1990s, and it is a much more competitive society than you might be used to," Antonia said tersely.

I took my time answering, hoping to avoid family holiday drama. "Yes, I suppose things are different. I only meant that there might be some value in permitting a baby to be a baby and a toddler to be a toddler."

I could almost see the hairs on the back of Antonia's neck rise. I could tell she was irritated with me, and I instantly regretted wading into the issue that seemed a bit fraught.

"How dare you question my mothering instincts. Just because I work long hours to ensure our family's comfort, I don't see how that makes me a bad mother for considering my son's future!"

I had said no such thing and hadn't thought I'd even implied it, but it was crystal clear at that moment that I wouldn't have needed to say it anyway. Antonia was saying it to herself. Once the outburst was finished, Antonia seemed to deflate. I looked at Tim, who was fiddling with his fork and appeared to be as much at a loss as I did, or at least he was trying to avoid wading into a misunderstanding between his wife and his mother. Jack, always the peacemaker, immediately began to fill in the void by discussing the latest show he was working on for the Halifax gallery. His usual approach was to distract if defusion didn't seem to be the way to go. And so, we moved away from the subject of Nicholas's preschool. I looked at my little grandson as he sat in his enormous highchair at the table between Antonia and me, sucking on a piece of baby biscuit, and wondered what he'd grow up to be.  I hoped an early foray into preschool wouldn't be too traumatic!

~

After our first trip to Nova Scotia in October before our winter wedding, we plotted and planned how to get back there as often as we could. We enjoyed the place that much. With the offer of a show in the new year, Jack worked feverishly through that winter to prepare for the show at the Kaufman Gallery as he had arranged on that first visit. Jack sent his paintings for the show by courier ahead of time, and four days before the show was scheduled, we got into the car again and drove to Halifax. As I contemplated my packing, I realized that I was excited to be returning. There was something special about the city.

Douglas and I had been to Halifax on several previous occasions. I realized that I'd felt this way before. I was drawn to the idea that a little city like Halifax was a cross between a big city like Boston (which it was not) and a sleepy seaside village like Bar Harbor (which it was not). So after the unmitigated success of Jack's first show, we began to visit regularly. Jack and Nigel became friends, and whenever Jack and he had meetings, I spent my time getting to know the city. I would wander out the door of the gallery to find myself on Water Street. Just below Water Street was the area they called Historic Properties along the harbourfront. I loved the boardwalk and could feel the excitement of the plans for its expansion that I'd read about in the local newspaper. I loved the old stone buildings and the sense of history at every turn. I would then walk up to Citadel Hill, a fortress in the centre of the downtown area—a defence that had never had occasion to fire a gun.

Then I'd take myself to the Public Gardens—an oasis of English country charm in the centre of the city. It was no Central Park, but I loved the winding pathways through cultivated gardens, the large duck pond at its centre and the swans. I would sometimes feel energetic and walk farther afield, strolling down Young Avenue past the most impressive houses in the city, observing the little architectural touches and the way the exteriors of the homes were decorated. There was an especially impressive stone mansion with a turret that I later discovered was owned by a brewery baron. I kept notes in a little Moleskine® notebook. As a designer, I could never be sure when I'd need such inspiration. Then, when I was energetic, I'd continue.

The stroll down Young Avenue led me to Point Pleasant Park, a point of land comprising almost two hundred acres of forest and walking trails surrounded on three sides by water. I don't remember the exact moment I realized it, but I suddenly had the feeling I should move to Halifax. The feeling enveloped me like a warm blanket. It felt nice, but it was somehow foreign at the same time. There was some unseen force drawing me to the city—something more potent than I'd ever felt before on any other trip. I told Jack about it that evening.

"You don't mean to say you want to move here, do you?" he said. "It's that much farther away from New York and your wee grandson, my dear."

I shrugged. I wasn't sure if I really wanted to move, but that tug at my heart wouldn't go away. There was just something about the place that made me feel like I belonged here.

Over the next couple of years, I felt the same every time I visited the city with Jack, whose business relationship with Nigel seemed to grow with each visit. When Nigel offered Jack a partnership in the gallery business, I was delighted. Then Jack asked me about Tim.

We were sitting down to dinner one evening when the subject of Tim's art came up.

"When Nigel and I were talking on the phone the other day," Jack said, "he asked me how Tim's doing with his art career. Remember that painting Tim had left in the gallery?" I nodded.

"Well, it seems that after a local collector bought it, the gallery had a noticeable number of people ask them about the artist. Nigel wants to know what to tell them."

"I honestly don't know," I said. "I've broached the subject with Tim, but he doesn't seem willing to share any of his work. I know he has had an occasional conversation with an old classmate from art school who is doing very well internationally, but Tim hasn't suggested he has a body of work ready for exhibition if that's what you're asking."

"You are perceptive, my dear. That is exactly what I'm asking. And so is Nigel. Tim showed me two of his new works not long ago when we were over for dinner, and they're terrific, but that's all he'd share—just two pieces. Anyway, I'm going to make Tim a proposition. He could begin his exhibiting at the Halifax gallery. That should be far enough away from the New York critics."

I looked at Jack carefully. "Do you suppose it's the idea of the critics that bothers Tim?"

"I can't be sure," Jack said, "but I do know that it's how I felt at one time. I also know a thing or two about starting small. This could be Tim's chance."

I was more than pleased that Jack had decided to offer Tim an opportunity. We chatted a bit more about how we might convince Tim to take advantage of the offer. Then Jack said, "By the way, Grace, my love, when are you planning to tell Tim that we've started looking for a small house in Halifax?"

I had told him about Tim's issue with Halifax, so he knew why Tim was reluctant to be involved with anything related to the city.

"I'll call him tomorrow," I said. And I was true to my word.

As expected, Tim was negative about everything I said about Halifax. If he thought I didn't notice how much he discouraged my growing affinity for the city each time I mentioned it, he didn't know his mother very well. It was crystal clear to me. This time, though, I'd had enough. It had been several years since his dalliance (for lack of a more precise word—mothers can never know for sure), and he had moved on to a new era in his life, but it was an era that was quickly stagnating. It was one thing to make a commitment to a child, but it was quite another to immerse yourself so completely in a child that you forget who you are—so that you disappear. I'd seen too many young women do it, and I wasn't going to stand there and watch my son do it. It was too much pressure for the child to make him your whole world. I didn't want that for Nicholas—or Tim. I told him it was time to get over it.

Now it was Jack's turn to call him to propose that Tim have his first real show in Halifax. As expected, Tim's first inclination was to say no. I had my work cut out for me.

~

I had given Tim a few weeks to stew over the idea. Just before I picked up the phone to begin my campaign to get him to change his mind, Kelly called me from Toronto in tears to tell me that she and Greg had broken up. I knew she'd had a miscarriage the year before (she had sworn me to secrecy, so I'd not shared this with anyone else—not even Jack) and feared she'd never have a child. So, she was feeling more than just the pain of a breakup. She asked me if I thought Tim and Antonia would let her stay with them for a couple of weeks so she could attend a yoga conference in New York and pull herself together. With both of my children facing a crossroads in their lives, I thought it might be a good time for Mom to visit. And since they were both going to be in the same city for a few weeks, it was ideal. I didn't tell her that I'd be joining them.

I arrived in New York on a cold day in November, a month before Nicholas would turn four. I checked into The Algonquin, then hurried out to find a cab to drop me at Tim's. I was anxious to see my little family. The moment Tim opened the door, I was greeted by a flash of red as Nicholas sped by the door, a dramatic cape flying out behind him.

"I'm Superman, Gran! Watch me go!" And he was off, swooping and soaring, his almost four-year-old arms straight out in front of him, leading the way.

I laughed as Tim embraced me. "Hi, Mom. How are you? I think you can see how Nick is." Indeed, I could.

I hadn't seen Nicholas in several months, and I was astonished at how much he'd grown and how much his energy level seemed to be mushrooming. He was maturing before my eyes. Nicholas was smart, funny and articulate, and a physically beautiful child with his floppy dark hair, brown eyes and creamy skin. But doesn't every grandmother think that?

Tim took my coat and handbag, and we repaired to the living room, as they say, where Tim had lit a beautiful crackling fire. As you do, I immediately went to the fireplace to warm my hands, although truthfully, they weren't that cold. It just seems like we're drawn to some images, aren't we? I turned back to Tim, who was pouring wine into two of the four glasses he'd laid on the coffee table. I presumed the other two were for Antonia when she returned from work in due course and Kelly, who hadn't yet materialized, although I knew she had arrived a few days earlier.

"Is your sister here?" I said, gratefully accepting the glass of red from Tim.

"She's out for a walk. Um, Mom, do you know why—"

"Do I know why she's here? Yes, I know that she and Gregory broke up." Tim looked like he was about to say something he couldn't quite get out. "I also know about the miscarriage." It was clear Kelly had finally revealed her secret to her brother. "I suppose she also told you she's now unable to have children?"

Tim nodded. "I don't know what to say to her, Mom. Brothers aren't so good at that kind of thing."

"I suppose not," I said, sipping thoughtfully for a moment. "The truth is, though, that Kelly made that diagnosis herself."

"What?"

"No medical opinion was involved in her conclusion about not being able to have a child in the future. You know your sister. She was always a child who would make up a story with only the slightest provocation. It was her way of dealing with things that upset her. Don't worry. When she gets over the breakup and meets someone new, she'll do an inventory of her strengths again and see that motherhood might well be in her future. Until then," I raised my glass, "let's drink to her speedy recovery." That elicited a smile from my son, who knew very well that the speedier it was, the better when it came to his sister.

When Antonia and Kelly had both arrived home, Tim ordered pizza, and we had a (somewhat) delightful Friday evening *à la famille*. It was delightful if we could all ignore that pout on Kelly's face—the one I thought she'd left behind in her teenage years. It was nice to have both of my kids in the same room.

The following day, I did a few shopping errands and ate a quick lunch at the Palm Court at The Plaza—what woman of a certain age and sensibility can visit New York without a luncheon at The Palm Court? And, if I'm being frank, I didn't want to ruin a perfectly good New York moment by inviting my mopey daughter. As I ate, I considered the possibility that I was being a bit harsh on her. But the truth is that Kelly's pregnancy had been unplanned and unwanted. I knew this because it was exactly what she had told me when she called to tell me what had happened after insisting I swear to keep her secret. Even then, she and Gregory were having second thoughts about the relationship, and she was hysterical about how she might procure an abortion. Before she had a chance to figure anything out—and before even telling Gregory about the pregnancy—she miscarried. The pragmatist in me couldn't help but think that it was for the best and that things have a way of working out. I suppose that kind of equanimity comes with age and experience, so I knew it would not do Kelly or me any favours if I relayed this perspective to her at the time. In time, she would come to that conclusion herself.

It was after lunch by the time I arrived back at Tim and Antonia's, only to find that Tim was alone in the house.

"Where is everyone?" I said, unwinding my new silk scarf.

"Antonia is having lunch with Nathan." I must have looked confused. "Remember Nathan? Our friend? Antonia's best person at our wedding?"

Finally, it clicked. "Oh, yes. His partner was that wonderful wedding planner. How are they both?"

Tim laughed. "Well, they weren't partners back when you met them, but they're still going strong as far as I can tell."

"And Kelly and Nicholas?"

"It's a bit weird, but Kelly and Nick are gone to see Annalise, Kelly's old friend."

"Annalise, the ballerina? How wonderful for Kelly to reconnect with old friends, but why is Nicholas with her?"

Tim shrugged. "That's the weird part. Kelly said she and Nick were dancing upstairs, and suddenly, she thinks Nick should see some ballet dancers. To tell you the truth, it was the first time I'd seen her smile since she got here this week, so I just let her take him."

"Interesting," I thought. But to myself, I was thinking it was *more* than interesting. Then I realized this was the opportunity I'd been waiting for. "Tim, I'd love to see your current work. Will you let me into your studio?" I was relieved when he smiled.

"You know, Mom, I'd like you to see some of it. The stairs to the studio are steep, though." He immediately clapped his hand over his mouth. "Sorry, Mom. I didn't mean—"

"You didn't mean that I'm old, right?" I laughed. "Well, as it turns out, I'm not, Timothy Sinclair. Lead the way."

Thus, I found myself sitting under the sloping ceiling in Tim's attic studio, lit by watery November sunshine through two skylights, surrounded by watercolour paintings and pastel drawings. The work was extraordinary.

Tim had captured so many aspects of the New York City's urban grit and the seaside idyl of the Bar Harbor of his youth. At least the coastal paintings resembled Bar Harbor. On closer inspection, I realized they were Tim's interpretation of many of the same parts of Halifax that had captivated me—the historic properties on the waterfront, the citadel, the harbour, the gardens, the park. They were all there. What was missing were people. Tim used to paint watercolours of people, and there were none. Before I had a chance to ask him about this, we heard the telephone ring downstairs.

"You stay here, Mom. I'll get that and be back. Hold tight."

When Tim had gone, I got up to see what else he had piled on the drafting table he kept by the round window that overlooked the street below. I did not doubt that there was a significant enough body of work here to mount a show. Jack, and especially Nigel, would be elated—if only I could convince Tim to let them organize it. That's when I saw it.

A large black leather portfolio was peeking out from where it was tucked beside the drafting table. It looked intriguing, and I wondered if Tim planned to show me what was in it. I drummed my fingers on the desk, thinking about whether I should open it without him. *What the heck*, I thought. *It probably contains his best work*. I lifted it onto the desk and opened it.

There was a lovely watercolour of the Halifax harbour ferry on top. I stared at it for a moment, then moved it aside. Beneath it, was the most extraordinary watercolour portrait. I picked it up carefully and took it over near a skylight, clipping it to the wall with one of the vacant clips Tim had installed. I stood back and gasped. Not only was the painting exceptional in itself, making the viewer feel as if the subject were alive in the room, but I felt I knew whose image it was.

"Mom! What are you doing?"

I turned toward Tim, who had come up the stairs and was now standing in the attic doorway, silhouetted in the light from the staircase. He began moving toward me as if panicked.

"Mom, please."

"It's Megan, isn't it?"

Tim sank onto the stool beside the drafting table and put his head in his hands. "No one was ever supposed to see that."

"Timothy, my darling son, if that were true, you would have destroyed it. But you know how remarkable it is, don't you?" He nodded sadly. "Tell me. Tell me everything." And so he did.

Tim had told me the bare bones of the story of how he had met Megan McMaster and how he had deceived her by omission. But he had not told me everything.

"Mom, that September, when I first came back to New York from Halifax, I planned to tell Antonia that we were finished—that I couldn't see a way forward for a life together. But Antonia and I seemed to have grown apart. We seemed to want different things. I planned to tell her that I was moving to Halifax even though, at that point, I didn't even know if Meg would ever talk to me again. I was also planning to tell Antonia I was giving up advertising to be an artist full-time. Isn't it funny how the last part came true anyway?"

"Something you're supposed to do?"

He nodded and continued. "I loved Antonia, but I had lost that feeling we had for the first few years where we just knew that together we could accomplish anything. She knew I was becoming more and more jaded about my work at the agency, but it was her whole life, and she couldn't understand how I felt."

"Did you ever really tell her how you felt about your work and your relationship?" I said softly.

Tim shook his head. "Maybe not in so many words. Looking back now, I don't think I ever did a very good job of trying to get her to understand. Then I met Meg, and everything changed. I mean, my whole way of thinking turned on a dime. My whole life up until then seemed to have been only about getting me to that point. I had such a knowing in my mind and my heart that we should be together that I was willing to give up everything here and take a chance. I was ready to jump, expecting with every fibre of my being that the net would appear."

I almost laughed. It was something Douglas had said to both Tim and Kelly when they were growing up. Whenever they seemed hesitant to pursue something that we, as their parents, could see was something meaningful to them, Douglas would say, "Jump. And the net will appear." I never knew who he learned that from, but it had always been good advice as far as I was concerned. They tried lots of new things that way. Not all of them worked out, but who lives a life where everything turns out perfectly? Now, that would be boring, wouldn't it?

"But Antonia's news took away your moment to jump, didn't it?"

Tim nodded. "Don't get me wrong, Mom. I love Nicholas and wouldn't change that part of my life for anything. And Antonia and I are building a life together."

"But it doesn't feel like enough, does it?"

Tim looked miserable.

"Tim, do you remember that stupid song from back a few years? 'Torn Between Two Lovers'?"

"Geezus, Mom, that was a cheesy song we used to make fun of when I was at art college. What about it?"

"Do you remember any of the words?" I could see him trying to hum a bit of the melody, just like I would do to try to remember song lyrics.

"Something about a woman who has two lovers."

"Um-hm, but it applies equally to a man, and there's a bit more to the cheesiness of it than that. I love you with all my heart, Tim, and I'm going to give you some advice, whether you want it or not." I took a deep breath. "The song lyrics were actually written by a man—Pete Yarrow. Peter, Paul and Mary?" Tim nodded. I continued. "It's all about knowing when you have to say what's on your mind, even if it hurts. I know Antonia knows about your interlude with Megan. But as far as I can tell, she has no idea of the depth of your feeling." I took a deep breath. "If you want to find peace in your life, Tim, darling, you have to tell her."

As horrified as he looked, I knew he understood.

# 20

# Tim

## 1993-1994



IT HAD BEEN YEARS SINCE I CRIED. I mean, really cried. Not a few tears that a guy tries to hide when a movie gets to him. I mean profound, heartfelt tears that come from somewhere so deep you have no idea you even had that kind of depth. I didn't know I had it. I'd begun to think that life would just continue as a superficial reflection of what I was supposed to do—of the people I was supposed to love, of the places I was supposed to live, of the work I was supposed to accomplish. Mom's words cut through me like a knife aimed straight at my heart. I knew she was right. Unless I told Antonia about my feelings, they would fester in my heart for the rest of my life. But I also knew it could hurt her. The question in my mind was this: would it hurt her more to know about my feelings or to find out someday that I hadn't been honest with her? I was at a loss.

The thing that bothered me most about everything my mother was right about was this: it *had* been several years, and it was time I got over it. But hardly a day went by when I didn't think about Meg and what might have been if that one little thing hadn't happened. My whole life changed in that instant when Antonia told me we were having a baby. Don't misunderstand. I didn't for a moment regret my decision or having Nick in my life.

I couldn't even imagine a life without him now. I just realized that I expected to have it all. I now knew this was impossible, no matter how much anyone wished it wasn't. I'd just have to man up.

After our heart-to-heart talk, Mom and I spent the rest of the afternoon in the kitchen together, making dinner for all of us. We had never done that before, mainly because I had little interest in cooking growing up. Now, necessity had forced me to learn, and I'd discovered that I loved to cook. I'd also discovered The Silver Palate, a fabulous food shop near us, where they made the most delicious food.  I bought their cookbook, which had become wildly popular, and I had learned to make several recipes from it, including Chicken Marbella. Mom had a few dishes she knew without a recipe—food from my childhood, like lasagna. So we made Mom's lasagna and my Chicken Marbella together that cold afternoon.

Kelly and Nick arrived home two hours later. I'd been getting increasingly nervous about where they had gotten to since Kelly wasn't that familiar with New York. I also wasn't sure about her experience with or tolerance for an almost-four-year-old. I needn't have worried.

When Kelly opened the door and announced that the two of them had arrived, Nick raced into the foyer, throwing his arms around Mom. "Gran!" he said excitedly. "Look what Auntie Kelly bought me!"

Mom leaned down, and I strained to see. It was a book. Kelly was hanging their coats in the front hall closet when she turned to me. "It's a book about *The Nutcracker*. You know, bro," she said, nudging me. "The ballet?" Of course, I knew what *The Nutcracker* was. I just had no idea why Nick would have a book about it. Or why he was so excited.

Kelly's grin was even wider than it had been the day before when she and Nick had come down the stairs after allegedly dancing. "Annalise sneaked us into a *Nutcracker* rehearsal. A dress rehearsal. It opens next week, and this was one of the last rehearsals. Nick was enthralled. Geezus, Tim, the costumes and sets are magnificent. Your kid is a real ballet fan."

I snorted. "Nick? Our Nick, who spends his time pushing around bulldozers and dump trucks?"

"Yup. That Nick." She headed up the stairs. "I'm going to change and teach him first position. I promised."

I had no idea what to make of this or what "first position" could possibly mean. More to the point, though, was that I had no idea what Antonia would think of this. Mom was no help. She and Nick were settled in the living room, and Nick was proudly showing his grandmother his new reading skills. I wasn't sure I'd ever seen him this excited—and this was a kid who was regularly excited about something.

Mom stayed in town long enough to convince me that I should take advantage of Jack's offer of a show at the gallery in Halifax. Finally, I reluctantly agreed on the condition that I didn't have to go to Halifax. I wasn't ready for that yet, and I still hadn't had a chance to talk to Antonia. Mom had called this the coward's way out, but she said she would honour my wishes. I got on the phone with Jack, who said he'd put the wheels in motion so the show could open in early April. Until then, I would make selections from my current works and complete a couple of new ones that I thought might work for the Halifax buyers. I was beginning to feel excited about it, something I seemed to be sharing with my son. Ah, yes—back to the ballet excitement.

Antonia was surprisingly contemplative later that evening when Kelly conveyed her advice regarding our son's future.

"He'll need to enroll in ballet class ASAP," Kelly said over dessert. "It's halfway through the year, but I think we can get him in for January. Annalise and I have another classmate who has a school not far from here. Mom, you remember Natalie Rodriquez?"

"I do, Kelly. Wasn't she in one of your ballet classes back in Boston? I seem to remember that she was a bit tall as ballerinas go."

"You could say that," Kelly said. "I think she's five-foot-eleven or so. She towered over all the men she ever partnered with."

"Did she ever do any modelling?" I said. I remembered her, too, from Kelly's ballet recitals Mom and Dad were always dragging me to when I was a kid. I had a vague notion that I'd seen her in more recent years among the scads of models' headshots I had to review at the agency.

"She did, "Kelly said. "She was in one of those Guess jeans ads a few years back. Anyway, when she couldn't get a ballet job, she stayed in New York City and did two Broadway shows—*Forty-Second Street* and *Starlight Express*. She's not a great singer, though, so she thought it was too limiting and went back to school to get her ballet teaching credentials. Anyway, I'm sure she'll take Nick. They don't get that many boys."

Kelly kept talking non-stop. In the end, Antonia, who had said surprisingly little about it, finally got up to clear the table, saying, "Well, then. That's it. That's how Nicholas will get rid of his extra energy. He can do it for a year and then move on to soccer or baseball. So, it's settled."

And so, it was settled. Sort of. It's funny how things have a way of taking on a life of their own, isn't it?

~

Two weeks later, Antonia and I had a night out—just the two of us. We finally had a reservation for dinner at Tavern on the Green. We had hoped to be able to have dinner at Windows on the World on the one-hundred-and-seventh floor of the north tower of the World Trade Center, but that bomb in the parking garage in February had closed it—temporarily, we hoped—and it was still closed. We'd both been up to the roof of the tower to see the views, but we'd never had a chance to have dinner there. Street level in Central Park would have to do this evening.

We hadn't done this date-night thing for—well, I couldn't remember how long. I only hoped this evening's conversation didn't put a stop to future nights out.

When we had almost finished our main courses, I took a sip of wine and sat back. "Antonia, we have to talk about something."

She put her glass down on the table and looked across at me. "Do *we* have to talk about something, Tim, or do you?"

"I do, then I hope *we* do."

Antonia took another sip of wine. "Is it about your upcoming show? Are you planning to go to Halifax after all?"

"No, I'm not. And it's not really about the show, but it is partly about Halifax."

"I thought it might be."

"I know you remember that day you arrived at my rental cottage in Halifax, and my friend Megan McMaster arrived for dinner."

Antonia started to bristle the moment I used the word "friend," but I had to get this out before she interrupted. I held up my hand and continued.

"You were right. Meg and I were more than just friends. And the truth is I fell in love with her. I even thought she was my…" I hesitated for a moment. "…my soulmate." Antonia rolled her eyes but kept quiet. "I knew I was being unfair to you, but I thought there was something there."

Antonia could hold her tongue no longer. "Why are you telling me all this now, Tim? Of course, I always knew you and she were more than friends, but I forgave you. I may never have said the words, but I have to believe you recognize that everything that's happened since then has been because I forgave you. It's water under the proverbial bridge. Why are you dredging it up now? You're not—"

"No, no," I cut her off before she could even put into words what she thought I might be doing. "No, I'm not doing anything related to that relationship. You're right. It is in the past, but I'd be lying to you if I continued to live with you thinking I'd forgotten about Meg. I think about her almost every day. I know I need to get over it, but I can't do it alone."

Antonia sat up straight, and I recognized the stance of a lioness about to pounce. "You can't do it alone? And you expect me to help?"

"No, Antonia, that's not what I mean."

"Then what *do* you mean? Do you think dumping your love-stricken confession on me that you'll miraculously get over your infatuation—an infatuation, by the way, that is more befitting of a teenaged boy with acne than a grown man with a home, a family and a career."

I knew she was right, and I was beginning to doubt my mother's wisdom in encouraging me to share this with Antonia. Then it struck me. Mom knew exactly how Antonia would react. She knew this would be a watershed of sorts for our relationship, and she knew we might not survive it. But she knew I couldn't live my life the way it was going, and if we did survive this, we'd be stronger than ever. I could feel it now as I listened to Antonia.

"Tim, if you expect me to wave a magic wand over you to absolve you of your guilt, well, I have news for you. Guilt is an inside job. If you still have feelings for this Megan person, then perhaps you should go to Halifax for the exhibition and see where that leads. Nicholas and I will be here in New York, and neither one of us is going to take on your burden. It's yours to carry until you're ready to put it down as I did. So, one way or another, the ball is in your court."

~

Nick started his ballet classes the first week in January. On that first Saturday morning, both Antonia and I accompanied him to the "In Motion Ballet Studio." I thought it was an apt name for our in-motion little guy.

We arrived by taxi at what looked like an old factory. Kelly had told us Natalie's father had been in the garment business and had offered her one of his vacant shops to turn into a studio. As we walked into the low-rise brick building, there was a small reception desk that led to three studios. But what I noticed more than anything was the sea of pink. There were little girls everywhere, each one seemingly pinker than the one before.

There were pink tights, pink leotards, pink hair scrunchies, pink ballet slippers. It was enough to make you think you'd gotten sick from cotton candy and started to vomit it all up. When I mentioned this visual to Antonia, all she could do was nod in agreement, her eyes wide. Finally, I spied one other lone little boy in a white T-shirt and black pants. At least Nick wouldn't be alone. However, judging from Nick's look of sheer delight, I needn't have worried. Being in a sea of little girls didn't seem to bother him at all.

"Where do I go, Mom?" he said to Antonia, his eyes shining with excitement.

I looked around and saw someone who appeared to be in charge. I made my way through the throng of tulle and tutus that was pouring into one of the studios and introduced myself to the teacher. She told me her name was Suzanna, and she'd be delighted to find Natalie for us.

By the time Natalie arrived, the corridor had cleared, and I could breathe again. Taking my son to ballet classes was going to be harder than I thought. Then I turned my attention to Natalie. She was just as tall and striking as we all remembered her.

We introduced ourselves, and Natalie told us that Nick would be in the first-level ballet class. He would be a bit behind since the rest of the students had started in September, but she offered to give him extra coaching after classes to get him up to speed.

"Kelly has already taught him a few things," I said.

"Oh, yes, of course. Kelly did mention that when she called. But we will want to be sure he has internalized the basics."

"He's only four," Antonia said. "Surely internalizing basics is something that takes time and is more for children who wish to pursue ballet in the long run. And after all, it's all just for exercise, isn't it?"

Natalie looked stricken. "Mrs. Sinclair—"

"Ms. St. John," Antonia corrected.

"Uh, yes, Ms. St. John. We do take ballet very seriously here, even for the very youngest ones. It's an art form we are conveying to a new generation of dancers. Even four-year-olds take it seriously in my studio."

I was starting to get anxious. But I wondered at that moment what was making me more nervous: the idea of Nick in this ballet world or that Antonia might just slap this young woman up the side of the head any moment.

"May we stay to watch the class since it's his first?" I said as warmly as I could manage while Antonia and Natalie stared one another down.

"We prefer parents to wait until parents' day," Natalie said, taking Nick by the hand. "We'll see you in an hour and a half."

Nick went along happily with this Amazon of a woman, and we were left staring after him. It was to become a way of life—we just didn't know it at the time.

# 21

# Grace

## 1994

*Opportunities multiply as they are seized.*
~ Sun Tzu


I WAS DELIGHTED TO HAVE BEEN ABLE TO NUDGE TIM into agreeing to show his work at the gallery in Halifax. In my view, his work was too important to keep hidden away. The world needs to embrace and nurture artistic talent wherever it might be and however it might differ from someone's plan. I'd always believed this, but sometimes, when it's your own family, the realities of what that means can be overwhelming. As the date for the exhibition approached, I thought Tim might have changed his mind about attending—surely it would be essential for him to start building bridges with his audience—but during our last telephone conversation in February, he seemed even more determined than before not to reconnect with Halifax or presumably anyone who might still be there.

"I told Antonia just like you said I should. She had already figured out that there was more to my brief relationship with Meg than I might have let on. But she didn't seem to be able to deal with the idea that I might not have completely gotten over the whole thing. She pushed me to find my own way out of this."

I usually found it much more difficult to respond to these kinds of things from my children when we were talking on the phone. I would have loved to be able to read his face and his body language. But I was stuck with his voice. "Tim, if Antonia is willing to stay the course, you've been given a massive gift."

"I know, Mom. I've been trying to work all of this through."

"Have you sought outside help?"

"Outside help? You mean a shrink? No, not a shrink. But…" Tim trailed off.

"But what?" I said, hoping he had found something useful.

"Well, you know Nick and I still go to a play group with the moms and kids we met when we first started getting out when he was an infant. I've gotten to know a couple of the moms quite well, and a few weeks ago, one of the moms, Dierdre, noticed I didn't seem to be myself. She guessed it had something to do with my wife and suggested a book for me to read."

I braced myself for some kind of oddball pop-psychology book. I wasn't disappointed.

"It's called *Men are from Mars, Women are from Venus*. Have you heard about it?"

I had heard about it but hadn't had the occasion to read it at this point in my life. I felt as if I might have been able to write it at this stage.

"Well, anyway, it's by this relationship counsellor, so I was hesitant. I kind of made fun of the idea of me reading a book like that when she mentioned it, but I finally picked up a copy when Nick and I were doing errands. It's not as creepy as I thought it would be. The guy who wrote it actually has a few insights that seem relatable—at least to me."

"Whatever works for you, honey."

"You know, Mom, I haven't highlighted anything in a book since I was in art college, but I'm finding myself with my yellow highlighter in hand, saying yes, this is good. I can hardly believe it."

"Anything specific?" I said.

"Let me find it here," he said. I could hear papers rustling. "Yeah. Here it is. 'Because she is afraid of not being supported, she unknowingly pushes away the support she needs.' I was thinking about that. I was so focused on myself these past few years I forgot about Antonia. I'm beginning to think I get how she feels."

"Do you think that if you 'get' it, you'll be able to get over it?"

"I'm working on it, Mom." I could hear pages rustling again. "This guy also says, 'Men are motivated when they feel needed while women are motivated when they feel cherished.' I never thought about that, but it's true. My plan is to appreciate Antonia more—because, you know, I really do, Mom—but even more important, I'm going to make sure she knows it."

I knew it was a tall order, but I had faith in my son. I sent a tiny prayer to heaven for support for Tim's challenge.

~

Jack and I arrived in Halifax two days before Tim's show. We had loaded several new works into the back of Jack's station wagon (he had long since sold the BMW for something more useful to an artist and art dealer who made frequent trips from Bar Harbor, Maine, to Halifax, Nova Scotia), which we delivered to the gallery before checking into our hotel. We were in a hurry and excited because we were meeting with our real estate agent. He was sure he'd found the perfect *pied-a-terre* for us in the city that we could call home whenever we were there.

Our agent picked us up in front of the hotel, and as we drove to the north end of the city, he filled us in on the area known as The Hydrostone. It was a neighbourhood of 1920s rowhouses built for people whose homes had been destroyed in a massive explosion in the city in 1917. The houses were laid out on ten streets, most of them with grassy, treed boulevards in the middle. Although it had been a working-class neighbourhood, it was quickly becoming a gentrified space where younger families were buying the houses and renovating. There were still lots left to renovate, and our agent thought that might interest us. I could feel every interior design bone in my body come alive.

A short drive from the gallery (or a long walk if we preferred), the house, as it turned out, was perfect for us. It still had the original wide, plank floors and ceiling beams. Although the owners had done some updating to the kitchen, I could reimagine it as it might have been (except with modern conveniences). It had two bedrooms and two bathrooms, the second bathroom added by a previous owner. Everything needed some TLC, but we could see the potential, and it would be such fun to do together. We made an offer on the spot, and the sellers accepted it the next day. We were on our way to being Halifax homeowners! Then we had to focus on Tim's art show.

By seven-thirty on the evening of the event, The Kaufman Gallery was filled with eager art lovers from the area and some even from beyond. As I mingled with the guests, I encountered several visiting businesspeople and two of Nigel's art friends from Montreal. It turned out they were both gallery owners themselves, one of them a partner in Nigel's Montreal enterprise. They were excited about what they were seeing.

*"Mon dieu,"* one of the Montrealers said, gazing rapturously at one of Tim's renderings of two sailboats silhouetted in the setting sun. *"C'est extraordinaire!"* I quite agreed.

Before I had a chance to boast about being the artist's mother—which I fully intended to do—Nigel rushed over to me excitedly. "Grace," he said breathlessly. Nigel did very little without that breathlessness, or so it seemed. "I have someone who wants to meet you."

I turned to see a striking older woman with sparkling silver hair gazing toward me. If I had to describe the look on her face as she contemplated me, I would have said she looked slightly bemused. She was smiling, wasn't she?

Nigel gently pulled me toward this woman who stood slightly on the periphery of the throng in front of one of my favourite of Tim's watercolours: a back-on portrait of Nicholas picking up shells on the beach in Bar Harbor. Of course, you couldn't tell it was Nicholas.

"Grace, I'd like to present Dr. Ellen McMaster. Ellie, this is Grace Sinclair." I hid my slight startle and stared into Ellie's eyes as I took her hand. She gently squeezed my hand and nodded almost imperceptibly. Nigel wouldn't have seen it, but I did. He continued. "Grace, Ellie is the artist whose work you admired on your first visit. She is also the art lover who bought Tim's piece from me a few years ago." Nigel looked around at his full gallery and smiled broadly. "We have Ellie to thank for the buzz here this evening. You know, Grace, we're planning an exhibit of Ellie's sculptures here this summer, and now that you and Jack have a home here in the city," it was Ellie's turn to look startled, "you will, of course, be here for it."

I took a deep breath and smiled. "I wouldn't miss it. Dr. McMaster—Ellie—I believe you know my son, the artist."

She nodded and turned without a word. I watched her walk away in the crowd. I had to talk to that woman.

# 22

# Antonia

## 1995

*You may give them your love but not your
thoughts, for they have their own thoughts.*
~ Kahlil Gibran (*The Prophet*)

SO MUCH IN MY LIFE WAS SO CONFUSING, and I hated the feeling.
First, there was my unexpected jealousy of Tim's bond with
Nicholas, then there was Nicholas and the ballet, and then there
was Tim and his confession. I was working on my jealousy, and I
was getting used to Nicholas and his ballet classes—but I'll get
back to that. I was still perplexed, though, about how Tim would
handle my reaction to his so-called confession. Of course, I had
known all along that he and Megan had been more than friends.
Sometimes when I allowed myself to think about it, I
remembered that Tim was a philanderer, and I wondered if he'd
ever stray again. At other times, I remembered that he had chosen
me—and Nicholas—and realized that this was a gift that I ought
to consider nurturing. Maybe the ball wasn't entirely in his court.

Tim had chosen not to go to Halifax for the exhibition, and
even after the show was a massive success, selling out, he seemed
humbled in a way that I hardly recognized in my long-time
partner and husband. Tim had never been as arrogant as I knew
I was, but we had both been part of a larger community of
snobbish, self-centred young adults in a business that seemed to
cultivate snobbery and narcissism. When the Montreal gallery

owners started calling him regularly, he accepted it all with a degree of equanimity I thought could teach me something. Finally, when Nicholas went to school and Tim had more time, he worked feverishly, eventually landing a show in New York—a show even the critics loved. And now, back to this whole ballet thing.

What was going on there? I fully expected Nicholas to want to get out of those classes packed with little girls as soon as he could. I never expected him to want another year of dance classes. So, I let the idea of soccer or baseball go for a later time, and we put him back into Natalie Rodriguez's school for both ballet and jazz dance classes.

Sometime during his second year at the school, I happened to be the one picking Nicholas up one Saturday around noon. As far as I could figure out, there were only two other little boys in the entire school, although when I asked Natalie about this, she assured me that she had older male students we didn't see on Saturdays. That day, I waited in the small lobby area and noticed another mother who was also picking up a boy. I knew she was waiting for a boy because I'd seen her before.

She suddenly turned to me. "Do you have to drag your son here every week?"

I assured her I did not.

"I have to bribe Xavier every week to get him here. It's getting harder and harder."

The idea of having to bribe my child to do anything was perplexing to me at the best of times. Why anyone would bribe a five- or six-year-old child to do something like this when he so clearly wasn't interested was absolutely mystifying.

"Why don't you just let him give it up and find something else?"

Her eyes widened in what could only be described as abject horror. "Something else? My whole life is about ballet, and my son is going to be a star."

I looked at her more closely. The erect posture. The slight turn-out of her feet. The ballet-bun hair. And it was clear to me that this was a mother who was going to push her child into something because that was what she wanted—perhaps something that she had not been able to do herself for one reason or another. Then I looked toward the studio where the students were beginning to emerge and realized I had just been given a gift. I realized I could come very close to doing the same thing if given a chance. When I saw the bright eyes, rosy cheeks and wide smile on my own little guy as he made his way toward me, I knew that from that moment, if he wanted to be a ballet dancer, then that's what I would support. I had no idea what I was doing, but Nicholas Sinclair would be what he was supposed to be.

~

The OJ Simpson trial was all over the news that fall. Would he be found guilty, or would he walk away? This pending verdict seemed to permeate so many conversations of so many people I'd previously thought more intelligent than to have nothing better to talk about. It was almost unavoidable, but I had other things on my mind.

I'd spent the past few years trying to get used to the fact that Ken Berger, my former boss, was now my partner. Just when I felt comfortable in this partnership, Ken announced that he was retiring. So, I clearly had better things to talk about (and certainly to think about) than the trial of a celebrity football player who so clearly wasn't going to get what he seemed to deserve. What would happen at Moffatt, Green, Berger, St. John and Partners?

Ken owned the largest number of shares in the partnership. Moffatt had died several years before I even joined the agency, but since it had been his company from the beginning, they had left his name on the letterhead. That would leave only Stanley

Green and Antonia St. John as partners. I wasn't sure I could cope with Stan Green by myself without Ken there as a buffer.

Stan Green was one of those Madison Avenue ad guys who seemed to think it was still the 1960s. He certainly wasn't ready for the new millennium that loomed. He was old enough to have been weaned on lunch-hour martinis and women who were happy to stay in their places as secretaries and errand girls. He was skeptical when Ken decided I should be offered a partnership, but since Ken owned a larger share of the company, he was outvoted, so to speak. I always felt that Stan had never really gotten over that.

At every opportunity, he had tried to undermine me. Stan second-guessed every client I took on and questioned every campaign that received the green light from me. He even complained that several young women on my team seemed to have gotten "above themselves" for sharing ideas at meetings. In a word, he made me furious. So, the fall of 1995 was stressful for me, to say the least—so stressful that I'd begun having fantasies about leaving my job and staying home with Nicholas. Of course, Nicholas was now in school, dancing, playing soccer when he wasn't dancing, taking piano lessons and learning about astronomy—his latest obsession—so my role would be reduced to ferrying him around from one activity to another. I had missed so much. And, of course, there was the small matter of money—money my career provided.

On the Tuesday of the second week in October, a week after OJ Simpson had been found not guilty, Ken called me into his office. I had been dreading this meeting since it was the one where I'd have to bare my soul to him about how I felt about working with Stan. I had never really been honest with him about the depth of my dislike for that man. It would probably come as something of a surprise to Ken. However, I was the one who was surprised.

After Ken's assistant told me I could go in, I knocked lightly on the door and then turned the knob. As I opened the door and stepped inside, I noticed Ken was not alone. To my complete shock, Nathan was sitting on the sofa with a bottle of champagne in a silver ice bucket on the coffee table in front of him. He had his arm stretched across the back of the sofa, his legs crossed and a broad grin on his face.

"Come in, Antonia. Come in and join us," Ken said, smiling broadly, something I had rarely seen him do in all the years I'd worked with him. Perhaps impending retirement was having a genuinely positive effect on him. But there was something else about his expression. If I had to put a finger on it, I'd say it was a bit of the expression I'd seen on my own son's face whenever he was trying to hold back on me.

"What's going on, Ken?" I said and then turned to Nathan. "And what in god's name are you doing here? You didn't mention you'd be in the building today."

Nathan had long since left the agency to work with a rival and had managed to leverage his business acumen into a vice-presidency. We still saw each other about once a month for drinks, but he hadn't mentioned he'd be in the office to wish Ken a happy retirement.

"Well, I don't tell you everything, Toni," Nathan said. Ken's eyebrows raised at the sound of the nickname. He continued. "Sometimes, I leave things to be a surprise. And I hope a good one."

"Champagne?" I said, gesturing to the ice bucket as I sat down in one of the two chairs opposite Nathan. Ken sat in the chair beside me.

"I hope we'll pop that cork," Ken said. He turned to me. "Antonia, I know it will come as no surprise to you when I tell you that you've managed to impress me at every turn since the day I hired you. That was the day I told Stan my prediction: that you would own the firm one day."

I rolled my eyes. "That must have gone over like a lead balloon."

"You could say that. I won't subject you to a verbatim recollection of his exact words but suffice it to say he is a bit old-fashioned."

"A bit," I said. "Always the master of understatement, Ken."

Ken and Nathan both laughed before Ken continued. "Antonia, I have long suspected that you've often had to grit your teeth and put up with Stan and his anachronistic advertising ways, but you have always been smart enough to know when just to let things go. I was probably more offended than you were on many occasions."

Once again, I was surprised. "I didn't realize you knew how I felt."

"I did, and Antonia, you could always have talked to me about it."

"I don't think so. You know as well as I do that it would have been career suicide for me, which brings me to something we *do* need to discuss. I'm not sure I'll be able to continue here with Stan once you're gone." I looked at Nathan, and suddenly an idea popped into my head. "Did you bring Nathan here today so he could offer me a job with his company? Are you suggesting we dissolve the partnership?"

"Antonia, my dear, if you'd let me finish my speech, all will be clear." Ken cleared his throat. "As I was saying, when I hired you right out of school twelve years ago, I told Stan you'd one day own the firm. And if you'll consider my proposition, my prediction is about to come true."

Nathan handed me a piece of paper that was blank except for the letterhead. I looked at it and noticed something odd about the design and the colour. Then I read the name and was confused for a moment. Etched at the top of the page in an art deco font were the words "The St. John Harrison Agency." And suddenly, the fog began to clear.

Ken began talking again, but it was all I could do to tear my eyes away from the letterhead. Suddenly I realized that Nathan was talking.

"Ken always knew we wanted our own agency, Toni. We never fooled him."

I looked from Nathan to Ken. "You knew. Why didn't you say anything?"

"What was there to say?" Ken said. "Don't poach our clients? I just hoped we'd keep you around long enough for this day to come."

And what he meant by *this* day was that he and Nathan had begun a conversation some months earlier about Nathan and I taking over the agency. It turned out that Stan had grudgingly agreed that if I left the firm, they would be in trouble, so he decided to retire himself. Nathan and Ken put together the package for Nathan and me to take over the firm, realizing that the clients would be more than happy to stay the course with the two of us as principals. He was right, of course. The financial details seemed secondary, but they filled me in. When they were finished, Ken took the bottle of champagne and handed it to Nathan.

"Why did you put my name first?" I said to Nathan as the cork flew out and hit the wall behind me. He had never managed to master the art of smooth uncorking.

"Toni, you and I have been friends for so many years," Nathan said. "I just thought I'd save us both a lot of time since we both know your name would have ended up first anyway."

Nathan knew me so well.

~

Tim had laughed at the irony that Nathan's and my dream of having our own agency had finally occurred—not by leaving the agency, but rather by taking it over. And he was happy for me. He knew very well that this was what I'd been aiming for. It was the glass ceiling I had planned to shatter. I could almost see it in pieces.

Nathan and I spent the rest of that autumn reorganizing ourselves and the firm so that we could launch on the first of January. Then we gave our staff the week between Christmas and New Year's off and decided we both needed a break. I was nervous about leaving the office for a week, but it was just as well since Tim and I were going to be busy over the holidays. We had family holiday preparations.

Tim and I were working together and chatting about how my career had blossomed.

"What's next?" Tim said as he polished wine glasses in preparation for welcoming the family for a New Year's Eve celebration again. Kelly had already arrived from Toronto on Boxing Day to spend a few weeks with us to visit friends in the city, and Grace and Jack were driving down from Maine.

"What's next?" I repeated his question. "Does there have to be a next?"

Before the words were out of my mouth, I wondered where they had come from.

"There's always a next, Antonia," Tim said.

Of course, he was right.

# 23

# Tim

## 1996–2000

*The central struggle of parenthood is to let our*
*hopes for our children outweigh our fears.*
~ Ellen Goodman

I WAS HONESTLY ELATED FOR ANTONIA. It was everything she'd always wanted. At least, that's what I always thought. Antonia was the embodiment of the 1980s power-suited woman clawing her way up the ladder. And now, she'd arrived. The only little nagging thought at the back of my mind was this: if a woman reaches her career nirvana at the age of forty-three, what happens then? As her husband, I was terrified by this question—or, to be more precise, the potential answer to the question was the frightening bit.

After I posed the "what's next?" question to Antonia, we welcomed the family for a New Year's Eve celebration. This was the first time in six years that we'd all been together to see in a new year. The last time we did this, Mom and Jack had announced their engagement. This year, we would celebrate Antonia's new venture. Since Kelly had taken her favourite (only) nephew for an outing, and Antonia was having her annual New Year's Eve lunch with Nathan, I was once again alone in the house. I decided we had much to celebrate.

I threw on my coat and scarf and slammed the door behind me, heading for the liquor store on the corner three blocks over. I would buy the most expensive bottle of champagne I could find there. As I walked the three blocks, I thought about the past year. It was true: there was much to celebrate.

First, Nick was happy in school. He had even learned to sit still long enough for his teachers to realize that he was actually a very bright little boy, reading far ahead of his grade and understanding science in a way that put me to shame. I was the one who had introduced him to astronomy, and he could run rings around me already in naming planets and solar systems. He had played soccer all summer, and although he had a bit of difficulty making contact with the ball, he looked magnificent doing it. And then there was the ballet.

He'd been taking classes from Natalie since the beginning, and she often murmured that he was good. Antonia and I knew very little about what constituted "good" in the ballet world, but whenever we attended a ballet school recital, it seemed to us that he was "good." At least he seemed better than the girls dancing alongside him. In fact, it was hard to keep your eyes off this little guy. I remembered the first time we'd seen him on stage with a bevy of pink-clad girls in his white T-shirt and grey tights. I had turned to Antonia and said, "My god, Antonia, he's a dancer." And the thought worried me more than a little. I just wasn't sure why, but I think it had something to do with how I felt about the difficulties of being an artist. And I should know.

When I returned to the house carrying not one but three bottles of champagne (I'd had difficulty deciding between the Veuve Clicquot Grand Dame and the Taittinger Brut Reserve when I spied the 1989 Perrier-Jouet Belle Epoque), Kelly and Nick had returned from their outing. Kelly called to me from the living room.

"Tim, have you got a minute?"

When I walked into the room, Kelly was sitting there with three books beside her on the sofa. "What's up, Kel?"

"Your son, that's what's up." I shrugged and sat down beside her. "I have some books here I think you should read," she said, patting the top of the pile.

I picked them up one at a time. The books were all about ballet. Two of them were what I'd call primers, and the third was a new biography of Rudolph Nureyev that had just been published. I'd read about it in *The New York Times*. "Okay, sis. I give up. Why would I want to read about ballet? I spend quite enough time in a ballet school as it is."

"Bro, you haven't seen anything yet. I predict you'll be spending a lot more time at the ballet."

Then she explained. She had arranged with Natalie for Nick to have a private lesson with her and a friend of hers—a male member of the corps de ballet at the American Ballet Theater in the city. It was the first time Nick had ever had a class with a male teacher. Natalie and Kelly had watched. All of this was because Natalie had told Kelly that she had never seen such promise in a little boy as young as Nick. In fact, she had never seen such promise in any of the girls she'd taught over the years—even the ones who went on to professional careers.

"So, Tim, what I'm telling you is that Nick is a ballet dancer."

"Kelly," I said, waving at her as if I could swat her thoughts away like an annoying housefly, "that's ridiculous. Nick is far too young for anyone to be able to say that. And I don't think that's what he'll want from his life."

"How do you know what he'll want in the future? But I suspect you *do* know what *you* want for him in the future." She pushed the books toward me. "Read them, Tim."

It wasn't until a few days later that I had a chance to tell Antonia about this exchange. When I mentioned Kelly's prediction, Antonia laughed. "Well, you have to admit that he likes it."

That was not what I'd been expecting from my wife, the biggest promoter of a solid university education I'd ever known.

When we first met, she had barely been able to contain her disdain for my own major—art—although she did see how it could be applied to the advertising world. In recent years, the successes I'd had with my art had given her a different perspective. Anyway, we both agreed it was too early to give this much more thought, and we left it at that. Some time passed before Natalie began her campaign in earnest.

~

"Nicholas should be attending the SAB summer school here in New York this year."

Antonia and I were sitting across from Natalie Rodriguez at a meeting she'd called to discuss what she'd referred to as "an important consideration for Nicholas's future."

"I'm sorry," I said. "you've lost me. What's SAB?"

Natalie looked at me like someone might look at a daft child. "It is the School of American Ballet, of course."

Of course. How could I not have known? Give me a break. Anyway, now I knew.

"A few years ago, the school's director, Peter Martins, set up a tuition-free program for boys in their children's division. It's been a marvellous way for them to increase the number of boys at the school. Nicholas needs to learn with more boys and from male teachers."

"But ballet is just one of the things he does, Natalie. Why can't he stay here and continue to take classes from you?"

"He could, Tim," she said, "but in a few years, he'll be into full-time training and getting a foot in at SAB almost guarantees they'll offer him a place when he's ten or eleven."

Full-time training? Ten or eleven? This was too much for me.

"Have you mentioned any of this to Nicholas, Natalie?" Antonia said.

"Not directly. I wanted to discuss it with you first."

"What did you say to him indirectly?" Antonia was a wise woman.

"We've talked about schools where there are more boys and where the students have an opportunity to dance in productions like *The Nutcracker* with professional dancers. That's all."

"I suspect that was quite enough," Antonia said under her breath.

# 24

# Grace

## 2000-2001

*There are only two lasting bequests we can hope to give our children. One of these is roots, the other, wings.* ~ Johann Wolfgang von Goethe

TIM AND ANTONIA WERE WONDERFUL PARENTS, as far as I could tell. They were loving and kind yet had expectations about acceptable behaviour. They opened doors for Nicholas and generously made sure he had opportunities. But whenever I visited my grandson over the years, it became increasingly clear to me that they had their own plans for Nicholas—plans that often seemed to reflect Antonia's, and perhaps even Tim's, personal perspectives on education and careers. Their direction was so clear I wondered if little Nicholas would have a chance to do his own thing—whatever that turned out to be. And I found this puzzling, given that Tim was now making a very good living as a fine artist.

He exhibited in New York and London regularly, but even as his reputation as an artist grew internationally, he still prepared pieces for our gallery in Halifax. I mention it as "our" gallery because a few years after Jack and Nigel became partners in the gallery, Nigel sold it completely to Jack and moved away to live full-time in Montreal. That was when Jack told me he was renaming the gallery—which, of course, was to be expected. He told me about it one afternoon while we were in Halifax, standing in the middle of the gallery half an hour before we were scheduled to receive guests for an exhibit of his own paintings.

The caterer had arrived, and the three servers had begun pouring wine into glasses in preparation for the guests' arrival. Jack went to the bar at the back of the gallery and brought two glasses. We stood near the door where I was admiring one of my favourite pieces in his collection. It was an oil on particleboard of the beach our house in Bar Harbor overlooked. Anyone here in Halifax who looked at it would probably think it was somewhere in Nova Scotia. It was our little secret. We clinked glasses, and then Jack looked serious.

"Grace, my love, I have another wee secret to share with you."

I was all ears.

"I'm going to make an announcement this evening, but I didn't want you to be completely taken by surprise."

"Should I be worried?" I said.

Jack laughed. "Not at all, my dear. I'm going to announce the gallery's new identity."

"Well, then," I said, raising my glass, "let us drink to the new Lawrence Gallery."

Jack shook his head. "I suppose that's what everyone will expect, but I have a different idea completely. Grace Sinclair, you are the love of my life, and I would never be here if it hadn't been for you." I started to interject, but he shook his head slightly, and I stopped. "It also seems clear to me that Timothy Sinclair has been an important force in putting this little gallery on the map, so to speak." Jack began to raise his class. "For those reasons, tonight, I will be introducing the art community to the new Sinclair Gallery." He smiled broadly. "And I will be announcing my new partner, Grace Sinclair. This gallery is now officially half yours, my love." He handed me a piece of paper.

Indeed, it was the business ownership papers. There it said it in black and white. I was a full co-owner. I was astounded.

~

In June of 2000, just after we all recovered from fear of Y2K, I travelled to New York for a ballet recital. Nicholas was still at Natalie's school, despite what I knew was Natalie and Kelly's campaign to get Antonia and Tim to permit him to audition for a full-time school. Natalie had suggested the School of American Ballet in New York, but Kelly had other plans.

She had called me at least half a dozen times to recruit me to her plan. She was now situated in Toronto permanently, with a new man in her life, and was the proud proprietor of what was becoming a very successful dance and yoga studio. She had used her small inheritance from her father to buy a building and had made contacts with enough of the right people to support her growing reputation. It seemed that she and Natalie had talked at length about Nicholas, and they were on the same page about one important thing: Nicholas was a ballet dancer, and the world needed him. The only ones who thought he would get over his growing obsession with dance were his parents.

Kelly's plan was simple: convince her brother and sister-in-law that her nephew had to attend a full-time ballet school—and soon. Natalie had almost convinced them that he should audition for SAB in the fall, but Kelly had other plans. She wanted Nicholas to travel to Toronto to attend Canada's National Ballet School.

"Good heavens, Kelly. That seems like it might be a bridge too far, doesn't it?" Kelly and I were having our regular mother-daughter telephone conversation a week before I was scheduled to travel to New York for the recital. "Perhaps you could join forces with Natalie on the New York school thing."

I was as convinced as Kelly that Nicholas should be given the chance. I'd talked with him briefly on the phone recently, and it was clear his passion was starting to become laser-focused. He had talked to his parents about SAB and hoped to convince them to let him attend their summer school at least. He'd been offered a space months ago and was keen to go.

"Mom, SAB is great, but the NBS here in Canada is better. I think he should be here. And besides, I'd love to have him near me," Kelly said.

I was sure Antonia and Tim would never let him leave home to attend a foreign school at his young age, regardless of its stature in the ballet world. I felt strongly that Antonia in particular, still expected Nicholas to follow in her footsteps into business—although she had expressed the opinion that Nicholas would make an equally good doctor. The fact that Nicholas had not expressed a single  bit of interest in being a doctor—or a business person, for that matter—didn't seem to matter in the least. "He isn't even in high school yet," she had said to me when I questioned her. "No one knows their own mind at age eleven." I disagreed with her on that subject.

Nicholas had started his own campaign to obtain his parents' approval to attend the SAB summer school. He had told all his ballet school classmates and his classmates at the private school he attended that he was going. When we arrived at the auditorium for the recital that June evening, Tim and Antonia were suddenly surrounded by parents congratulating them either sincerely or—and this seemed equally evident —enviously. I could tell from their faces, and through the years, I'd perceived that a competitiveness permeated the ballet-parent world, so it was what I would have expected. In any case, Tim and Antonia were ambushed.

The recital was lovely, but Nicholas was amazing. And he went to summer school at the School of American Ballet. When I arrived back in New York in late September, my grandson was transformed. He could talk of nothing else but what summer school he wanted to attend the following year. But before we could spend much time on that conversation, we had a date. He and I were going to see a new movie.

It was a movie that had debuted at the Cannes Film Festival in May. When I visited New York for Nicholas's June recital, I told him about what I'd seen on the news, and we had made a date. When the movie opened in New York in September, I would come for a visit, and we would go. Now the day had arrived for us to see *Billy Elliott*.

Anyone alive in 2000 has heard of *Billy Elliott*. It seemed like a small, British movie at the time, but it would, of course, go on to have a life of its own in cinemas and eventually in the theatre. But that afternoon, as I sat in the dark cinema beside my almost eleven-year-old grandson, the dancer, I could feel something emanating from him. He was almost vibrating. When on-screen Billy danced for the audition panel at the school he wanted to attend, I could feel Nicholas vibrating even faster. When we walked out of the theatre, Nicholas said, "Gran, I could feel it."

"What exactly, darling?"

"The electricity. You know when they asked Billy how he felt when he danced? He said electric. That's how I feel."

I could feel that electricity through him and knew, one way or another, that my grandson was going to be a ballet dancer.

The following summer, he once again attended the SAB summer school, and I could tell that Tim and Antonia's resolve to steer their son in a different direction was crumbling. Nicholas finally called me in ecstasy one afternoon in August to tell me that his parents were going to let him audition for the full-time school in the fall. Kelly had suggested to him that he go to Toronto to audition for the NBS in Canada as well, but he said they had vetoed that idea, although he thought going away to school might be the best thing. But he was happy anyway.

Then it happened.

~

I awoke early on the morning of September 11, 2001. As usual on a warm, sunny morning, I was outside on the deck, sitting in a comfortable Adirondack chair, reading the newspaper with a cup of coffee, when Jack hurried out.

"Grace, you need to see this," he said. I was alarmed at the panic in his voice. "Something is happening in New York."

"New York? What kind of something?"

"I don't know. Maybe a bomb? Something bigger?"

All I could think about was that my family was in New York. I scrambled up from the chair and followed Jack into the family room, where the television was tuned to the news report.

"What in god's name is going on?" I said, sinking into the sofa, my hand over my mouth. The camera was trained on the twin towers of the World Trade Center. I could see thick, dark smoke billowing out of the north tower. Then, suddenly, I saw a jet. It looked to me to be out of control. It was heading straight for the south tower. I almost screamed. I checked my watch. It was just past nine.

"What is going on, Jack?" I wailed. I watched in horror as the jet that had appeared in the frame only seconds ago plunged into the south tower. There was another massive, black, billowing cloud of smoke, and I could see burning debris as it fell from the building on what I imagined were people in the streets below.

I lunged for the telephone and punched in Tim's home number. There was no answer. I could feel panic rising. "Where are they, Jack? Where are they?" Then I punched in Antonia's office number. There was no answer at Antonia's office either.

What was happening to the people in those buildings? What was happening to the people in New York going about their usual morning business on the streets below?

We sat there, arms around one another, watching with growing horror what the news people were now calling a deliberate attack. A terrorist attack. Tears streamed down my face as we watched the south tower collapse just before ten o'clock. We couldn't even imagine what was going on in the streets of New York. And it was killing me.

Finally, the phone rang. I answered after the first ring.

"Mom," came Tim's voice, "are you watching the news?" I told him we were. "I'm in Boston, so I'm far from the disaster, but I just talked to Antonia—you know we use those cellular phones these days—and she's with Nick. They're okay. We're all okay."

But, of course, nothing was really okay. Nothing was ever the same.

# 25

# Antonia

## 2001-2002



THE NEW OFFICES OF THE ST. JOHN HARRISON AGENCY were located near West 38th Street and 6th Avenue, not far from Bryant Park, just over three miles from the World Trade Center. On the morning of September 11, 2001, I had a breakfast meeting scheduled for eight am in the Windows on the World Restaurant—on the 106th floor of the Trade Center's north tower. After the 1993 terrorist bombing of the World Trade Center garage, the restaurant was closed for three years. Since it had reopened, Tim and I still hadn't gotten there. So, I was excited. Not only did I have a chance to meet with a potential new client, but I'd also be able to see what the buzz was all about. Finally. I couldn't really call myself a true New Yorker until I'd eaten there, could I?

My plan was to go directly from home to the restaurant after dropping Nicholas off at school. I called a cab for the two of us and asked the driver to make a detour to the school before taking me downtown. We dropped Nicholas off at seven-forty-five and inched our way south. I knew I was cutting it close, but who could predict Tuesday morning traffic? Two blocks short of the door where I'd asked the cabbie to drop me off, I heard the Brring-brring of my cellular phone ringing from the depths of my purse.

"Sorry," I said to the cabbie by way of apologizing for distracting him. "Antonia St. John."

It was one of the early morning teacher-monitors at Nicholas's school. "Ms. St. John," she said over the chatter and clatter of pre-teens in the background. "So sorry to bother you. Nicholas is sick. You need to come and get him."

Any other week, I would have been able to call Tim and ask him to take on parent duty, but Tim was in Boston this week, meeting with a gallery owner, so there was only me. I sighed and called the restaurant to ask them to tell my guests that I couldn't make it but that they should enjoy their breakfast, and I would take care of the bill. Then I asked the cabbie to take the next side street, and we returned to the school.

As the cab pulled up in front of the school at about 8:45, I could hear what sounded like a plane flying far too low for Manhattan airspace. Then there was a roaring sound, like thunder in the distance. I scrambled up the school steps where Nicholas was waiting in the foyer, looking slightly green. I bundled him into the car, and as the taxi made its way through yet more traffic on the way back to the house, we heard another loud crash, like a bomb going off. We had no idea what could be gong on. Half an hour later, the two of us were sitting together on the sofa, a blanket wrapped around Nicholas as he sipped ginger ale, watching with growing horror, the nightmare unfolding practically outside our door. I had never felt so vulnerable in my entire life. But I tried not to let Nicholas feel my fear.

By noon it was clear that Manhattan was a disaster zone, and my fears had multiplied by the hour. My mind was racing with all kinds of possibilities for the future—and for my son.

"Nicholas," I began as we sat down together to a bowl of soup, the only thing he felt he could keep down.

"Mom, can you stop calling me Nicholas, please? I'm Nick now," he said, and I could see he was feeling better.

"Nick," I started again, and he smiled. "Nick, you remember Aunt Kelly talking to us about the ballet school in Toronto?"

"Mom, it's not just a ballet school. It's *the* ballet school," he corrected me.

"Yes, well, anyway, I seem to remember her saying there would be auditions in Toronto for next year. Are you still interested?"

Nick's eyes lit up, and he stared at me. "Mom! Are you for real? Are you saying I can go?"

I thought for a moment to see if I could figure out precisely what I *was* saying. "I guess I am, Nick. Yes, yes, I am."

What I was really saying was that I wanted him out of this city and out of this country as much as possible. Canada looked very attractive at that moment.

~

I had always considered myself a strong, modern woman who had the capacity to prevail over just about any obstacle. For the first few weeks after the attacks, as I watched the events that unfolded to try first to save victims and then recover as much human remains as possible, I felt helpless—a feeling that was previously unknown to me. Of course, the office remained closed for the time being—no one would or could come to New York for meetings anyway, so we held telephone meetings and tried to pretend the world was still the same. Air space was closed immediately after the attacks, so Tim rented a car and drove home as quickly as he could. We huddled up in the house every evening, watching what had become of our city both physically and emotionally. Tim and I talked quietly every evening about how close I'd come to the end of my life.

"What if Nicholas hadn't been sick that morning?" I said to him more often than he needed to hear it.

"But he was," Tim said. "And you're here where you're supposed to be."

I knew he was right, but that didn't make it any easier to deal with what I suspected was a bit of survivor's guilt. I had arranged the breakfast meeting. I had invited the clients. And now they were dead, and I was still here. Sometimes, I found the thought overwhelming.

Grace called us almost every day. It was a funny thing: I found her telephone calls soothing. For the first time in our occasionally strained relationship, I found the composure of her voice and her ability to move me away from the horrifying images without diminishing their importance to be just what I needed. She was my saviour during that first month. The moment I was able to return to the office, I felt energized, almost my old self. And I credited Grace with helping. Then there was Nicholas—Nick.

Nick's school was closed for several weeks, and he was only mildly interested in the unfolding tragedy in his city. He was more focused on arranging his audition in Toronto and ensuring he was ready. We set up a makeshift ballet studio in the guest bedroom, and Natalie came to give him extra tutoring, which she said he didn't need, but that Nick wanted. Nick spent every other evening on the telephone with his aunt in Toronto, who sent him the required documents. The audition was to be in Toronto at the National Ballet School in November. I was most assuredly going with Nick, but I didn't want to fly.

It was an eight-and-a-half-hour drive from Manhattan to Toronto. All three of us—Tim and I and Nick—piled into the car early on a cold, clear November morning and headed to the Canadian border. As we took the ramp from the Gardiner Expressway into downtown Toronto at six that evening, snow flurries swirled in the headlights, but we had made it safe and sound. I felt a kind of relief I hadn't expected when I realized I was no longer in New York.

The audition was set for the following afternoon. Tim planned to visit with Kelly while I accompanied Nick to the audition. I had no idea what to expect.

As Nick and I approached the school the next afternoon, I realized I was quite out of my depth even after all these years. I wasn't like the over-involved ballet moms I'd observed at Nick's school, and although I'd read the materials Kelly had sent us about the school, I still felt like a fish out of water. Nick, however, felt right at home. I could tell by his excitement as we mounted the few steps to what appeared to be an unprepossessing building on an unprepossessing street in downtown Toronto.

The main building where the entrance was located was one of several old, attached houses—not unlike New York brownstones—that I would eventually discover housed the boys' residence where Nick would stay if they accepted him. To the left of the entrance was what I'd read was an old Quaker meeting house built in 1911 that was also part of the school. It was the most impressive-looking part, with its massive pillars flanking the doors that led directly onto the sidewalk.

We checked in at the desk, and a pleasant young woman directed us to what she called "Studio A-B," which turned out to be in the Quaker meeting house. As she passed Nick two cloth patches with the number sixteen, she smiled and said, "Good luck." Then she directed us to pin them on him once he was ready.

We made our way through a labyrinth of narrow corridors and emerged in another small hall outside the studio. I stood outside the doors to the studio with a bevy of other nervous students (and mothers—there was only one father I could see) and helped Nick get ready. Then the parents were directed to sit silently in the chairs set up inside the studio. I was delighted since I wasn't aware I'd be permitted to watch.

I took a seat and noticed a long table where four people, who I figured must have been teachers at the school, sat. To the side of the table was a large video camera on a stand. There were about twenty dancers, all but three of whom were girls. There seemed to be more nervousness in the audience than among those auditioning. Finally, the kids were lined up in rows and an older woman—clearly a long-time teacher—appeared and began conducting a class. Nick was inches taller than the rest of the auditioning students and was in the back row. It was fascinating. I tried to figure out precisely what they were looking for, but since I wasn't a dancer, it was difficult for me.

When it was all over, we waited for the panel to call out numbers. The numbers they would call would be asked to stay behind. The others were thanked for their enthusiasm, but could leave. I held my breath. The first number she called was "sixteen." Nick. It was as if I'd just been selected. I had no idea I'd feel this way.

It was the beginning of a journey for which this was merely the first step. Nick was accepted to attend the summer session the following July. It would be a four-week audition. At the end of that period, selected students would be invited to attend the full-time program beginning in September, a little less than a year from now. It was nerve-wracking.

In June of the following year, as I sewed tiny labels into each T-shirt, each pair of underwear and each individual sock belonging to my son so that they wouldn't get lost in the school laundry, I considered how far I'd come as a mom. And I cried when we left him at the school residence the first week in July. It was just another beginning.

Of course, at the end of the four-week audition, Nick was accepted, as Kelly, Natalie and everyone else who knew anything about Nick and dance had predicted. So he began his ballet journey away from home that September, and Tim and I returned to our lives. Then there was something the school called "Parents'

Day," which took place the last weekend in November. It would give us an opportunity to observe a class and to chat with Nick's teachers, both his dance teachers and his academic ones. Tim and I couldn't wait.

~

I missed Nick more than I could ever have imagined. We talked once a week, but this didn't seem nearly enough. He had come home for the weekend that Canada celebrated Thanksgiving in October, but we hadn't seen him since then.

He had met so many new people that I found it hard to keep track. There were the other boys in his ballet class, something new for him. And there were the girls in his academic classes. One week when he called, he was particularly excited about a new class he had started. It was called character dance—boys and girls together.

"Mom, it's great," Nick said, and I could hear the excitement in his voice across the telephone wires. "I get to dance with a girl."

I thought this an odd statement coming from a boy who had been in classes almost exclusively with girls up until now. However, he had never been actually dancing "with" any of them. Then, every time he called, he mentioned dancing with a girl. Then it clicked —*a* girl.

"What's her name, Nick?" I said, feigning a nonchalance I couldn't really capture.

"Oh, Mom. Well, her name's Alex—short for Alexandra."

So, my son had his first crush. I hoped she wouldn't break his heart.

"We look forward to meeting this Alex when we come for Parents' Day, Nick," I said. I could almost feel him rolling his eyes.

Finally, it was time to fly to Toronto. Tim and I arrived at the school for Parents' Day with plenty of time to spare. We weren't

permitted to wander around much, but we did visit the boys'
residence with Nick before the class. There was only one word for
that building: Dickensian. I expected Oliver Twist to come
around any corner at any minute. It was old, dingy and Nick
loved it. He shared a room with three other boys—two sets of
bunk beds, four small desks and a mixture of clean and not-so-
clean clothing peeking out from every corner. I found it hard to
believe that a kid who had grown up as he had in a pristine room
of his own would be so comfortable here. What I didn't realize
was that it was the whole package—the whole was assuredly
more than the sum of its parts in this case. The teachers, the kids,
the residence staff and the ballet. Always the ballet. Finally, Nick
said it was time for us to get going. Class would start shortly, and
we needed to get into the studio before all the chairs were taken.

"The studio is pretty small," he said, "so you need to get
there early to get a good seat."

Of course, we needed a good seat. So, Nick pushed his feet
into the big, quilted warm-up boots we'd brought for him (as
directed by Nick), picked up his ballet bag and headed out the
door. We followed like a couple of lemmings.

When we arrived at the crowded central hall onto which at
least three studios opened, Nick said, "You'll have to wait here
for a few minutes, guys. I just need a minute to say hi to someone
before class."

I nodded, thinking this would be a terrific opportunity to
observe the other parents and their ballet kids. There was a
distinctly different feeling here in this elite ballet school than the
one we'd gotten used to at Natalie's school. I couldn't put my
finger on it, though.

"I'm just going to run to the men's room," Tim said, "if I can
find it." His eyes darted around, and then he headed off down a
narrow corridor.

I then turned to watch Nick as he made his way to the
opposite side of the hall, dodging parents and students. He

looked around for a moment, and then I saw what he was looking for. He began chatting with one of the girls who had just emerged from the hall on the other side, presumably from the girls' residence. *This must be Alex*, I thought. *I wonder if this would be a good time to go over and introduce myself.* I considered this possibility for a moment, but on second thought, I realized it was probably a bad idea. Nick would introduce us when he felt the time was right, but it was all I could do to take this mature view. I needed to see who my child was so smitten with because it was clear to me that he was smitten.

I watched Nick's face as he talked to her. His eyes shone with a brightness that put to shame even the shine I'd seen over the years when he spied a new present under the Christmas tree or when he first saw *The Nutcracker*. And there was something about his smile—a smile he had obviously reserved for this kind of person. As his mother, I'd never seen it. Was I jealous?

I tried to get a better look at her, but all I could see was the dark head with its inevitable ballet bun tilted slightly toward Nick's face. I was so curious to know if she had the same love-struck look. As I struggled to see better, I moved slightly too far to my left and bumped into a woman who was also gazing vaguely in their direction.

"I'm so sorry," she said. I was the one who should have apologized, but, of course, it was likely that she was a Canadian. They always beat us to the apology. "It's a bit crowded in here, isn't it?"

There was something slightly familiar about her voice. I turned toward her to make my own apology when I froze. She stood less than an arm's length from me, staring. I could feel the stare pierce my forehead, and I thought my head might explode.

"It's Antonia, isn't it? Antonia St. John, as I recall," she said. The woman had stopped staring, and I could see her take in a deep breath. "Remember me?"

I looked at this woman with dark-almost-black breezy, ear-length razor hair cut and her cream-coloured sweater coat that she held tightly around her. My heart stopped for a split second, and I felt my stomach lurch. "Yes," I said. "Yes, I do. You're Megan McMaster." She nodded, her face a complete blank. I had always taken pride in my skill at figuring out what people were thinking. It had often been hailed as one of my most valuable business assets. I could read the faces of clients sitting in a boardroom so well that I could anticipate their next thoughts and give them just what they wanted. But that skill seemed to have left me. I had no idea what she was thinking. "What are you doing here?" I said finally.

"Probably the same thing you're doing," Megan said. I noticed Megan's eyes begin to flutter off to the side as if she might be looking for something. Of course, she was looking for Tim. Who else?

At that moment, Nick looked over toward me and smiled as Tim turned the corner from the hallway. Tim looked at me, smiling, then he froze. The smile on his face looked like an ice sculpture slowly beginning to melt. He was looking at Megan, who had turned her head. I could see the moment when they locked eyes, and I had to look away.

Suddenly, my life seemed to fade into slow motion,

Out of the corner of my eye, I could see Nick saying something to the young woman he'd been talking to, and the two of them looked toward where the three of us were standing. They were both smiling. They began to move toward us as I willed them to stay where they were.

Megan was staring at Tim, who had begun slowly advancing toward us. Tim, Nick and the girl arrived beside Megan and me at the same time. Tim hadn't yet said a word.

Nick finally broke the silence. "Mom, Dad. I'd like you to meet Alex."

Young Alex looked at me, then up at Tim, who towered over her and said, "I'm so happy to meet you both. I'm Alex McMaster."

# 26

## Tim

### 2002

*Life can only be understood backwards; but it must
be lived forward.*
~ Soren Kierkegaard

I WAS FINDING THE WHOLE BALLET SCHOOL THING overwhelming.
As my son grew up, I always thought we'd have a lot in common,
but he'd chosen a different path. It was a path so foreign to me
that I sometimes struggled to find common ground. But he was
my son, and I loved him, so I learned.

As I stood in the men's room just before the Parents' Day
class, I looked in the mirror and told myself to get over myself.
Nick did have something in common with me—we both had the
soul of an artist. Anyway, it was his life, and I'd support him
wherever his talents took him. *After all*, I thought, *he probably
inherited his artistic bent from me.* I finished washing my hands and
headed back into the fray.

When I rounded the corner back into the hallway, I expected
everyone would have gone inside the studios by then and hoped
that Antonia had been able to save me a seat. I was partially right.
Most of the parents and students had gone into the studios, but
there were still a few stragglers, my wife among them.

I could see Antonia just outside the studio door. Her face
looked serious as I watched her speaking to a woman whose back
was to me. I wondered who Antonia might have struck up a

conversation with and why the excitement we'd both felt to finally see our son's class at the National Ballet School was no longer reflected on her face when she saw me. Her face was a blank mask—a pale blank mask. The woman chatting with Antonia now turned slightly, and I could see her face. My heart stopped. I couldn't breathe, and I couldn't take a step. My body wouldn't respond. It was Meg. But it couldn't be. She was long in my past.

*What the hell?* I thought. *How can she be here? Why is she here? She can't be here. I'm seeing things.* When I started to breathe again, I looked at Antonia's face once again and understood. I told myself I was a grown-up and could handle this. Of course, I could.

I walked toward them slowly, arriving just as Nick, with a young ballerina at his side, reached the group.

I didn't have a chance to say anything before Nick began introducing the girl, who I assumed was the Alex he'd been talking about for months. If I had expected Antonia to be riveted on Meg's face, I was wrong. As if in a trance, she was staring at Nick's friend as she introduced herself as Alex McMaster.

I was confused for a moment. Then the wheels in my brain started slowly moving round and round. *Oh. My. God.* I thought. *Nick and Alex.* Then Alex McMaster looked directly at me, and I knew. I knew why Antonia was staring at her face. I looked at my son and then back at Alex, and as I looked at this young woman, I knew. I was looking at a reflection. Of me.

~

There are moments in life when the world seems to stop spinning. When we finally wake up from our dream, nothing is ever the same again. Our worlds turn on a dime. All I could think about was that crazy quote about how life-changing events are a bit like having the rug pulled out from under you. They don't announce themselves. They just happen. I just wasn't sure what was happening or if any of us would ever be the same. These thoughts were running through my head as another young woman about Nick's age ran around the corner into the small quadrangle toward us and breathlessly said, "Am I late? I hope I'm not late." She looked at Alex. "Hey, sis, let's see what you've learned."

Nick's eyes brightened up. "Hey, you must be Ava. Alex has told me all about you. And whoa! You sure are identical! I'm Nick Sinclair."

Ava stood back for a moment and looked at Nick with the critical eye that only a thirteen-year-old girl could perfect. "You know, you're not half bad, Nick Sinclair."

I was staring at Ava. I couldn't help myself—she was the spitting image of Alex. There were two. I turned toward Meg.

"Yes, Tim," Meg said quietly as if reading my mind. "They're twins."

Before anyone could say another word, a ballet teacher popped her head out of the studio where we were crowding the door. "Class is about to start, everyone." She looked at Alex. "Alex, come on and get ready for warm-up. You're late." Alex smiled, shrugged and followed her teacher into the studio. Ava trailed behind her, and Meg took up the rear.

"I suppose we need to talk," Meg said quietly as she closed the studio door behind her.

"Hey, Dad, I'm late, too. You and Mom should come in and get a seat before Mr. Stephanopoulos sees I'm late, too."

Nick went in, and Antonia and I moved slowly toward the door.

"Talk?" she hissed at me. "She thinks you need to talk?" Antonia shook her head. "I think you need a whole lot more than talking." She turned away from me and took the last seat on the end of the first row of chairs that had been jammed into one end of the studio. I found a vacant chair three rows behind.

I sat down heavily in the empty seat against the back wall beside another couple of parents. They looked at me, nodding and smiling. I forced a smile, then looked out into the centre of the studio and saw that the boys—Nick and his classmates—were taking their places at the barres that took up the three remaining mirrored walls.

"Prepare," Mr. Stephanopoulos said, and each of the boys stood tall, side-on to the barre and placed a hand gently on the worn wooden rail. They were ready to begin.

I watched the barre exercises, the exercises in the centre of the room, and the bits of actual dance that each dancer did individually and in groups of two or three. I was vaguely aware of the power and grace that both seemed to reside simultaneously in my son. I even had a moment of marvelling at his strength and flexibility. But the undercurrent of all these moments where I should have been only proud of my son for his single-minded pursuit of his talent was the feeling I could not shake—the feeling that my life had just been altered dramatically. I was way off balance. How could this have happened? There was no way this wasn't going to be a problem—and that problem would start with how to tell Nick that his new girlfriend was his sister.

Before I knew it, it was time for *"révérence,"* that moment at the end of a ballet class when the dancers line up to bow to show respect for and thank their teacher and class pianist.

"What'd you think, Dad?" Nick said, coming toward the rows of parents while pulling on his sweatshirt.

I knew it was important to Nick that I learned to love what he loved so much. Ballet was growing on me, but I still had a long way to go. "Looking great, man," I said finally. "Looking great."

Nick smiled broadly and finished picking up his things. There would be a small performance that evening in the Betty Oliphant Theatre, named for the school's founder, in which we'd get to see all grades perform. I'd been looking forward to it until I realized that Meg would be there, too, and I began to feel a cold sweat break out between my shoulder blades. I'd have to sit in the same darkened auditorium with her, and I didn't know how I'd be able to concentrate on the performance. And, of course, there was Antonia. For her, this had to be a disaster of proportions I couldn't even begin to understand.

Antonia and I returned to the hotel between the afternoon class and the evening performance. We walked silently down Yonge Street and across to Bay Street, where we were staying at the Marriott, as was becoming our habit.

As I held open the door to the lobby for her, she looked at me and said, "You have to work this out, Tim. You can't ignore it, as much as I'd just like to close my eyes and hope it all goes away. It won't, and, most important of all, you have to talk to your son." Antonia went through the door and kept on walking straight toward the bar. I knew she was right.

~

"Did you know?" Antonia took a deep drink of the gin martini the server had just put on the table in front of her and then sank back into the cushions on a sofa in the lobby bar by the fireplace.

"Did I know?"

Antonia sighed deeply. "Dear god, Tim, are we going to play this game? It's clear Alex and Ava are yours. They look just like you, and the timing works. Did you know? Did you deliberately keep this from me?"

"Antonia," I said, reaching for her hand. She pulled it away. "How could I have known?"

"You went back to Halifax to see Megan after I told you I was pregnant. She could have told you then. You could have decided to keep it a secret from me and the rest of your family, thinking you'd never cross paths again."

"What kind of person do you think I am, Antonia? How could I not have wanted to be part of my children's lives, in whatever form that might have taken? No, I didn't know. But..." I trailed off, racking my brain, trying to remember something.

"But what?"

"It's just something my mother said once. I wonder—"

"You wonder what? If she knew and didn't tell you? How could she have known?" Antonia took another sip of her drink, a daintier one this time. "She and Jack have spent a lot of time in Halifax over the years, haven't they? And Halifax is a small city." Antonia sighed. "But your mother, the sainted Grace Sinclair, would never have kept that from you."

I frowned. I never liked hearing Antonia talk about my mother in her just-short-of-sarcastic way, but she did have a point. Mom had opportunity, that's for sure. But how could my mother have kept something like this a secret? *No,* I thought, *we're reaching. Mom would have told me.* But I knew I'd have to talk to her.

By the time we'd had dinner and returned to the theatre, I had still not formulated any way forward. My stomach felt like it was burning, and I had half a headache.

As we took our seats in the auditorium, I couldn't see Meg or her daughter Ava. I have to admit I kept my head down as much as possible until the lights went down, and the school's artistic director emerged from the side of the orchestra area and stood beside the grand piano just below the stage. After introducing herself and telling us it was her privilege to be the artistic director, the massive curtain rose and the performance began.

I stared unseeingly at the stage through the grade six presentation of perfect technique (at least, it looked perfect to me) and the grade seven classes of boys and girls doing something called character dancing. I couldn't focus. Then the flamenco began.

Nick was leading the group. He stood tall and handsome, his hands clapping above his head while his feet moved impossibly fast. The grade eight girls massed around him in their flowing, brightly coloured dresses and I was transported to an evening Antonia and I had spent in Madrid watching an impromptu flamenco show in the middle of a street in the light of the street lamps. Then Nick reached for his partner. It was Alex.

I could feel Antonia sucking in a deep breath beside me as we watched them. As far as the audience was concerned, they were moving as one, as if they were meant to dance together. To us, they were two young people whose bonds of trust they now had with us, their parents, were about to be stretched, if not broken.

We then watched Nick and his class of boys display their newly learned moves. Alex's class followed. We then sat through the displays by the students closer to graduation, and it was clear to us we were seeing the next generation of professional ballet dancers. Antonia had been right to let Nick choose this school.

When the lights came up and I stood to find my coat, I saw Meg and Ava three rows behind us. I turned to Antonia.

"Antonia, I'm going to ask Meg to join us for coffee tomorrow morning. We need to get some things sorted out."

Antonia nodded. "Join *us*?" she said. "I'm not going to be part of this. I can't be part of it. You two need to figure out this debacle." She wound her scarf around her neck and moved toward the aisle behind the rest of the parents filing out. "I'll wait for you and Nick in the lobby." We were taking Nick to a late dinner.

I caught up to Meg as she neared the door to the lobby. "Meg, can I talk to you for a moment?"

Just then, Nick came up the stairs from backstage and said, "Hey, Dad. I didn't know you knew Dr. McMaster."

I was slightly jarred by the Dr. McMaster moniker, but of course, she would have finished her doctorate within the year after our—encounter. I coughed slightly. "Yes. Dr. McMaster and I knew each other a long time ago." Meg narrowed her eyes and shook her head so imperceptibly that I barely noticed it. She needn't have. I had no intention of blurting out my secret to my son without some serious preparation.

# 27

# Antonia

## 2002

*Adapt or perish, now as ever, is nature's inexcusable imperative.* ~ H. G. Wells

THE MOMENT I SET EYES ON ALEX across the quadrangle, smiling up at my Nick, I felt my world fall away. The earth beneath my feet, which had felt solid and stable a second earlier, gave way as if I had been standing on a precipice without realizing it was so fragile. I didn't need to see that Megan was there, too, to know that I was looking into the face of my husband's daughter. I didn't have to be told the circumstances of the situation to know that my world had been set on its head. I didn't have to be told that my son was in love with his sister. I could see it as plain as day. Alex could be no one's daughter except Tim's.

Nick looked over and smiled at me, and my heart melted as it always did when my son smiled at me that way. But all I could see was my son standing across the hall with a young woman who could never be his girlfriend. All I could think was how heartbroken he would be. And how he would blame his father. I had no idea what to do.

Then I looked at Tim's face as he caught Megan's eyes. *Oh my god*, I thought. *This can't be happening. After all this time.* But it was happening. Then Ava appeared, and it was twice as bad as I thought.

I turned away and staggered into the studio, allowing my body to fall into the first empty chair I saw. My mind and body seemed to have separated. I spent the entire class riveted on my son so much that I didn't see a single other dancer in the studio that morning. I couldn't trust myself to look in any other direction than directly at Nick, or I knew I might cry. I had made up my mind about one thing, though. Tim and Megan would have to figure this out between the two of them. My only concern at that moment was for Nick. I couldn't even bring myself to imagine what it would be like for Alex and Ava to come face to face with a father who had been absent from their lives for thirteen years. They were not my concern.

# 28

# Grace

## 2002

*Time is the longest distance between two places.*
~ Tennessee Williams, *The Glass Menagerie*

SOMETIMES TIME SEEMS TO PASS IN THE BLINK OF AN EYE. Other times, it is so exquisitely slow as to be extended moments. That late November day when young Ava McMaster walked into the Sinclair Gallery was one of those moments that stretched so agonizingly that it seemed frozen in time.

It was late in the afternoon, and the sun had already set that late November day. I had my back to the gallery's front door, standing shoulder to shoulder with Jack as we tried to determine if the three paintings now claiming real estate on the back wall were appropriately grouped. Our opinions diverged.

I thought the painting in the centre, a bright abstract piece ostensibly representing a raging hurricane, was too dramatic, hanging between two quiet, impressionistic watercolours.

"A rose between two thorns, as it were," Jack said. "I like it."

"More like one thorn in the middle," I muttered.

Before Jack had a chance to ask me to repeat myself (because I was certain he would do so), the gallery door opened and slammed shut, and a voice behind us said, "Excuse me. I don't mean to interrupt."

I turned with a smile. "No interruption at all."

The young woman in front of me was but a child, no more than twelve or thirteen, with a broad smile poking out from under a wild mass of dark curls that tumbled onto her shoulders. But the words of welcome that were forming on my lips fell away as I was caught by her arresting blue eyes. They were eyes I'd seen before—eyes I knew as well as I knew my own. And her face! It was as familiar to me as my own—or as my son's. I was looking at young Ava's face, but I was seeing my own child, Tim—as a teenager. I couldn't speak.

"Well, then, what is it we can do for you, young lady?" Jack said, coming to my rescue.

"I'm looking for Ellen McMaster. The artist? We're supposed to meet here at five-thirty. She's going to show me her newest sculpture, all lit for the exhibition."

"She is, is she?" Jack said, smiling while I stood there beside him—still mute.

"Yes," said the young woman. "I'm Ava McMaster. Ellie's my mentor. I'm an artist, too." She stopped for a beat. "I'm also her great-granddaughter."

I nearly collapsed.

~

Jack's gallery assistant returned from the store room, where she'd been tagging new pieces, and said she'd be happy to look after Ava and Ellen when the elder McMaster arrived so we could leave. I grabbed my coat and fled.

Before long, Jack and I were sharing a bottle of wine at a harbourfront restaurant. I was staring out into the darkness, watching the lights of the harbour ferry as they passed the window.

"What's going on, Grace?" Jack said. "You've been acting peculiar ever since you laid eyes on young Ava."

Jack knew me well. I sipped my wine slowly and then carefully placed the glass on the table. I toyed with the stem for a moment. "It's a long story," I said. "But I think it might only just have begun."

"Well, you know I'm a good listener. Start at the beginning, and don't leave anything out."

So, I started. "You remember way back when we first came to Halifax, and you met with Nigel Kaufman?" Jack nodded, his face registering slight surprise at where the story had begun. "That was the first time we heard about Ellie McMaster."

"Yes, and from our success at the gallery and beyond with her work, it was damn good news."

"Yes, of course," I said. "But you might also remember I mentioned to you that when Tim spent some time here in Halifax earlier that year before he and Antonia were married, he had something of a dalliance."

"Oh, I see." Jack's eyes widened. "I seem to remember you mentioning the name of the woman involved was also McMaster. You seemed to have some odd notion that this young woman and Ellen McMaster, the sculptor, might have been related."

"Yes, I did. The young woman's name was Megan, and as it turned out, they are, indeed, related. We've even met her, Jack."

His eyebrows raised in surprise. Then he cocked his head slightly to the side as if trying to remember something. "We have? I have? Yes, I suppose I did meet Ellen's granddaughter at a gallery opening a few years ago. I don't really remember much about her—there were so many people milling about. In any case, I hadn't remembered you mentioning her as Tim's paramour." Jack's forehead furrowed even more as if he were trying to remember something.

It was my turn for raised eyebrows. "Hardly a paramour, Jack. More like a fling. But here's the problem." Just then, the server passed and offered us more wine. We both nodded, and the server poured.

"You were saying?" Jack said as the server walked away.

"I was saying there was a bit of a problem even at the time. Tim was in love with the girl."

Jack pursed his lips. "Oh, dear. That certainly must have posed a problem for the impending nuptials of Tim and Antonia. But what does this have to do with what's on your mind today?"

"Well, the day Nigel mentioned Ellen McMaster, and I asked him if Megan might be related to her, he said she was. He also told me Megan was a scientist. Tim's Megan was also a scientist, and this isn't a very big city."

"I seem to remember suggesting that you cease any notion of sleuthing to determine that direct connection. My sense was that it could only lead to problems." He sipped his wine and stared me down. "You didn't heed my advice, did you?"

"Perhaps I might have taken a little trip to the university where Megan was studying. And I may have found her department. I may have told a bit of a white lie about why I was there. I must admit I never expected to actually see her, but as fate would have it, she happened to come into the department chair's outer office while I was there."

"Grace Sinclair!"

"I know, I know. But I didn't speak to her. All I heard was the secretary say hello to her and pass her a form. I might have noticed the name on the form. And there was something else." I took a deep breath. "I suspected she might be pregnant."

"Oh my god, Grace. You don't think…"

"I don't *think*. I *know*. That young woman we met today is Tim's daughter—my granddaughter. I'm as sure of this as I have ever been of anything in my life."

Jack took a moment to reflect on what I'd been telling him and then asked me if I'd ever considered telling Tim about my suspicions at the time. I had not. In my view, it would not have been in anyone's best interests for me to pass on speculation. Because that's what it was—pure speculation and gossip if spread. I thought she looked pregnant, and it occurred to me that it was possible Tim might be the father. I had no way of knowing the truth of any of this. It wasn't my story to tell. So, I kept it to myself. But now—now, I was confronted with a reality too big to ignore. And there was another issue.

Suddenly alarm seemed to fill Jack's face. "Didn't that young Ava mention she and her mother were flying to Toronto tomorrow to see her sister at the National Ballet School?"

I swallowed hard. "She did."

"Isn't that Nick's school and the exact place where Tim and Antonia will be this weekend?"

It was. The question was whether I should warn them or leave it in fate's hands. Perhaps I should try to give them a heads-up about it before Tim and Antonia stumbled on Megan and her daughter Ava in Toronto. I told myself I'd call the house, and if they had already left, that would be a message to me to leave it alone. I wouldn't try to track them down by their cell phones on the road. I'd leave it to fate.

There was no answer at the house. They'd already left. It was all up to the fates.

~

Jack and I drove back to Bar Harbor two days later. It was less than four weeks until Christmas, and we wanted to be settled back in our beach-side abode before we welcomed the family for the holidays. I tried to concentrate on the festive decorating I'd be doing as soon as we got home, but I could feel the anxiety mounting as I wondered what was happening in Toronto. Before we closed up our Halifax house, I jumped every time I thought I heard a telephone ringing.

When the phone finally rang, it was the middle of the next week, and I was sorting through Christmas decorations and trying to spruce up the wreath for the door. Jack was in his studio painting and would help me with the decorating after lunch. I picked up the phone.

"Did you know, Mom? Please tell me you didn't know." Tim's voice pleaded with me over the telephone line.

He told me what had happened in Toronto, and I told him I didn't know. Then he told me that Ava's sister at the ballet school was her twin. There were two. My head was spinning.

"We'll have to tell Kelly, you know," I said.

"First, I have to tell Nick. I haven't found a way to tell him yet. I'm going back to Toronto again this weekend to do it in person," Tim said.

"Is there anything I can do to help?"

I heard a deep sigh at the other end of the telephone line, and all I wanted to do was hug my son. And I also wanted to hug my granddaughters. My granddaughters! But how would they react to that? Tim said he'd call me after he told Nick.

~

I could hear the fatigue in Tim's voice when he called me again the following week. He had told Nick that he had twin sisters, and evidently, Megan had told her daughters that they had a brother and a father and that their father's absence for thirteen years had been her decision. None of the explanations mattered—to anyone.

"Mom, it's a disaster," Tim said. I could hear profound dejection in his voice. "Nick isn't speaking to me. Antonia isn't speaking to me. Ava and Alex aren't speaking to their mother, and certainly not to me. It's a catastrophe of biblical proportions. I've blown up so many lives."

"Well, my darling boy, you could see it that way. Or perhaps you could look at it another way. Just think how many lives can now be richer for the knowledge?"

"Richer?"

"Of course, Tim. Nicholas has sisters. How wonderful could that be if we let it? His sisters have both a father and a brother—not to mention another grandmother and an aunt. Four new wonderful people for them to have in their lives. Kelly has two nieces—one of whom is a ballet dancer as she was herself." I stopped myself. "There is only one problem that we probably can't fix."

"Antonia," he said. "Dear god. How will she ever be able to forgive me?"

"Forgive you?" I said. "For what? Not knowing you had daughters? No, Tim. Antonia's problem is far more fundamental and difficult to solve. How is she going to figure out where she fits?"

There was only one solution as far as I was concerned. Everyone—and I mean everyone—would have to come to spend Christmas with Jack and me in Bar Harbor. I would not take no for an answer from anyone. And I didn't.

# 29

## Tim

### Christmas, 2002

*The loneliest moment in someone's life is when*
*they are watching their whole world fall apart, and*
*all they can do is stare blankly.*
~ F. Scott Fitzgerald

I HAVE NO IDEA HOW SHE DID IT. I mean, three weeks before Christmas, I thought Antonia might never speak to me again and that my only son might never forgive me. I had two daughters I wanted to get to know and a former lover who had kept a years-long secret from me. Now it was Christmas Eve, and as I pulled the car—stuffed to the roof with Christmas "things"—into the driveway, I was too exhausted from the long drive (almost nine hours) and the silent treatment I'd received from both my wife and my son (they spent the entire trip with headphones on apart from the three hours in the middle where Antonia drove) even to care how Mom had pulled it off.

Mom opened the door as I got out to stretch, and I could see her smile was as wide as the Bar Harbor shoreline. Antonia and Nick both got out of the car and started to remove boxes and suitcases.

"Antonia, you didn't have to come. We could have stayed in New York—just the three of us," I said as I helped remove presents from the trunk.

Antonia stopped her sorting for a moment and looked at me. "Tim, I'm here now. And only because your mother coerced me. Let it go, and let's all just get through this."

I didn't know how Mom strong-armed her, but a small part of me, buried deep inside, was hopeful that Mom might be right—that we could somehow come out on the other side of this holiday with a future that didn't consist of recrimination and regret.

"I hope this isn't going to be like one of those stupid Christmas family movies," Nick said as he passed by me on the way to the open arms of his grandmother.

I watched as Nick dropped the suitcase and boxes he was carrying and allowed himself to be buried in Mom's arms. I kind of agreed with Nick. When I walked in the door, Kelly was coming down the stairs. The minute she saw the three of us, she hopped down with a broad smile. How in the world could my sister be so happy when my world was falling apart?

"Geezus, you guys," she said as she hugged and kissed all around. "This is going to be the best Christmas ever! I've already got my present—you three here and two new nieces. Way to go, bro!"

Bro? Still bro at her age? I sighed, and for the briefest of moments, her wild enthusiasm for this family debacle gave me hope. I was just wondering where everyone was going to sleep. I needn't have wondered. Kelly and Mom had it all figured out.

Mom and Jack would, of course, remain in their room. Antonia and I would have the guest room upstairs next door. Nick would sleep in the small room on the third floor since that was his favourite room in the whole house with its widow's walk and one-hundred-and-eighty-degree view of the ocean, and it had been his room ever since he could climb the steep stairs. Kelly would sleep in the Murphy bed in the den, and Megan, her grandmother Ellen and the girls would share the two guest rooms with the Jack-and-Jill bathroom on the lower floor with its walk-out under the deck. Mom and Kelly had agreed that Meg, Ellen, Alex and Ava would be most comfortable with their own separate space at this point.

I had been surprised to hear that Ellen McMaster was coming, too. As it turned out, when Mom told me she would make this Christmas gathering happen, her first call was to Ellen. It seemed they had met briefly at the gallery in Halifax on one occasion or another. Now, it seemed they quickly bonded over their shared offspring, and the absurdity of the situation, then settled on a plan for this grand intervention. Mom was telling us this as we sat in the living room with the fireplace roaring, having our first (of many) festive cocktails while we waited for Meg, her grandmother and the girls to arrive. I was still fairly sure they wouldn't show up. As I gulped my first drink, I realized I was suffering from serious cognitive dissonance. On the one hand, I wanted all this to work out; on the other hand, I was terrified that they might actually show up, and I'd have to face everyone all at once.

"Just going to check the weather again," Jack said, getting up from his chair, presumably to check the little weather station he had set up in the kitchen.

I had seen a few flurries as we drove into Bar Harbor earlier, and now I could see that they had turned into light snow.

As Jack returned to the living room, Mom said, "You look worried, Jack. What's the weather situation?"

"Snow's coming faster, and the wind is picking up. I'm a bit worried about Ellen and Megan and the girls. The roads can get slippery quite fast. I'll be happier when they're here."

I wondered if Jack was beginning to think this family Christmas wasn't such a good idea. But those worries soon disappeared, only to be replaced by my whole other set of things to be anxious about as we heard a car pull into the driveway. They were here.

Antonia and I were sitting side-by-side on one of the sofas. I took her hand and squeezed it silently. She pulled it away, her face a mask of foreboding.

Nick stood up. "Show time," he said as he headed toward the door. "My *sisters* have arrived."

~

I waited until Mom and Jack had welcomed the newcomers to their home before I poked my nose into the front hallway.

"My word, this is a beautiful house," Ellen McMaster was saying as Mom hung coats in the closet and Jack took drink orders. "Thank you so much for the invitation, Grace. I just know we're all going to have a memorable Christmas." Her old eyes were twinkling. Mom hugged her, and all I could think was that memorable was probably apt.

"I'll show you guys your room," Nick said as he helped Ava and Alex with their suitcases. "A movie later, maybe?"

They both nodded, but I could see the sadness in Alex's eyes. I wanted to go over to her and tell her I'd be there for her, but I knew she'd think I was lying. But I wasn't. I was her father, and that thought was just beginning to sink into my brain. Then I saw Meg.

She stood in the foyer, staring. I wondered what she was thinking, but I didn't have the courage to approach her and ask. Antonia came up behind me. "Tim, talk to her," she said.

I turned. "I'm surprised you think that's a good idea."

Antonia sighed as if she had the weight of the world on her shoulders, and she might very well have—at least the full weight of her world and mine. "It's inevitable, Tim. I know that. I'm a big girl. Although I have no idea how I'll manage it, I know I'll move on eventually. Just go."

I walked up behind Meg and said, "Welcome, Meg. Merry Christmas."

She turned, her arms wrapped around herself as if to protect her. "Thank you, Tim."

# 30

# Antonia

## Christmas, 2002

*Your children are not your children. They are the*
*sons and daughters of Life's longing for itself. They*
*came through you but not from you, and though*
*they are with you yet they belong not to you.*
~ Khalil Gibran

THE ONLY COURSES I'D TRULY ENJOYED when I was a student were the ones I thought would get me the career I knew was rightfully mine. So, why did a quote from a writer I studied in an obscure course on American-immigrant literature I'd taken as an elective as an undergrad so many years ago flit through my mind as I watched Nick disappear down the stairs with Alex and Ava trailing behind? As I watched Tim and Megan chat quietly for a moment, I realized that Khalil Gibran was right. Our children do not belong to us. Nick did not belong to Tim—or to me, either. Neither did Alex and Ava belong to Megan—or Tim. But Nick, Alex and Ava all came through Tim, and there had to be a reason for that. Perhaps someday, I'd figure out that reason. But tonight, to distract myself, I was going to concentrate on helping Grace with Christmas Eve dinner.

An hour later, everyone was settled, and I'd spent the hour in the kitchen with Grace. At some point, Ellen joined us. I had always thought I'd never met anyone quite like Grace, but Ellen McMaster—Ellie, as she told us to call her—was a whole new dimension. I didn't know many older women in my life, but if I could cultivate half the passion for life I felt from Ellie at her age (I judged it to be late seventies), my dotage would be happy. When I'd arrived earlier with Tim and Nick, I thought I'd have to grit my teeth and force a smile as we progressed through the next couple of days. But Ellie and Grace had me laughing as we worked together around Grace's giant-sized kitchen island. I usually hated these situations of forced camaraderie with women—I much preferred the company of men—but I could get used to this. Then it was time to serve dinner.

Grace had planned a veritable feast. I wondered if she subscribed to the view that "families" eating together would bring them closer. I doubted that, but I was hungry by that time, and the wine I'd had earlier was starting to go to my head. I'd forgotten to have a few nibbles. We all sat down.

The starter consisted of lobster sliders, so delicious I thought I'd died and gone to heaven. That was followed by oysters Rockefeller. The main course was beef bourguignon and chicken biscuit pot pie accompanied by crispy Brussels sprouts and garlic mashed potatoes. I was so looking forward to those potatoes since I'd given up on carbs almost entirely over the past year in an effort to keep my weight and Tim's cholesterol under control. But before we had the main course on the table, just as everyone found their place at the table, the lights went out. I heard a collective intake of breath.

Jack was sitting beside me, and I heard him mutter something about a generator, but I could see in the light of the candles Grace had placed in the middle of the large table her hand gently pull him back into his seat and shake her head almost imperceptibly. I could hear the wind whistling and snow whipping against the windows. Did she not want him to fire up the generator?

"Let's get the candles, girls," Grace said, addressing Alex and Ava, who were sitting across the table from her. "We have lots."

And so Grace, assisted by Ava and Alex, her newfound granddaughters, lit the candles while Jack put a few fresh logs on the fire in the living room. They placed candles everywhere, causing me to worry slightly about the potential for fire.

"Let's eat in the living room by the fire," Grace said. "Everyone take their plates. Jack and I will bring the wine." She looked at Nick and the twins. "A sip for the three of you, perhaps?"

I was going to object, but I could see her shining face and the smile playing around her lips. Grace Sinclair knew what she was doing.

There's something magical about candlelight, isn't there? We took our plates as directed, and each found a place in the living room—on chairs, sofas and the floor. Nick, Alex and Ava found cushions to sit on and sat on the floor at the coffee table in front of the fireplace. I found myself sitting beside Megan on one of the sofas. We ate silently for a few minutes, bathed in the forgiving light of the candles' glow. Then out of the darkness from the other side of the room, I heard Grace say, "Megan, tell us about the day the girls were born."

In the darkness, I could feel Megan's hand on my arm. She squeezed lightly. "It's okay," I whispered. And she told us the story.

~

I sat in the darkness as Megan warmed to her story. She began hesitantly, her voice catching, no doubt self-conscious about telling this story to this odd group. But she seemed to want to tell it. She did as Grace asked and began with the story of the day the girls were born. I had hoped she might start the story some months before the birth. What I wanted to hear most from this woman who, in my mind at least, had been my competition so many years ago was why she had decided not to tell Tim about his daughters. When she had finished with her story, there was silence in the candle-lit room. I wanted to ask her about the months before Alex and Ava were born, but I didn't think anyone would welcome my input at that moment. I was also unsure I dared to voice the insecurities I'd spent years trying to hide. In the end, I didn't have to suffer in my ignorance. A small voice from the other side of the coffee table did it for me.

In a strained voice that sounded a lot like someone choking down tears, Alex said, "Why didn't you ever tell us, Mom? Why didn't you ever tell us who our father was? Or that we had a brother? What right did you have to keep it from us?"

I could hear the anger in her voice alongside the anguish. I'd spent my career learning to hear what people were saying between their words, and that skill was on full alert. As much as I was wallowing in my own discomfort, this was a confused and angry child whose life would never be the same again. I wondered if Ava shared her sister's sentiment.

"I'm sorry, Alex. You're right. You and Ava had a right to know, and I deprived you of that right. But there was a lot more at stake, " Megan said. Then she turned to face me, and I could see her silhouette in the dim light. She continued. "There was Antonia to consider."

I was stunned. Me? She was considering me? Someone was considering me? It didn't seem possible. Then I realized I was being unfair to Tim, who, for the past several weeks, seemed consumed by little else than how I felt about it. Truthfully, I was getting tired of hearing him ask how I was. But now, Megan McMaster was considering me.

"When Tim came back to Halifax in September of that year," Megan continued, "I was prepared to tell him he was going to be a father. I loved him with all my heart in a way I never thought I'd ever love anyone. I had even forgiven him for not telling me the whole truth about his career, which seemed so at odds with my passion for the environment. But before I had a chance to tell him, he told me Antonia was pregnant. As far as I was concerned, there was only one decision a man like Tim could make." She reached across the coffee table to search out Alex and Ava's hands. "The only decision a man like your father could make was to be a father to the child he knew was coming. There was no more point in me being a part of his life. I was devastated but so very proud of him." She swallowed hard. "I remember a poster I had on my dorm room wall when I was an undergrad. It was a picture of someone's hands holding a butterfly. The caption said, 'If you love something, set it free. If it comes back, it's yours. If not, it was never meant to be.'  I'm afraid that at eighteen, I had no idea at all about what that could truly mean. It wasn't until that day in Halifax that I knew. I set Tim free and wondered if I'd ever see him again." Megan put her hands back in her lap and bowed her head slightly. "Hate me if you have to—all of you. But I have never regretted a moment of ushering these two fantastic young women into and through the world. It has been the greatest privilege of my life. And I'd make the same decision again if I had it to do over. I'm sorry."

With the fireplace lighting Megan in silhouette, I saw a single tear escape her eye and realized there was more than one escaping mine.

# 31

# Tim

## Christmas, 2002

*Love sought is good, but given unsought is better.*
~ William Shakespeare, *Twelfth Night*,
Act 3, Scene 1

I REALIZED I WAS HOLDING MY BREATH as Meg told her story. When we'd had coffee in Toronto just three weeks earlier, she told me the part about her plans to tell me back in 1989 and how I had derailed them. At the time, sitting in that café in Toronto the day after the shock at the ballet school, I felt like someone had pierced my heart—and not only because I'd missed thirteen years with my daughters (arguably the best years of their lives—they were now teenage girls). I also realized that I'd missed her. After all these years and how far Antonia and I had come as a team, I knew that a part of me was still in love with Megan McMaster. I could feel my jaw tighten as I sat there in the dark on that Christmas Eve, not knowing what to say or even if I should say anything. I didn't trust myself.

"What the hell are we supposed to tell everyone at school?" This was Nick's voice. I'd never heard him quite so belligerent. "How can we just tell them that suddenly we're brother and sister? Everyone will think our family is seriously messed up."

Out of the darkness, I heard someone snicker. I was surprised when I realized it was Ellie. "To paraphrase Tolstoy, if I may be permitted, she said, '"Happy families are all alike; every dysfunctional family is dysfunctional in its own way.'" Then she giggled like a schoolgirl.

Mom then joined in. "I'll see your Tolstoy and raise you one George Bernard Shaw. 'If you cannot get rid of the family skeleton, you may as well make it dance.'"

Nick groaned. "Grama, really?"

Then Antonia, who had been extraordinarily silent throughout the evening, said, 'Family love is messy, clinging, and of an annoying and repetitive pattern…like bad wallpaper.' Nietzsche."

"Antonia wins the prize!" Ellie said. "Yes, family love, it is. Messy and often annoying. But when you're offered a bigger helping, I say, take it."

"Here, here," Mom said. That's when the lights popped on, and we sat there looking at our empty glasses, trying hard not to make eye contact with anyone. At least, that's what I was doing. "We need some champagne. Jack," Mom said, "get those champagne flutes from the china cabinet, will you please? Timothy, go to the wine cellar and get that bottle of Grande Dame we've been holding onto. And bring two bottles of the regular Veuve." She looked at Alex, who was sitting on her floor cushion, still looking sullen and angry. "Kelly," she said, "why don't you tell Alex about your friend Annalise Stevens."

Alex looked up at Mom and then over toward Kelly. "Annalise Stevens from the New York City Ballet? The corps member who danced a solo part two years ago and got promoted to principal dancer just like that? You know her?"

Kelly nodded, smiling. "I sure do. We've best friends since my ballet days. We do need to talk. Tomorrow, after we open our presents, you and I will huddle and talk about Annalise and her career. And I'll make sure you get to meet her before long."

~

Finally, it was midnight and no longer Christmas Eve. It was officially Christmas Day, and I had never been so tired in my life. I had thought the nine hours of driving were exhausting enough, but I realized that the family drama that had just played out, directed like a Spielberg movie by none other than my mother, Grace Sinclair, had completely drained me.

The kids had gone to bed, as had Ellie and Jack, the seniors among us. After directing the clean-up, Mom also said good night and left the three of us alone. It was just Antonia, Meg and me—an odd group if ever there was one.

"Anyone want another drink?" I said wearily, hoping no one did because I'd have to get up from my comfortable seat in front of the fire that was beginning to wane, just like the rest of us.

"I'll get us some tea," Antonia said, heading toward the kitchen. "Chamomile work for you, Megan?"

"That would be wonderful." When Antonia had left the room, Meg turned to me. "Tim, I don't know where all of this is headed, but now that the girls know about you, I'd like them to get to know you. Are you up for that?"

"Up for it? I'm not sure you could keep me away, although they might not feel quite the same way about me. I'm also still a bit worried about Nick and Alex in particular."

"Alex is a bit broodier than Ava. I'd say it was the artist in her, but Ava is every bit as much of an artist as Alex is. In fact, I think you'll be stunned at how much her watercolour style is like yours."

"I thought she was a budding sculptor, like her great-grandmother."

"She is, but she's been doing watercolour painting since she was five or six. When she was ten or so, Gran took her to what's now the Sinclair Gallery," Megan rolled her eyes, "and she happened to see one of your paintings. She came home raving about this artist called Timothy Sinclair. It was almost more than I could cope with not telling her right there and then. But I didn't.

Just before we left to drive here, she remembered that, and it dawned on her that you are that Timothy Sinclair. I think she's ready to get to know you. Alex? Well, that will take more time." Meg laughed. "You know, now that I think about it, Alex is a lot more like Antonia than she is like me. Maybe that's what drew Nick to her."

My eyebrows raised as I tried to take in this preposterous thought as Antonia returned to the living room with a tea tray.

"What's going on?" she said. I wondered if I detected an edge of suspicion in her voice. But maybe I was just projecting.

~

Christmas Day was oddly pleasant—and a bit subdued. As we sat around the Christmas tree sipping hot chocolate the next morning, looking out at the snowdrifts the night's blizzard had left behind, I wondered if everyone else felt as odd as I did. I mean, here we all were—unwrapping presents from people we hardly knew and politely acting as if we were enjoying ourselves. But as I looked around at the faces, I realized that there were only three of us who appeared distant—cool even. Or maybe we were just reserved, biding our time to get to know the lay of the land before we jumped into the fray. Antonia, Alex and I were the wary ones.

I suddenly remembered what Mom had said to me that day when we sat on the deck at the house in Maine, overlooking the angry ocean. I had just told her the whole sordid story about Antonia, the pregnancy and my romance with Meg. She told me the most important thing a father can do for his children is to love their mother. I didn't suppose anything had changed in the intervening years.

Mom and Ellie seemed like they had known one another forever, swapping funny stories about their careers and even a few recipes. There was also a lot of laughing. Kelly and Ava were talking about Ava's art, and I hoped Kelly could work her magic on Alex later when they planned to talk ballet. Nick and Jack were working together to figure out something called an "Xbox" that Antonia and I had given Nick for Christmas. He had asked for it—I had no idea what it was. As it turned out, Antonia and Alex were sitting side-by-side on the sofa, directly across from me, both looking exceedingly uncomfortable.

"Alex," I said, "did you know that Antonia was a patron of the American Ballet Theater in New York?"

Alex raised her eyebrows slightly as she turned to look at Antonia. "I guess Nick's interest in ballet must have pushed you to donate." Ouch. She was entirely correct.

"I suppose it was," Antonia said, "but the truth is that I've come to love the ballet. I truly enjoyed seeing you and Nick dance together at the Parents' Day performance. You're good together."

"We *were* good together," Alex said. "Everything's changed."

"Really?" I said. "Everything? Nothing about your talent or Nick's has changed. I think it might be cool for a sister and brother to become dance partners."

Kelly piped up from the other side of the room. "Tim, that might be the most insightful thing you've said for the past twenty-four hours. Think about it, Alex. There hasn't been a brother and sister dance team since Nijinsky and his sister."

"I'm not sure they ever actually danced together," Nick said from his position on the floor. It seemed everyone had tuned into the conversation.

"So, you could be the first ones ever," Kelly said, her voice gaining in enthusiasm by the moment. "Just think about it. Nick Sinclair and Alex McMaster, the newest *pas de deux* sensation of the ballet world. I can already see the posters."

Alex and Nick both rolled their eyes at precisely the same moment, but I could see something in the hard edges around Alex soften. Was that an upturn at the corner of her mouth?

"Well, that would be interesting," Antonia said, breaking her stone-faced silence.

~

After dinner on Christmas day, we all spent some time outside shovelling snow. Mom and Jack had a guy with a plow on the front of his truck who they had contracted to clear snow, but he didn't arrive until late. By then, we'd dug out the cars and moved them to the road so he could clear the driveway.

The next day—Boxing Day— we all piled into our respective vehicles and hit the road. Meg and I had spent a bit of time after the snow shovelling planning a way forward. I could visit the girls in Halifax during March break, and we'd see how things went. I hoped they'd come to New York in the summer, but that was a long way off. I had a lot of time to make up.

Nick fell asleep less than an hour into the drive. Antonia glanced into the back seat. "Tim, I think it might be time."

"Time for what?"

"Time to move out of the city."

Antonia and I had begun talking about selling our brownstone and moving to Connecticut for the past few years, then Nick went away to school, and it didn't seem so important anymore. In any case, Antonia had mixed feelings about the prospect.

On the one hand, she longed for more space around her and some quiet at the end of the day. On the other hand, she wasn't sure she was ready for the commute to Manhattan.

"Why now?" I said as I maneuvered the car onto our exit at Bangor toward the I95 South.

"We're probably going to need the space," she said.

# 32

# Antonia

## 2003-2005

*…last year's words belong to last year's language.*
*And next year's words await another voice.*
~ T.S. Elliott

BY THE TIME I WALKED BACK INTO MY OFFICE the first week in January, I felt as if I'd aged a decade. It wasn't so much that I felt older, but I felt much wiser. I had managed to weather the storm that was Grace Sinclair's Christmas intervention and made it out relatively unscathed. Truthfully, I was beginning to get excited about the prospect of a new house. It had been a long time since Tim and I had moved out of our perfect little home in the sky into our Manhattan townhouse, and we were no longer the same people. I had brought my new baby home to that townhouse, and Nick had spent his early years there, but now he was off at school in the wilds of Canada (oh, perhaps Toronto wasn't really the wilds). He could come home for only a month in the summer and a week or so at Christmas. Even March break this year would be spent away since he planned to go to Halifax with Tim to spend some time with Ava and Alex in his new role as a half-brother. I demurred, looking forward to a week of solitude—perhaps even in the company of a real estate agent. But since I wasn't going to see Nick during March break, I flew to Toronto in the middle of another snowstorm in February, and the two of us spent the weekend together. He and Alex seemed to be weathering their new relationship better than I expected.

"Mom," Nick said as we sat down to a feast at The Old Spaghetti Factory, one of his favourite Toronto restaurants, "everyone at school was so cool when Alex and I finally told them we're brother and sister. Yeah, they had a few questions about how come we didn't know and about Dad, but it was like they thought it was a fairy tale or something."

I smiled as I looked dubiously at the plate full of carbs the server had just placed in front of me. Tim and I were still trying to cut down on carbs—or perhaps more accurately, I was cutting us both down—and I'd just put myself on the waitlist for a new book due out this year by a cardiologist in South Beach, Florida. From what I'd read about this cardiologist's diet, he wouldn't be pleased to see this mound of pasta. "I'm so happy that you and Alex seem to have found your balance, and speaking of balance, will you and Alex be dancing together at Spring Showcase this year?"

Nick expertly twirled a length of spaghetti onto his fork without the aid of a spoon and popped it into his mouth. After he finished chewing and swallowing, he looked at me with that impish grin I'd seen more than once when he was much younger. I was delighted to see it once again. "Not sure. Guess we'll all just have to wait to find out."

And in late May, when Tim and I arrived at the theatre for the showcase performance the students did every year, we opened our programs to find that, yes, Nick Sinclair and Alex McMaster were dancing. Together. It was magical. It was also the beginning of something extraordinary.

~

By the end of June, we had moved into our new house. The sale of the city house had gone smoothly, garnering more money than we had expected, making the move all that much sweeter. The house was a four-thousand-square-foot Cape Cod on a large corner lot with a fishpond in the backyard and birch trees all around. The only thing missing was a swimming pool, but there was room for one, so it would come later in the summer. After all, we had to do something with that extra money! I only hoped the pool and the yard would be ready in time for Alex and Ava's visit in late August.

When the girls finally arrived, the pool was, indeed, finished, and I had the odd experience of running a household with three teenagers in it for two weeks. I had decided to take the two weeks off, allowing Tim to spend time with the kids and not have to take on any housekeeping duties. Unaccustomed as I was to this kind of domesticity, I called Grace. She was only too happy to give me some pointers about cooking larger portions and generally keeping people happy.

The visit went well. It went so well, as a matter of fact, that the girls planned to come back for New Year's, which they did. We began 2004 as a kind of motley crew of a family, and I thought I could feel the girls starting to accept me, albeit grudgingly. At least, I hoped so. Ava seemed more open to the idea of a stepmother than Alex did—she even referred to me as such once during their visit. I suspected that Alex's notion of a stepmother was more akin to Cinderella's experience than anything the twenty-first century might have to offer.

The winter melted into spring, and it was May again and another Spring Showcase. This was the first year we planned to spend time with Megan and the girls in Toronto. When I saw her at the theatre on the first evening, I noticed Megan had deep circles under her eyes—she looked tired. I remembered this when she called later that summer.

"Antonia," she said when I answered the phone one Saturday afternoon in August, "I have to speak urgently to Tim."

"He's not home, Megan. Can I help?"

"Only insofar as I'm going to have to ask your indulgence for something."

"Sounds mysterious."

"Not really so mysterious." She seemed to hesitate for a moment. "It's just that I need Tim to come to Halifax."

"Are the girls okay?" I said, suddenly alarmed at how Tim might react to a problem just when things were going so well.

Megan laughed lightly. "No, the girls are fine. I just need him to come to Halifax. Can you get him to call me when he gets back?"

I told her I would and hung up. If it wasn't about the girls, what could possibly be so important that Tim had to go to Halifax? Whatever it was, I was sure he could handle it from here. I found myself feeling bothered that she would presume he'd just drop everything and come.

Later that evening, Tim went into the den to call Megan. I couldn't help myself. I stood outside the door, eavesdropping like a spoiled child.

After a few quiet exchanges, I heard Tim say, "Meg, are you sure? I mean, I know you're probably sure, but how could this have happened? Aren't you too young to have cancer?" My hand flew to my mouth to stifle a gasp. Then he listened for a moment and said, "Oh, god," he said, "of course. I'll come."

Tim hung up the phone and slumped into the chair behind my desk. I moved into the doorway so he could see me. "Oh my god, Antonia. It's Meg. She has stage-four ovarian cancer."

# 33

# Grace

## 2005



*Being deeply loved by someone gives you strength,*
*while loving someone deeply gives you courage.*
~ Lao Tzu

IT'S DIFFICULT TO DESCRIBE HOW I FELT when Tim called me with the news. "Meg has cancer, Mom. And it's bad." And I knew Tim's life had again begun to spin on a dime. Again.

Once I got him to calm down, I managed to get from him the few details that he had at that point. I was shocked and saddened, of course, but I also felt something else. It was fear. There hadn't been many things in my life to truly fear, but this was one. I was afraid for Megan and how she would get through this. I was afraid for Alex and Ava—my granddaughters—who faced losing their mother. And I was afraid for Tim, who had spent the past couple of years carving out a space for himself in his daughters' lives and in Meg's. My mind began to move immediately into the arena of the "what ifs." The primary "what if" was what if she dies—and that what if seemed all too likely. What would happen then?

Tim told me he would immediately fly to Halifax to see Megan as she had requested, and I told him to get the key to our house from our Halifax neighbour, who looked in on it when we weren't there. There was no need for him to stay in some sterile hotel. I wished I were there and not happily enjoying a Maine summer. Then I picked up the phone and called Ellie McMaster. I knew she would be devastated. Perhaps I could help in some way.

"Oh, Grace," Ellie said when I finally got her on the phone, "this is a nightmare of disastrous proportions. I keep hoping I'll wake up. I'm so glad Tim is coming."

Then she told me about Megan's prognosis, and it wasn't good. "Grace, Meg tried to sugar-coat it with me when she told me about it. I may be over eighty now, but I'm a retired physician, as you know, and she couldn't keep the details from me. Her medical team has told her to put her affairs in order. The most important of those are the girls."

"Do the girls know?"

"Not yet—at least not how severe it is—but Megan plans to tell them before Tim arrives."

I was trying to imagine how Alex and Ava would react. How would any teenage girl react to the news that her mother is dying? "What about you, Ellie? How are you? Will the girls stay with you?"

"I wish I could say I'm fine, Grace, but I'm not really fine. I lost my daughter—Meg's mother—many years ago, and I'm not sure I ever really got over it completely. Who gets over the death of a child that easily?" She sighed. "I'd like nothing more than to have the girls live with me, but I'm not as well as I once was. I'm afraid we might have to lean on Tim."

And I knew Tim would be there for his daughters as I would be there for him. But there was nothing I could do on that front at the moment, but I could be there for my daughter-in-law and grandson. After we hung up, I called Antonia.

Antonia and I'd had our differences over the years. I'd be the first to admit that when I first met her, I thought she wasn't good for Tim. Over the years, we hadn't seen eye-to-eye on many things. Still, since that fateful Christmas when we all realized we were going to have to become some sort of family—as dysfunctional as it might be, as Nicholas had suggested—Antonia and I seemed to have developed a mutual respect. I was proud of how she handled the unsettling news that she had two stepdaughters and how she had taken them into her home more and more often. Now would come the real test.

"Antonia, how are you?" I began as carefully as I could.

"I'm okay, Grace, but I have no idea how we're all going to get through this. I've learned to love Alex and Ava, but they're still wary of me. And I don't know if I'm prepared to be a full-time stepmother."

As I thought about this, I began to realize that there would be so many complications ahead—and they were probably only the tip of the iceberg. "Antonia, I've learned something over the years about stepping up when we're needed. I know that facing what needs to be done is much easier when you do it out of love. Please know that I'll be here when you need me."

# 34

# Antonia

## 2005-06

*You have to accept whatever comes, and the only*
*important thing is that you meet it with courage*
*and with the best that you have to give.*
~ Eleanor Roosevelt

WHEN TIM RETURNED FROM SEEING MEGAN in Halifax that August, as she had asked, I expected him to be devastated. He was sad—of that, there was no doubt—but he didn't seem overwhelmed.

Although it was unusual for us to meet each other at the airport since the traffic was so bad, when Tim arrived back from Halifax, I drove to JFK to meet him. On the way to the airport, I took advantage of the hour in the car alone to consider how my life might be changing. I knew Tim's decisions would play a large part in those changes.

"Did you and Megan discuss the living arrangements for Alex and Ava?" I said as we drove home.

"It's going to be complicated," he said.

We then talked at length about what would happen. Of course, Megan wished for Tim to take care of his daughters when she died. This surprised me a bit, although it probably shouldn't have. After all, although they'd come to know him over the past couple of years, they didn't see him often and, in some ways, were still in the early stages of a relationship. And, of course, they were teenage girls, I was their father's wife, and I had never quite been able to figure out how they felt about me. Then there were the practical issues.

The girls were diehard Canadians who grew up in a small city on Canada's east coast. I was sure they wouldn't want to move to Connecticut, although since Alex spent most of her life away at school in Toronto, it was less of a consideration for her—at least in my view. Surely Ava would want to finish high school in Halifax, and Ellie was there. Nick and the girls had one more full year to go before they would all graduate from high school.

"Meg and the girls have moved in with Ellie. She has a huge Victorian in the south end of the city," Tim said.

I knew that Megan and the girls had lived in their own house somewhere in the city near the university where Megan taught until she took long-term sick leave recently. According to Tim, Ellie would be there for the girls in the short term, but he was to be the official parent. Megan wanted Tim (and me) to spend some time in Halifax over the next year and a half so the girls could have some continuity until high school graduation. That made sense to me, but it didn't stop me from reeling with the feeling of responsibility that fell over me like a lead blanket.

"We'll have to get Nick on board with all this. How's he doing?" Tim said.

"He's distracting himself with his new video games and getting ready to go back to school." I glanced at Tim, who was nodding as if that was exactly what he would have expected. "I plan to fly with Nick back to school next weekend as usual," I said.

The following weekend was Labour Day, the weekend I traditionally accompanied Nick back to school in Toronto since he'd first gone. I always stayed overnight for one night in a hotel, ensuring we picked up all his school supplies when we got there. The next day, I'd leave him at the boys' residence and fly home. I didn't think this year should be any different.

"Yes, of course," he said distractedly. "Back to school as usual."

We drove in silence for a while, then I said, "Tim, I want you to know that I'll do whatever I need to do to make this as smooth as possible for Alex and Ava."

"I know you will, Antonia," Tim said. "I know you will."

~

Megan died in the middle of January in 2005 as a blizzard blanketed the northeast Atlantic coast. It was a Saturday. Ellie called to give us the sad news and when Grace called later that day, we had just come into the house after more than an hour with the snow blower and various shovels. I answered.

"Jack and I are going to pack the car and drive to Halifax as soon as the roads clear," Grace said. Ellie had called her with the news as well.

"Oh, Grace, are you sure that's a good idea? The driving will be bad for a few days." But Grace was adamant. I passed the phone to Tim.

I watched Tim as he listened to his mother, and I saw a single tear escape each eye and trickle down his face. That's the moment when I started crying—as softly as I could.

"No, Mom," Tim was saying, "it's okay. I'll drive up to Bar Harbor and meet you. I know it's a full day's drive, but it'll do me good, and then we can go together."

It sounded like Grace was arguing with him, but Tim wasn't having any of it. He'd made up his mind. When he hung up, he said, "You arrange to fly to Toronto to pick up Alex and Nick and then fly with them to Halifax. I don't want any of them to be alone right now." Nick and Alex were now in grade eleven at Canada's National Ballet School and had just returned to school following Christmas break. They had been so excited to be dancing together again at the Spring Showcase, and Nick had told me Alex hoped her mother would be well enough to travel to Toronto for the show. Now that wouldn't happen.

I agreed to do as Tim wished and began packing for the two-part trip.

Tim left the following morning before it was even daylight. The roads had cleared, and I realized he needed to get his thoughts straight as he embarked on a new phase of his life, so I didn't argue with him about driving. I spent the rest of the day making flight arrangements and listening to Nick as he cried on the phone. He was doing his best to help Alex but felt like he was losing. I felt helpless. There was nothing I could say that would make things better. I just hoped Alex wouldn't see me as an interloper when I arrived in Toronto to accompany them to Halifax and all that would bring. I was on an early morning flight from JFK to Toronto, so I hoped I'd get some sleep, but I also hoped Tim would call before I fell asleep. I needed to know everyone in my family was safe—or as safe as anyone could be.

The call came from Grace just after midnight.

"Antonia, I'm sorry if I woke you up, but I was wondering what time Tim left today."

I was confused for a moment. What day was it? I must have been dozing. "Hello, Grace. Well, he left before sunrise." I sat up straight, suddenly aware of what she was saying—or not saying. "What time did he arrive in Bar Harbor?"

"That's just it, Antonia. He didn't. Yet."

I looked at the clock. It was fifteen minutes after midnight. "What's the weather like there? Maybe he decided to stop somewhere."

"I suppose so," she said slowly, "but wouldn't he have called all of us?"

Grace was right. Something was wrong. I began to feel the icy fingers of dread creep up my spine and settle just under my hairline. I got out of bed and wrapped myself in a robe to keep out the chill that was as much from alarm as it was from the temperature in the bedroom. "I'll call his cell phone, Grace and get back to you."

"Oh, thank goodness he has one of those," she said. "I'll be waiting here by the phone."

I punched in Tim's number. I just hoped he had it turned on. Sometimes he turned it off when he wanted to think. I listened as the phone rang and rang. Finally, his voicemail told me to leave a call-back number, and I punched in our home phone. Now what? I called Grace to tell her I couldn't reach him, and I could hear the panic rising in her voice.

Grace and I agreed we'd sit tight for an hour or more. What else could we do? If we hadn't heard from Tim by then, I'd call her, and we'd do something. But I had no idea what.

I went downstairs and made myself a cup of coffee, expecting it to be a long night. I pictured Tim's car in a ditch somewhere, with no one on the road to help him. I was driving myself crazy. Finally, two hours later, I knew.

~

I felt like a zombie as I dragged myself into the departure area at JFK at nine am. Without any sleep, I wasn't sure I could get through the day. I stared lifelessly at the pretty young woman at the check-in counter. I stared through the agents at the security line. I stared past the gate agents as I boarded. Once I was settled into my seat, the dam broke, and I started to sob.

Alarmed, the in-charge flight attendant came over. I suppose it wasn't a good look for embarking passengers to see the woman in the front row of business class sobbing. It might not reflect well on the airline.

"Ma'am," she said, "what's wrong? How can I help?"

"No one can help," I said. "No one can help me find a way to tell my son that his father is dead." And I knew I'd have to tell his daughters, as well.

~

There had been an accident. As the sun set early on that January evening in southern Maine, light snow had begun to fall. It happened just after Tim turned off the interstate onto Route 1A south to Bar Harbor. An oncoming transport truck slid across into Tim's lane. He had swerved to try to avoid it, but the truck slipped directly into his path. There was nothing he could have done. That's what the crash investigators surmised. That was the thinking when the police had arrived at my door at three am. Tim never had a chance.

# 35

# Antonia

## June 22, 2007

*Bad things are not the worst thing that can happen*
*to us. NOTHING is the worst thing that can*
*happen to us.* ~ Richard Bach

IT WAS OVER A YEAR SINCE MEGAN AND TIM HAD BOTH DIED. I was again in Toronto, where the June sun was shining brightly outside the auditorium. I sat nervously in my seat with Ava by my side. The curtain rose on the stage of the Betty Oliphant Theatre, and lined up in their gowns and suits were the graduating students of the class of 2007 at Canada's National Ballet School. I looked from one to another, remembering the time Nick's best friend Stewart and his girlfriend Melanie had procured vodka for all and passed out tiny cups to their classmates at the back of a school dance. That had resulted in a telephone call from the head of the student residence. I remembered trying to keep a straight face while I scolded my son for his behaviour while Tim sat across the room from me, laughing his head off. That was the one time when Tim and I had realized the school's counsellor had been right all those years ago when he told us our children weren't "normal kids." There was nothing normal about a life fully dedicated to an art form at the age of eleven or twelve—but perhaps they did behave normally when given the chance. No, they weren't normal—and that was a good thing. They were special—so special.

As my eyes moved from one to the other, they finally rested on the two who were the reason Ava and I were sitting here on this beautiful day. Nick Sinclair and Alex McMaster. Two shining stars who were about to graduate.

This was no ordinary high school graduation. There was little doubt in anyone's mind about that. The artistic director took to the microphone to prepare to distribute diplomas. For each of the twenty-one graduates, she told a story. For some, it was a brief story of the past two years since they'd transferred from an elite school in Tokyo or Vienna. But for others, it was a story of a child arriving at a young age to live away from home for the first time, blossoming over the years into these beautiful, talented young men and women. That was the kind of story she told about Alex first, then Nick. As she spoke, each graduate stood and listened to their own story while we watched.

I watched Alex's face as she stood at her chair on the stage in her fiery red chiffon sheath that brushed the floor. Her wild hair was upswept on one side, and her dark eyes sparkled, just like I'd seen Tim's eyes sparkle when he knew he'd just sold a painting. We all listened while the artistic director told Alex's story, briefly mentioning the loss of her parents and how she had returned to school more determined than ever to make them proud.

My eyes filled with tears remembering how difficult it had been for her to lose her mother, only to have to face the loss of her new-found father as well. Then, in the end, she was forced to accept her stepmother. And that was a role I'd found so difficult to grasp. How did I know how to be a stepmother to two teenage girls? I didn't. It was a struggle at first, but with Grace's help, I'd come to realize that nothing worth doing is ever easy. And it had been worth doing.

Grace. *She should be here today, as should Ellie*, I thought. The grandmother and the great-grandmother. They should be sharing this moment. But when Ellie had told me she wouldn't be able to care for the girls, she already knew she wouldn't be around for long. She had died six months earlier. And Grace, whose coolly practical wisdom I'd come to cherish, was caring for Jack, who wasn't well. I realized as I sat there that everyone's story had to come to an end. We just couldn't know when or how.

Then the artistic director moved to Nick. Nick had found it so difficult to return to school after his father died, but he, too, had personal reserves I'd not recognized until then. Part of each graduate's story was what lay in store for them next year, and Nick and Alex had two of the most exciting prospects. They were the only two members of this year's class who had been accepted to join the National Ballet of Canada as apprentices. I was so proud of both of them.

As each of them accepted their diplomas from the director, I could feel Ava squeeze my arm. I was almost overcome. I loved Alex and Ava as if they were my own because, in a way, they were.

After the ceremony was over, we stood outdoors in the sunshine while the graduates posed for more photos in front of one of the new school buildings. It had come a long way from that Dickensian boys' residence and rabbit warren connecting small studios when Nick had first arrived in Toronto. Now, it was a shining example of extraordinary architecture, melding the old with the new. The new buildings didn't happen overnight, though. It took hard work and persistence to get there. It was a bit like my life, I thought. I smiled as I realized this was an apt metaphor for my own life—melding the old me with the new and unexpected role I found myself in. That had taken time and endurance, too.

As I watched their smiling faces embrace their futures, I thought about my younger self. What would she have thought about this situation? I realized she could never have imagined an ending quite like this one. Oh, I know, each ending is merely a beginning, but I'd always thought I'd go out with a bang. I thought that was how it would have to be for me to be happy. I was wrong.

I remembered the famous lines from the T.S. Eliot poem *The Hollow Men* that I'd studied and tried to understand as an undergraduate:

> *This is the way the world ends*
> *This is the way the world ends*
> *This is the way the world ends*
> *Not with a bang but a whimper.*

I had always thought that a whimper was a bad thing. Now I knew better. *This*, I thought, *is how the story ends.*

# Charlie

## Today

*Overcome space, and all we have left is Here.*
*Overcome time, and all we have left is Now.*
~ Richard Bach, *Jonathan Livingston Seagull*

IT WAS GIRLS' NIGHT OUT. My sister Evelyn and I had ditched our husbands, who were now on childcare duty with our offspring back at Evelyn's "pile." That was how she referred to the five-bedroom-four-bathroom-Frank-Lloyd-Wrightish mansion she lived in with her family in Rosedale, a chic, old-money neighbourhood a short drive north of where we were at that moment. Tom and I were visiting from Halifax, and Evelyn had decided we didn't need the men with us to attend the ballet here at the Four Seasons Centre for the Performing Arts in downtown Toronto.

After the eight-course tasting menu at Canoe on the sixty-fourth floor of the TD Bank building, the restaurant in the sky, we'd arrived just in time to take our places in the centre of the grand ring (Evelyn had splurged on her season's tickets this year) before the curtain rose on this evening's performance of *Romeo and Juliet*. I had always loved Prokofiev's music and had looked forward to seeing the choreography by the Russian-American choreographer Alexei Ratmansky. I didn't know much about ballet, but I'd Googled this one, and it looked amazing. Now it was intermission, and Evelyn, after much sighing, had gone in search of a couple of glasses of champagne, leaving me shoulder-to-shoulder with the rest of the audience in the crowded lobby area. The sighing had been prompted by the fact that the patrons' lounge was closed for renovations, and she—a long-time patron of the ballet company—had to line up with the masses for her champagne fix.

I was staring pensively at the program I had open in my hand when she returned.

"What's so fascinating about the R and J program, Charlie? We all know how it ends!" Evelyn said, laughing.

"It's not about the story," I said. "It's the dancers' bios that caught my eye."

Evelyn looked over my shoulder. "Who are you reading about?"

"These two," I said, pointing to the photographs of Alex McMaster and Nick Sinclair. "It's just the names that seem familiar. Sinclair and McMaster. It's like the characters in the book I wrote based on great-grandmother Frannie's unfinished manuscript. And what's more," I said, tapping on the open page, "Alex McMaster is from Halifax."

"Oh yes. Alex McMaster and Nick Sinclair. We are so lucky to be seeing them tonight as leads. They've been away a lot. It seems they're something of the international 'it' couple of the ballet world these days." Evelyn handed me my champagne flute. "You know, I read that they're brother and sister. Isn't that remarkable to see the kind of chemistry they bring to the stage? It's such a great story, isn't it? Just made for a writer like my little sister." She jabbed my arm with the elbow on which her Birkin was hooked, causing me to back into the woman behind me.

"Oh, I'm so sorry," I said, wiping champagne off the front of my new dress. I looked up to find a young woman staring at me intently. She looked familiar.

"Charlie Hudson?" she said. "CK Hudson, the writer?"

"Yes," I said slowly, trying to figure out where I'd seen her before.

"Remember me? Ava McMaster. We met at the Sinclair gallery in Halifax a few years ago."

"Of course," I said, remembering I'd visited the gallery while researching my last book—the unfinished manuscript my great-grandmother had written before she died in 1989. "What are you doing here?" The moment the words left my mouth, I realized how stupid they must have sounded. Of course, she was here for the same reason I was: to see a ballet. *But what's with all these McMasters?* I thought.

"To see my sister dance," she said.

I was stunned. Evelyn butted right in. "Alex McMaster is your sister? Well, then, Nick Sinclair must be your brother."

"Yes," Ava said. "He's my half-brother." Then she turned back to me. "Charlie—may I call you Charlie?" I nodded. "I'm a big fan of your books. Your last one—*Something I'm Supposed to Do*—was surprising, though."

"In what way?" I said, not liking where this was going. I'd visited the gallery to do some research on the people Fran—my great-grandmother—had based her story upon and then ended up going my own way.

"Well, when we talked that day, you said you'd come back to hear how the story ended."

"I did, didn't I?" I remembered that much.

"Would you still like to know how the story ends?" Ava said. I nodded, and she continued. "I'm going to wait for Alex and Nick at the stage door after the show. Why don't you join us there? We'll tell you how it really ended."

Because stories end the way they end.

# Author's Notes &
# Acknowledgements

THIS BOOK IS THE FIFTH in the "almost-but-not-quite-true" stories where Charlotte ("Charlie") Hudson appears. I can't promise that she'll never show up again, but I can promise that this part of the story has come to an end. What happens next is anyone's guess (although I may have a bit of a clue!). But before I move on to new stories, I want to take a minute to tell you about the "true" parts of this "not-quite-true" story.

Truth: I am a ballet mom. I have been a ballet mom since my eight-year-old son, who already had a list of professional television credits, performed in his third musical theatre production and asked if he could learn more about dancing. Fast-forward to 2007, when he graduated from the professional ballet program at Canada's National Ballet School before going on to a career as a ballet dancer and eventually a faculty member at his alma mater—which leads me to my thanks.

First, I'd like to thank Ian for providing me with more background material than any author could possibly hope to find for an eventual novel.

I'd also like to thank all the students who graduated with Ian in 2007. Knowing them and sharing a small part of their experience has inspired me and made my life richer.

Finally, as always, I don't know how my books would make it into your hands without the support and assistance of my always-first beta reader (and editor and so much more), my husband, Art, who was also part of this ballet-parent experience.

Together, through this book, we've relived a wonderful part of our lives.

Always remember that you create the life you have through every decision you make—and every decision has consequences both near and far.

# About the Author

PATRICIA J. PARSONS has written more than twenty books, including health and business books, a memoir, two historical novels, and women's fiction. She has been a fashion design and sewing fanatic for most of her life, a passion she writes about online at *The GG Files* at gloriaglamont.com. She lives, writes and sews in Toronto.

Connect with her on Instagram @patriciajparsons or @pjparsonswriter

Join her on Facebook @patriciaparsonswriter and in her group "12 Dresses" at facebook.com/groups/12 dresses

Visit her website at www.patriciajparsons.com.

www.ingramcontent.com/pod-product-compliance
Lightning Source LLC
Chambersburg PA
CBHW031938210726

48290CB00006BA/1818